BREATHING IN WATER

BREATHING IN WATER

BY

GRACIE WEST

DEDICATED TO YOU,

DEAR READER OF THIS BOOK.

ACKNOWLEDGMENTS

Thank you, dear children, for
sharing my attention with fictional
characters.

Thank you, dear husband, for feeding me
when I spent entire days writing and also
for helping me polish these pages.

Thank you, David Davidson, for your
generous gift of skillful editing and
meaningful conversation.

Hugs and love to
all of you!

CHAPTER ONE

She veered away from the old woman sitting on the sidewalk, who had locked eyes with her and was tracking her as she passed.

"Come on," her friend begged, grabbing her arm.

"No, way!" she protested.

"Why not?"

"Because it's a scam."

River tried releasing her arm from her friend's grip, but Olivia yanked her into awkward proximity to the fortuneteller, whose eyes were still fixed on her.

The dirty fingernails taking Olivia's five-dollar bill confirmed for River that this would be wasted cash. But the exchange of money effectively stifled her resistance to the humiliating pretend-game of palm-reading. The bedraggled woman took River's hand in hers, turning her palm to the sky, all the while staring right through her.

River swallowed.

A calloused finger moved across River's palm. Some time passed before the seer said, "Where is your fate? This line is missing on your hand." The woman shivered and said, "A strange force has fixed its eyes on you."

YOU, River thought.

The old woman continued in a trancelike state. "Maybe it's bad luck, or God. But it stalks you like a cat with easy prey."

River would have rolled her eyes if the seer weren't looking directly into them. She imagined this charlatan giving the same apocalyptic speech to every fool whom she'd ensnared.

"There's a storm coming. A wicked storm!"

A cold sensation crawled up River's arm and across her scalp like an ice-cold tarantula. She tried pulling her hand away but the seer squeezed it tighter.

"Beware of a gift that comes too late!" the seer warned.

River jerked her hand out of the old woman's grasp and scratched her palm, as if removing the creepy sensation that lingered. She shot big eyes at Olivia and said, "Gotta go, now!"

Olivia followed. "You didn't let her finish! How do you know she was done?"

"Because I was." River was rubbing her hand on her jeans as Olivia caught up.

"What do you think she meant by a gift?"

"I think she meant, 'Thanks for the five bucks, ladies!'"

Olivia shook her head. "You're such a skeptic!"

"Seriously, though? Fate? God? A storm? She couldn't have been more cliché or vague. It's a scam! But, hey, you can feel good about donating to a homeless woman."

"You know, Riv, someday you'll believe in energies and different realms and things."

River looked over at her eccentric friend who had multiple tattoos claiming the curves of her white skin. She wondered, for a moment, how she and her old college roommate ended up being such good friends. They had Harvard in common. That was about it. Well, that and the fact that both women orbited the world around 5'3". River decided a topic change was needed. "So, how's your friend Xander doing? Did he ever transition? Should I say 'she'?"

"No. Xander goes by Xandi now and didn't identify strongly enough with male or female, so zie's non-binary now."

"Did you say zie's?"

"Yes. Xandi's pronouns are zie, zim and zir." Olivia seemed proud to announce this.

Maybe it was the writer in her, but River questioned the latest trend of people owning their own set of pronouns and making people feel obligated to say them. She wasn't sure how to ask the next question, but she continued anyway, "Did his dad kick him out?"

"*Zie's* dad hasn't kicked *zim* out yet."

Olivia's emphasis on correct pronouns felt chastising. The conversation had become laborious. River didn't know how to formulate the next sentence about Xandi, so she moved on, asking Olivia how her search for a new roommate was going. Olivia gave River a review of various shady characters she'd rejected in the search, one of which actually admitted to stabbing his previous roommate. He'd tried reducing Olivia's shock by saying, "I didn't kill the guy. I just stabbed him up good." They laughed as they walked below buildings consumed by dark-green ivy along the historic streets of Boston. A suitcase bounced violently on the stone sidewalk behind Olivia.

There was just enough time to grab coffee before arriving at the station, so they dodged into a retro cafe pulsing with people needing their caffeine fix. The phone in River's hand buzzed, notifying her that a text had come in. After ordering, she moved to the end of the counter where a tall man didn't bother going around her to get his coffee; he reached right over her petite frame. She stepped aside to give him the room he needed and brushed her jaw-length, black hair away from her round face.

"Man-spreading," Olivia whispered, loudly.

River leaned in, "I thought man-spreading was when men take up three seats, one for their ass and one for each knee."

Olivia didn't bother trying to whisper this time. "Man-spreading is anytime a man takes up more space than he needs." She looked sideways at the man stirring cream into his coffee, hoping he'd heard her.

Remembering that she had an unread text River looked down at her phone. Her stomach tightened. She'd hoped it was her recent ex, Brian. Her shoulders dropped a little when she saw her curly-haired mom on the screen. Loretta spoke her texts and never verbalized punctuation, which meant her messages were run-on sentences that needed some translation.

> Hey baby doll were leaving for the air heart first thing in the morning I'm so excited to visit my little curl in the big city I have some important news I'm nervous about giving you a gift we'll talk about it when I get there love ya

River wondered what her mother meant by "important news." Loretta often overstated the ordinary, so the fact that she had "important news" didn't give River much pause. River's mind fixated on Brian. She wondered what kind of an asshole breaks up with someone by leaving a post-it note on their pillow? Even though the potent aroma of coffee grounds dominated her senses, she could still smell the expensive cologne that lingered on his side of her bed. She went cold as that yellow note appeared in her mind.

I'm going home Riv. This is goodbye. Thanks
for good times. B~

She shook her head without realizing it. She hadn't
expected to be discarded like the designer jeans he'd
forgotten were laying on her bedroom floor that final
morning as he left for the gym. She swallowed down the ball
that had formed in her throat. The fact that he hadn't
promised her anything consoled her only slightly. The truth
was, in their few months of dating, neither one of them
could have imagined a shared future together. They sprung
up in very different soils—he uptown New York City, and
she small-town Oklahoma. She was more upset about how
he left than the fact that he did. It felt wrong for him to leave
like that.

Brian had talked about dropping out of Harvard to follow
his dream—acting on Broadway—but she didn't think he
was brave enough to do it. She remembers her stomach
tightening one night as they lay in bed and he told her that
his last relationship was with a guy. Guilt nagged her
conscience when she felt disgusted by this idea. She didn't
care if men slept together. But it bothered her to wonder if
Brian thought she was better in bed than a guy was. Plus,
she couldn't imagine swinging both ways; but she never told
him that, of course.

"Hello? You in there?" Olivia waved her hand in front of
River's face. "You're thinking about Bastard again, aren't
you?"

"No. I'm not." She scratched her nose. "I was thinking
about the internship."

"Then why do you look sad and not terrified? Hasn't it
been a week?"

River nodded.

"Then it's time to stop thinking about him. Seriously! He's not worth it."

"I know. I'm not." She regretted telling Olivia she was giving Brian one week to call her, and if he didn't, she would never think about him again. If there was one thing River knew how to do it was think. And apparently Olivia could read minds.

Olivia picked up her steaming-hot latte, then opened the lid to put cinnamon on top.

River went back to thinking about Brian. Even though they only hooked up a few months ago, she had met him three years before in an undergraduate class at Harvard. She remembered being surprised when, during a discussion on Marxism, the professor had said that Brian was a "person of color" and therefore an "oppressed class." It kind of amused her when her professors used the phrase, "people of color," because River's mind automatically translated that to mean "everyone except white people." But her amusement was short-lived. It got replaced by guilt from an unknown source, which is why she never questioned aloud the strangeness of categorizing people as not-white. Still, grouping people by their skin color, putting all non-white people into a single category and then making sweeping statements about their condition was strange to her. It was too simple. Especially for Harvard professors. Since there were never-ending shades of skin color she often wondered exactly where the line got drawn between "white-people" and "people-of-color." Especially given the melting-pot of modern America. But it seemed like the line ran right between her and Brian. His skin was only slightly darker than hers, but apparently just dark enough to be called a person-of-color, or "a POC," as Olivia called them.

She understood the need to analyze race-relations in the U.S. It was urgent. Crucial! But River's intellect could rival her Harvard professors', thus her admission into the university, and she was never satisfied with discussions that used a version of Marx's economic theory to analyze race. As far as she could tell, Karl Marx was singularly interested in economics. In fact, she thought, Marx would roll over in his grave to hear someone say that Brian was part of an "oppressed class." His family owned a good chunk of New York City! Plus, she figured, once a person gets admitted into an Ivy League school you can't really call them oppressed. She wondered how Karl Marx had become the anthem theorist for analyzing arbitrary physical features. But she kept these wonderings to herself, of course. Vocalizing them would have been like waving a flag that says, "I AM A RACIST."

"RIVER?" someone yelled. Her attention was catapulted back to the coffee shop where she stood staring, unknowingly, at a barista making drinks. He had blue hair, more tattoos than skin, and metal coming out every orifice of his face. He was looking at her from the corner of his eyes. Her cheeks darkened as she grabbed her drink and joined Olivia at the door. When she got outside, she shot a quick reply to her mom.

> "Excited to see you, mama. Curious about your news."

The next morning her mom would leave Stillwater and drive to Oklahoma City, where she and her boyfriend of three years would fly to Boston for a week. Kenneth Kirskowski was a retired conductor for the Oklahoma City Philharmonic. River didn't know him very well, since she'd been away at college for the past five years, but he seemed like a nice guy when she visited at Christmas. He definitely had more class than the other men Loretta had dated over the years. There was just one thing River didn't like about him: his face. He had a habit of scrunching his face to move his glasses up onto the arch of his nose, which momentarily warped his expression. It was distracting. But despite a couple of quirks, she liked Kenneth. Loretta was never terribly successful with long-term relationships, but River hoped this one would last. She was glad her mom was happy. And not alone.

Olivia looked at River, "Are you ready for tomorrow?"

River's stomach flipped at the thought of her first day at the competitive internship she'd secured at The Boston Globe. She breathed through narrow lips. "Ready as I'll ever be."

"So, next time I visit you'll be a big-time journalist?"

River let out an audible huff, "Hardly. But I'll have my foot in the door. Just glad I won't be writing obituaries like I did as an undergrad."

River had decided to major in journalism when she became fully swept up in a professor's stream of consciousness one day in history class. This professor explained how it is not great people who make history, but great writers who do. He explained how history doesn't actually shape the future, our perception of it does. Basically, he explained, the past can only bring us to the present, but it's the stories we tell about the past that determine how the future will unfold. That's when River decided she wanted to be a journalist. She could literally make history, and would never need to stand directly in the limelight.

Her attention was grabbed by a young man walking toward them on the sidewalk who was taking up more space than he needed. His eyes kept darting in her direction as he approached. It seemed as though he would run right into her. *Man-spreading*, she thought, just as he brushed past her. She felt her purse slide off her shoulder. She grabbed onto it, but he yanked it out of her hands and ran down a narrow alleyway to her left. River stood completely still for a couple seconds, absorbing what had just happened. She finally screamed, "HEY! He stole my purse!" By the time Olivia realized what had happened, the man was halfway down the alley. Some other people nearby stopped and looked, but no one ran after the kid. He turned the corner at the end of the building, and she knew they would never catch him.

River squatted down with her hands over her face, memorizing what the guy looked like and trying to remember what was inside of her purse: her wallet, about twenty dollars, miscellaneous stuff like chapstick and tampons. NO! Even more devastating than losing her wallet was losing her phone, which had the contact information for her supervisor at The Boston Globe. WAIT! She grabbed her back pocket. She had slipped it in her pocket after texting her mom.

"Call the police!" Olivia yelled.

River considered what needed to happen next. She needed money for the bus, and Olivia needed to catch her train back to New York. She stood up. "Okay. I'll call 'em, but we need to keep going."

"I can catch the next train, Riv! I'm not leaving you like this."

River walked ahead. "You'll miss your chance to meet your new roommate."

"Potential roommate." Olivia followed behind her.

"Exactly. If you don't find one soon you'll end up homeless in New York City."

Olivia didn't argue. She dug through her pocket as they walked, "Here. You'll need this to get home." She handed River two twenties. River accepted the cash. She would need it to get through the next twenty-four hours.

River called the police while they sped-walked to the station. Just as she was finishing the call Olivia squeezed her neck, kissed her cheek, and ran to the train. She was the last passenger to board.

CHAPTER TWO

That particular day had a sort of weight to it, like the atmospheric pressure on a dark Oklahoma day when the sky touches down and carves a path through the red dirt. She stood looking at herself in the mirror, relieved to own slacks with pockets large enough to hold her passport, her new ID. She stuffed the blue, textured booklet into her pocket, then wiped her perspiring hands down the front of her slacks.

She'd been working toward this moment for years, and here it was. Over eighty people had applied for this paid internship but only she and one other person were selected for it. Big-city prestige seemed to offer itself to her, despite her small-town beginnings. By the end of summer, she could possibly start a progressive career in journalism in the great city of Boston. When River moved to Boston five years earlier, she'd abandoned her Okie accent. Blending in meant survival in the city. She mercilessly lopped off her long hair at the chin, exposing her neck and added bangs to cover her unusually high forehead. Her wardrobe was likewise transformed: big-city appeal demanded slimmer jeans and high-quality shirts. The new style suited her, and she wondered why she hadn't done that years ago. She gave herself one last scan, turning and looking over her shoulder in the mirror, before heading to the bus.

She stared beyond the grease-smudged window as the blur of fast-walking people and vintage brownstones passed by. Her new boss made it clear that she'd be working closely with the other intern, so she was curious if that person would be pleasant or pompous. She decided the latter was likely if chosen from among Harvard's elite.

Her unceasing conscientiousness dictated that she arrive thirty minutes early. The anorexic-looking supermodel behind the desk seemed bothered to do her job. With a forced smile and wave of her wrist she told River to take a seat in the lobby. River sat on the edge of the stiff black sofa. Not long afterward, a chocolate-skinned young man in a gray suit arrived. The supermodel gave him a flirtatious smile when she directed him to sit down. He pulled his collar away from his neck with one finger as he took his seat in an armchair. When her new potential colleague glanced over, River became aware that her legs were bouncing up and down. Their eyes met briefly, and they exchanged a forced smile. He wiped his palms on his thighs. It suddenly occurred to her that her new boss and this guy would have a natural bond, both of them being men. She would need to make sure that he wasn't getting perks or promotions just because he was male.

She noticed that the man's suit draped exactly over his seemingly perfect body. She couldn't decide if the suit made him look good or if he made the suit look good. She reasoned that even if he was pompous or had a bro-bond with the boss, his visual appeal would enhance the workplace. Her thoughts were interrupted by the outline of a tall woman with bobbed hair walking straight towards her. The large window behind the woman poured daylight around her slight frame, making her silhouette look like a Q-tip. River was surprised when the woman stopped in front of her.

"Sam Harkens," the woman said sternly, extending a hand. River stood and greeted her new boss awkwardly.

"Yeah, yeah, I know, you were expecting a man." Sam said dismissively.

River was surprised at her candor but knew the moment would only get more awkward if she acted like this wasn't true. She smiled and silently chastised herself for harboring an implicit bias, assuming her new boss was a man just because of her name. Sam turned and greeted the other intern with the same firm handshake. Apparently, his name was Travis, but River had already named him "The Suit."

Sam brought the nervous interns back to her office, which felt more like a lair: one glass wall perched over the city and another one monitoring a sea of cubicles. The room was perfectly sound-proof. River could almost hear Sam's stiletto-heels piercing the office carpet as she made her way around her desk. Sam spoke sternly and fast, and didn't pause to make sure they understood what she said. They were ivy-league graduate students. She expected them to catch on.

This was a job, she emphasized. They would be treated like every other employee at The Boston Globe. They were expected to produce the same high-quality work; and at the end of summer, if Sam liked what they produced, they'd secure a permanent position at the Globe. They'd be writing articles for online and print publications, and…

River's phone buzzed in her pocket. Sam stopped talking and stared at her. The Suit looked over, too. River reached into her pocket to stopped the vibration. "Sorry," she apologized.

Sam described the length of articles and time frames for various projects, when River's phone buzzed again.

Her cheeks radiated heat from their darkened color. The only person who would call her repetitively, even when sent to voicemail, was her mom. She knew her mother was traveling at that very moment, and that she'd never interrupt this meeting unless it was important. River couldn't help looking at her phone. She peeked at the screen she'd pulled halfway out of her pocket. It wasn't Loretta, but it was an Oklahoma number she didn't recognize. She pushed the call through to voicemail again and looked up.

Sam was staring at her with pursed lips and small eyes.

"I'm sorry." River squinted a little.

Sam picked up where she left off. She was describing what specific projects she had planned for them, and how they could go about finding primary sources to interview, when River's phone buzzed for a third time. River's eyes shot wide open when Sam slapped her chrome-lined desk and yelled, "Go, answer your damn phone!"

River's heart sank with the realization that she'd blown her first impression. She nodded and stepped out of the office through a floor-to-ceiling glass door. Her stomach tightened as she answered the call.

"Hello?"

"Hello, is this Ms. River Novak?"

"Yes," she said, holding her breath.

"Is your mother's name Loretta D. S. Novak?"

River's heart raced. "Yes," she said, still holding her breath.

"I'm calling from Stillwater Medical Center. Are you in a place you can talk for a moment, ma'am?"

River felt the seventh floor drop out from under her feet, and her heart clenched with sudden pain. "Yes," she said.

"I'm sorry to tell you, ma'am, that your mother was in a head-on collision on Highway 35 this morning, and she's in critical condition."

River grabbed her mouth.

"She's been admitted to the intensive care unit here. Also, I'm very sorry to tell you that the driver of the vehicle, Mr.

Kenneth Kirskowski, was killed on impact. I'm very sorry, ma'am."

River felt like someone had knocked the wind out of her. All the air left her lungs, but she couldn't breathe in.

"Ma'am?... Miss Novak are you there?"

River swayed.

She was already weak from not eating breakfast that morning. She was running on adrenaline and caffeine. Her nervous system was already on high alert from the encounter with Sam. The lack of oxygen dimmed her vision. The world went black.

CHAPTER THREE

It had been a long and quiet drive with a stranger. The Uber driver looked at River every so often through the rear-view mirror, trying to figure out why she wore sunglasses at night. If it weren't for her roommate who was willing, though begrudgingly, to loan her the money for a spontaneous flight, she wouldn't have made it to Oklahoma so quickly. Unlike Massachusetts, Oklahoma was strikingly flat and plain, the sky being the most dramatic part of the landscape, stretching itself out across the flat expanse of earth where the grass grows tall and brown. Most days, the sky put on a show at dawn and dusk, splashing colors over the clouds like a messy artist. But the Oklahoma sky came to a dramatic crescendo on days when a tunneling cloud touched the earth and indiscriminately twisted through towns and farmlands, displacing entire communities of people. But, other than a sometimes-angry sky, Stillwater was a typical small town in America. In fact, it was downright cliché. American flags and pick-up trucks lined the streets. Everyone knowing everything about everyone. And if you hadn't found Jesus yet then you were the one who was hiding!

She leaned against the window and let the tears roll down her cheeks from underneath her sunglasses. The driver turned onto the flat, straight expanse of highway 35 and River couldn't help imagining where her mother's life had almost come to an end and where Kenneth's life did end.

The sprinkling of lights in the distance made Stillwater look like the tiniest dot on the map. Stillwater had been River's entire world as a child. It seemed big to her then. But the biggest thing about this town was Oklahoma State University, which made up more than half of the city's population with its 25,000 students. The town seemed to empty each summer when most students returned home to their families. Just like the other locals, River enjoyed Stillwater more during the summer, precisely because the students were gone.

As they entered the edge of town, they drove past Penny Stone's house. A chill crawled up River's back. The scariest moment of her life happened in that part of town. River was barely a sophomore in high school when it happened. Penny's parents had left town that weekend, and she invited a bunch of kids over for a party. Most of them were high school girls, but she also invited some college boys because they promised to bring alcohol. It was a typical teenage party: kids were drinking and the music was loud. The college boys were trying to get laid, but they would take what they could get from a high school girl. However, there was one bad seed who took what he wanted from Penny. At some point, Penny had gone missing. By the time River and her friend Jules went looking for her, it was too late. They found her in the corner of an upstairs bedroom sobbing, crouched in the fetal position. When she looked up, Penny's bloodied face was darker red than her curly hair that framed it. River vividly remembered Penny smearing blood across her cheek when she wiped her nose with her arm. River sometimes still flashed back to that traumatic night, wondering whether there was anything she could have done to stop it. Or, whether this could have happened to her just as easily.

Penny got pregnant that night. It was then that River decided to get on birth control and she never again attend another high school party. She became unrelentingly focused on her studies at age sixteen.

BREATHING IN WATER

CHAPTER FOUR

An image of Penny's bloody face still lingered in River's mind when the angular brick building came into focus. The Uber driver was left counting a wad of cash as River ran through the sliding glass doors of the emergency unit. She surprised an older woman by the indiscriminate way she tossed her luggage near a chair in the lobby. Navigating Stillwater Medical Center was second nature for her. The distinct smell of bleach and decay reminded her of the many evenings she'd spent in grade school finishing homework in the lobby during those months leading up to the passing of both of her grandparents. She ran past the check-in station and down the hall to the ICU, where she was lucky enough to get through the door before it closed behind a nurse who was entering. There it was, Loretta's name on door 103. She had no way of knowing what to expect when she saw her mom, but what she'd imagined was downright elementary compared to what she did see lying in that hospital bed. Loretta's bandaged head was watermelon-sized, and the part of her face that was visible could have been the inside of a melon. It took River a second to recognize that the slits on her mother's face were her eyes, swollen shut. The plastic tubes sticking out from her bandaged body looked like the legs of a sea-creature attached to a mummy. What stood out most was something that wasn't there at all: Loretta's right arm.

The edges of River's vision darkened and the wall proved to be a useless support. Stumbling out of the room to the nearby bathroom, she dropped to her knees and projectile vomited. Nurses argued nearby, trying to decide who failed to warn her before letting her into Loretta's room. Jules Thompson's voice rose above the others. Jules rushed in and held River's short hair away from her cheeks while she emptied what remained in her stomach onto the bathroom floor.

"Where is she," River cried. "Where's my mama? That's not my mama!"

"That is your mama, darlin'. That's your mama. You can do this, River."

"I can't! I can't do this!" she sobbed.

"Yes, you can. You're stronger than you know. And your mama needs you right now."

River slumped down the wall outside of the bathroom, sobbing as if she were the only one in the ICU. Eventually, her cry became a hitched breath and she stood as the doctor approached. Jules took her hands while the doctor explained Loretta's condition.

"Your mother has sustained a number of life-threatening injuries, including a diffuse axonal injury, the tearing of brain fiber. Her liver has a laceration, which we've operated on. We did exploratory surgery to identify vessels needing repair and we've done those, so internal bleeding seems to be under control. But we're watching for any signs of continued bleeding that might indicate she needs further surgery."

River muffled her cry enough to hear what the doctor was saying.

"I suspect your mother has multiple broken bones. We're about to do x-rays to identify and repair those. You may have noticed that we've removed her right arm."

River grabbed her mouth, not sure whether noise or vomit would come out. Jules held her tightly, as if to keep her upright.

The doctor hesitated before continuing. "That arm posed an immediate risk because of uncontrolled bleeding, which is why we had to remove it without your consent. She's been through high-risk surgeries and given her condition she's lucky to have survived them. She's in a comatose state..."

A strange calm settled over River and everything around her took on a dream-like state; nothing looked real. She questioned whether the doctor was really standing in front of her and whether or not her small frame really did stand encompassed by the hospital walls. Even though she was looking the doctor in his eyes, she didn't hear him say,

"Ms. Novak, we'll do everything we can for your mother, but you should know, I don't expect her to survive the next 48 hours. But even if she does survive and regain consciousness, I expect she'll have permanent brain damage and physical impairment."

River couldn't recall the hours that passed immediately after this conversation. When she came back to herself, she was sitting in her mother's hospital room, unsure how she got there. Her only company was the hissing machinery connected to Loretta's body. When River realized that the liquid moving through a tube she was looking at was the fluid draining from her mother's head, her eyes darted away. She was determined not to leave that room until her mother's condition had stabilized. Thanks to Jules' advocacy, the ICU manager agreed to this, although against his better judgment. He was moved to learn that Loretta was River's only family.

She spent an uncomfortable night on an inhospitable cot next to her mother's bed. The only defense she had from the chill of a ceiling vent was a thin, coarse blanket. But, even if this makeshift bed were welcoming, she wouldn't have been able to sleep to the harsh soundtrack of nurses and machinery monitoring her mother's vitals.

CHAPTER FIVE

Like all small towns, this one had a few impetuous alcoholics who frequented dive bars on the outskirts of town. Carl Stenton was Stillwater's most infamous, and that night was not unlike others for him. He stumbled home from the bar in a drunken stupor and passed out within minutes of dropping into his worn-out recliner. One strap of his overalls dropped over his shoulder along with his head as he slumped to one side. His wife noticed this happening more frequently. Fifty-one years of life had provided him with more than his fair share of suffering. Like everyone else, he had moments of grace that provided him with enough courage to choose forgiveness and walk the path of healing. But he didn't. He chose the bitter pill of resentment and washed it down with alcohol. His feet wore a path on the road to destruction. He'd been treading this path for over thirty years and he had almost arrived.

His third-generation family farm would certainly soon fail, and he was entirely to blame. He drank most of the family profit away; they no longer had the resources to fix the aging tools needed to keep the farm going. And no one would bail him out this time. After acknowledging the ruined state of his farm and his life, he'd lost the will to live.

He wouldn't have admitted this to anyone, but it cut him to his core when his youngest daughter, his favorite, ran away at fifteen, leaving him an empty nest and a note that said, "Burn in hell, dad." Seared in the back of his mind by his fundamentalist upbringing, the question still haunted him, *Will I burn in hell?* When he was young, he believed in God, Satan, heaven, hell and everything else they preached at church. But that changed at age fourteen when a neighbor raped him. His troubled teens led him to the only thing that effectively numbed his emotional pain and confusion — alcohol. A bitter root deepened in Carl as he grew into a man. As time passed, the root developed thorny branches that agitated him from the inside. It grew so big it filled him entirely, wearing him like a glove. By the time his kids were born he could no longer contain these thistles. They extended far beyond his crawling skin, entangling everyone around him. The alcohol never left his right hand and he managed to create a hell of his own right here on earth. All three of his kids ran away from home before they were adults. And the only love he got from his wife was a façade. He craved her love. But he had beaten it out of her a long time ago. Yet he still believed she owed him her love and devotion, as his wife. Since life was no longer worth living, he had planned on killing himself once he got the courage to do it. He'd heard people say, *you can't take your possessions with you when you die,* but he disagreed. He could take Linn. And he planned on it. He'd be damned if he let her go on living, free from his watchful eye.

The dimly lit room was haunted by the sound of Carl snoring on his blue-felt recliner. His wife decided it was safe to gently lift his wallet off the side table and pull out the three-dollar bills inside. Linn's success invigorated and terrified her. She carried the worn-out bills into the bathroom and pulled out a tampon box out from underneath the sink. She began rolling up the bills but a shaky elbow knocked over a shampoo bottle which made a blunt noise. Beads of sweat formed on her forehead as she swung her head over one shoulder. Ears alert, listening, she took a deep breath but didn't quite exhale. Her heart kept up its frantic pace even though she still heard Carl's guttural sounds coming from the other room. He had blackened her eye and torn the house apart earlier that week looking for the slow leak of cash he'd rightly accused her of taking. Not even the pictures hanging on the wall escaped his searching hands. But Linn judged correctly when she decided he wouldn't look in the tampon box. She pulled one of the unused applicators out and replaced the tampon inside with the rolled-up bills. A mixture of excitement and fear rushed through her veins when she realized she'd almost saved enough money to execute the plan she'd made months ago.

BREATHING IN WATER

CHAPTER SIX

Jules came in to work the next morning to find River right where she left her the night before, lying awake on the cot next to her mom. "When was the last time you ate somethin', Sweetie?"

River shrugged, "Couple days, I guess."

"I'm gettin' you some food. You need to eat."

"I can't eat," she quickly replied.

"River, I'm a nurse. You're spending a lot of energy even though you don't realize it. You need to eat somethin'."

River lay staring ahead.

"Would you drink a protein shake if I brought you one?"

She shrugged.

When Jules left the room headed for the cafeteria, River realized Jules was becoming like her mother, Mrs. Thompson, who took great pleasure in filling the stomachs of the people around her. River had always appreciated this about Mrs. Thompson actually, since she spent summers with the Thompsons while Loretta worked full time. At the Thompson house, something delicious was always coming out of the oven: cinnamon rolls, breads or a casserole of some sort. It was a stark contrast to River's house. When Loretta took River home in the evenings they drove up to a dark and drafty farmhouse. They would turn up the heat and microwave frozen dinners before settling on the couch to watch Loretta's favorite sitcoms in syndication. River's home was different than the Thompson's, but it was home.

River often thought about the Thompsons when she recalled her childhood. She would join them at Broken Bow Lake each summer where they owned a large cabin. They vacationed with a couple families from their church every year. River and her mom weren't church-goers, but Loretta trusted the Thompsons to keep her daughter out of trouble on those long summer days while she ran her business.

River could still smell the attic room that her and Jules had bunked in for weeks at a time. After that top-story room had baked in the summer sun all afternoon it had a warm woody smell that lingered through the night. Jules' brother and some other kids ran around the lake those summer days as well. River remembered being annoyed by one boy named Andy who had a crush on her, he was always trying to get her attention. One day Andy got physical with River, trying to give her a kiss. Jules' older brother Luke happened to see this and he could tell that River didn't welcome Andy's attention. Before River even knew that Luke was watching, he had shoved Andy up against the cabin and told him that, if he ever touched River again, he would make a new window with Andy's head. Having no dad or brothers, River had no reference for this kind of behavior; in fact, the rules of male engagement were totally foreign to her. But she was happy to be rid of Andy. He never bothered her again. That was the first time River ever really noticed Jules' brother Luke. And he seemed to notice her as well, even though he had a girlfriend. One evening at the campfire, River noticed Luke staring at her newly developed breasts. When he realized River had noticed his stare, his eyes darted away awkwardly. Later, he tried to explain by telling River that she looked like Pocahontas at the campfire, with her dark hair draping over shoulders. She didn't buy his cover story because it was obvious to her that he was looking at her breasts. But she found his explanation amusing.

Jules walked into the hospital room with a strawberry shake in her hand, dripping with condensation. The cold drink soothed River's churning stomach. She was thankful to have kept it down.

Over the next couple of days, her appetite picked up pace at the same speed that her mother's internal swelling went down. Miraculously, Loretta stabilized rather quickly, providing River with desperately needed hope. On the morning of the fourth day, the hospital staff told her that she could no longer stay in the ICU, and she didn't argue because she recognized her desperate need of a shower.

Jules drove River home when her shift ended that evening. The smell of iron-rich dirt moved through the open window as they drove down Loretta's long, dirt driveway, welcomed her home. They carried her luggage up the planked steps and into the drafty house. The creaking wood beneath her feet made her think of the mama she'd known before the accident. When River visited home from Boston Loretta would always meet her at the door, throw her arms around her, kiss her forehead and call her "Baby Doll." A terrifying thought flashed through River's mind: she might never see that mother again. The roof seemed to float upward right off the house, and an endless expanse of sky took its place above her.

The cherry-wood staircase climbing up the wall didn't need elaborate woodwork to feel important. Its frame reflected the simplicity of life on a farm that generations past had appreciated for its utility, not its frivolity. But the open living space on the left was an invitation into the new century, thanks to Loretta's thoughtful renovation. She removed the wall that separated the living space from the real center of activity, the kitchen. A simple couch turned its back to the large kitchen island, which was a slab of burl wood with a tub-style sink nestled in the middle. The dining area joined the open space with an oversized bay window and a commanding solid-beam table. Above a wood stove framed by tall windows was an eight-point set of antlers that demanded attention. Jules carried in a box of Loretta's possessions that had been collected at the crash site.

After Jules left, River dragged her luggage into her childhood bedroom. The wood paneled walls would have made the space much darker if it had not been for the morning and afternoon sun that poured in through the south and east-facing windows. The open horizon spoke to her about endless potential for rejuvenation. She followed the pink hues shooting through the tall glass. But it was as if the sun sensed her grief. It quickly changed from pink to darker shades of gray with every second that passed. A gray wall of clouds formed in the distant sky and the wind picked up pace. The Oklahoma sky could turn on a dime and you never knew when it would form a funnel and turn through town. But River had learned to read its mood. She decided it was bluffing.

The overgrown prairie grass that lined the edge of the detached garage waved, catching her attention, reminding her that she needed to find transportation. Her mom's double-cab truck sat out front like it owned the place, but she really didn't want to drive that mammoth around town. The lopsided garage door creaked open, revealing the soft-top Jeep she'd driven around in high school. She kicked a chunk of dried mud off one of the rims and ran her hand over the dust on a plastic window. The summer air had warmed enough to keep the top down for the next few months, so she unzipped the windows, waving away the upset dust from her face. She stowed the windows and secured the canvas around the base of the roll bars.

That first night at the farmhouse her mind kept moving between images of her two mothers; the healthy, vibrant mother, and the broken, comatose one. River laid awake for hours trying to ignore the tangible emptiness that took Loretta's place in that house, but eventually, jarring sobs exhausted her into a deep sleep.

The next morning her puffy eyes adjusted to the invading sunlight that warmed her legs beneath the diamond-patterned quilt. The familiarity of home was a brief comfort, until an image of her mummy-wrapped mom appeared. She distracted herself by considering what needed to be done that day besides staying by her mother's side. That's when a wave of panic washed over her, like the fright she felt when coming back to school after being ill to find the class taking a test she hadn't studied for.

"The store!" she said aloud. Loretta had a business to run. And she wasn't running it.

CHAPTER SEVEN

River no longer felt the same kind of helplessness now that she had purpose. The Land & Cattle Co. was located centrally on Main Street, squeezed into a row of single-façade western-style buildings. The colorful storefronts ran along both sides of the street, featuring bars and restaurants, a drugstore, barber shop, and some boutiques. As she drove down Stillwater's main drag, she could see her younger self traipsing the sidewalk, weighed down by an over-sized backpack and a self-inflicted requirement to achieve Harvard entry.

She slid her Jeep into a diagonal slot out front of the store. It was strange to see it closed on a weekend, the red-lettered sign hanging crooked on the other side of the door. After an old couple passed by, she saw the handwritten note taped to the window explaining that the store would have reduced hours throughout the summer due to Loretta's accident. River was glad to remember the trick to opening the old glass door with the copper key she had found in the box of her mother's possessions from the crash. Leaning on the door produced a familiar bell-ring and the smell of earth invited her in like an old friend. Bags of animal feed and soil colonized the broad aisles directly ahead. Not even a few deep breaths of familiar air could fill the tangible void of being in the store without her mom. For the past fourteen years, Loretta had been like the metal pillars holding up the vaulted ceiling; an essential and permanent fixture of that place. If the store weren't devoid of customers, she would have felt self-conscious trying to figure out how to operate the register. She'd watched her mom handle the vintage machine many times, so she was confident in her ability to do it herself but hoped she wouldn't make a financial mess for her mother to fix.

That Monday morning River got to the store before it opened so she would feel prepared before the staff came in. There were only two names on the schedule: Skippy and Luke. She wondered who Luke was. The only Luke she knew was Jules' brother. But she'd heard about Skippy. Loretta had told River about the lanky young man who couldn't lift a single bag of animal feed, let alone two. But Loretta really liked his "vibe" so she hired him anyway.

The bell on the door rang as Skippy walked in. River introduced herself to the curly-haired man with a boyish face and happy demeanor. River was surprised when at the sound of the bell Jules' brother walked in. He still dressed like the country boy she remembered: faded jeans, boots and a T-shirt. But he was a far cry from the kid she remembered. His shoulders, neck and jaw had doubled in size. This was a full-grown man built strong from years of manual labor, and he towered over her at 6'2". Some of his light brown hair hit one eyebrow when he nodded and said, "Miss River Novak."

"Luke Thompson. It's been a long time."

"Yes, it has. I'm sorry about your mama. They aren't lettin' visitors in. How's Ms. Loretta doin'?"

Her stoicism failed; emotion threatened to take charge. "Not good. Still in critical condition in the ICU." Her lips quivered.

He meant to keep her emotions at bay, but what he said came out with little conviction, "She'll pull through. She's a tough lady."

River nodded with watery eyes, trying to keep them from dripping. She changed the subject. "Is this your name on the schedule?"

He walked around the counter. "Yes, ma'am. Your mama hired me to manage the store when Clara left."

"Where's Chris?" Her eyes scanned the store for the stocky woman who had worked at the store since River could remember.

He used a key to open the file cabinet below the register, "She retired."

"Retired? Who replaced her?"

"Yours truly. Guess your mama figured I got the muscle for Chris' job 'n the schoolin' for Clara's. Two-fer." He thumbed through the files as River scanned his arms and shoulders. It was clear he could do the muscle work, but she wondered if he could manage the paperwork too.

"Well, I've never helped my mama with the business, so I have a learning curve."

He couldn't help noticing that learning wasn't her only curve. River had fully bloomed since he last saw her, and her short hair tapped her neck when she moved. "Only been here a couple months myself," he watched her for the impact of discovering that he hadn't been there long either. "But I know some things. Looks like we'll be takin' this curve together."

River was glad Luke knew something about running the store, but was intimidated by the fact that he knew more about it than she did. In her opinion, Loretta's store depended too much on one man. One finger tapped after the other on the wooden counter, "Well, we'll see if I can put that one business class to use."

"That's right. You've been hidin' at Harvard," he said.

"Hiding?"

"Well, no one could find you 'round these parts."

She let out a little laugh. "Well, here I am. In Stillwater, Oklahoma." She was tempted to think about where she should be, The Boston Globe, but she couldn't bear it so she pushed the thought from her mind and shifted the focus away from her. "So, how's Ellie doing?"

"Beats me!"

That's when she noticed his wedding ring was missing.

Luke folded his arms across his chest and leaned on the counter, "I see the gossip gang hasn't gotten to ya yet. They'll tell ya all about it, no doubt."

"Sorry."

"Don't be," he said contentedly. "I'm lookin' up."

She thought it was strange that he said 'I'm looking up' instead of 'things are looking up,' but she nodded along.

Luke had been with Ellie since they were seventeen, almost eight years, until she left him five months ago. He could still feel the cold night air on his skin when they made love for the first time out by the lake.

Luke looked at the door with the ring of the bell. "Hal Henkins!" he said.

"Howdy! Is that your clunker out front?" Hal's shirt barely covered his large belly.

"My truck's in the shop," Luke answered.

"I got that ol' Ford sittin' 'round. Purrs like a kitten with 200,000 miles. You can borrow 'er anytime your Chevy dies on ya."

"Hal, you know I'd rather push a Chevy than drive a Ford."

Hal laughed, "I'd like to see ya do that, son. Teach ya' to buy a Ford next time your Chevy dies on ya."

Luke shook his head in playful disgust.

River had almost forgotten she came from a town where men sized each other up by the type of truck they drove and how many guns sat in its window rack. Her stomach sank when she remembered why she was back in town—her mama. She longed for the days when her greatest worries were exams and a burn from a steaming hot Americano.

As they were closing up shop that afternoon, Luke could see that River was out of her element. He sniffed. "So, how's the big-city treatin' ya?"

"Um, I would have said 'great' a week ago, but I got mugged the other day, like, just before I got to town."

"Damn! You alright?" he looked her up and down, as if he might find injuries.

"Yeah. The bastard just grabbed my purse and ran," River was glad this subject came up because she needed to ask Luke an awkward question. She hesitated, "Yeah, so, my bank in Boston won't send my new bank card to Oklahoma because I reported it stolen. They're sending it to my Boston address, so my roommate has to forward it to me." She rubbed the back of her neck and broke eye contact, "Actually, I'm wondering if you can sign company checks." She looked up again.

"Sure can."

"Well, I'm wondering if I could get a pay advance, just until my bank card gets here."

Luke had already pulled the checkbook out and flipped it open. "Course you can."

They agreed on an amount. River had never been so embarrassed in her life—her cheeks matched her red shirt. She had planned for every scenario in life, except for getting mugged and having her mother mortally wounded in the same twenty-four-hour period. That scenario had escaped her imagination.

As Luke tore the check from the book, he saw River's phone light up with a man's face. She grabbed the phone and stared at it like it was a venomous snake. He watched her consider whether or not to answer it. She finally did, on what must have been the final ring.

"Hi." Her teeth clenched together; her jaw flinched.

"Hey, Riv! How are ya?"

Brian was acting like his call was no big deal. She couldn't believe his flippancy. How did he think she was doing? Bitterness marked her words as they left her mouth, "I've been better."

He got to the point. "Hey, I was wondering if you've seen my stonewashed Ralph Lauren jeans? You know, the black ones with the knee-zippers?"

She knew which jeans he meant: the ones she'd found lying in a heap on her bedroom floor. He'd thrown them off the night they had slept together for the last time. He'd left for the gym the next morning in his shorts. Yes, she'd seen those jeans. She'd cut them up into a million pieces and then tossed them into the trash along with their relationship. River raised her voice, "Are you fucking kidding me?"

"Well, your place is the last place I ..."

CLICK. She huffed a breath in disbelief as she hung up on him. *What the hell was I thinking, answering the phone?* she asked herself. She answered her own question, she'd just needed some closure. *Well... that'll do it!*

"Who was that?" Luke asked.

"Nobody!" she grunted.

Luke watched as she changed Brian's contact name to "Nobody."

He nodded and thought, *no one escapes life's sucker punch.*

CHAPTER EIGHT

The evening sun streamed through the store window, warming her back as she closed out the register for the day. A buzz from her back pocket let her know that a text had come in, a message from Jules saying some high school friends wanted to show their support by coming by her place that evening. She wouldn't miss an evening of visiting her mother, so she told them to swing by later that night.

After grabbing take-out, River made her way to the ICU where the sterile aroma of latex gloves and disinfectant zapped a portion of her remaining energy. She was glad the nurse had finished changing Loretta's catheter so she could maintain her appetite for the pulled-pork sandwich she'd brought with her. The doctor told her that Loretta was recovering well from surgery and that her physical strength had increased over the past few days. He explained it was unlikely her mother could hear her talking, but River thought it was worth doing, just in case. She held out hope that Loretta could be prompted back into consciousness by hearing her daughter's voice, though she was fairly certain there was no science supporting this hope.

"I'm gonna figure out how to run your store, Mama." River took a big bite of her sandwich and chewed through the words, "I have no idea what I'm doing. But, apparently Luke does. Mama, that kid got tall! Well, he's not a kid, I guess. None of us are." She told her mom all about the customers who had stopped in that day and wished her good health and prayers. After finishing her food, she put a hand on Loretta's leg and told her she'd be back the next day.

On the way to her Jeep her empty fridge seemed to nag at her from a distance, but she didn't have time to grocery shop before her friends came by. She figured she could stop by the Get 'n Gallup corner store to grab something for breakfast. After a rushed search for a carton of eggs she turned around and nearly ran into a man. When she tried stepping around his large frame, he moved slightly in front of her, forcing her to stop, so she looked up. It was Quinn Schmidt. He and Luke had made it to the top of the food chain in high school when they'd won the state wrestling championships two years in a row. It appeared to her that they were still the biggest guys in Stillwater. Quinn's finely sculpted body had only perfected itself over time, and his dark hair had the kind of texture that made women want to run their hands through it. He was quite aware of his effect on women, and he usually got what he wanted from them. *Figures*, she thought, as she stood eye-level to his chest. He still wore t-shirts that emphasized his biceps.

"Scuze, me Darlin'." He stood looking down at her, immovable like a wall. "You grew up 'round here, right?"

Her voice lacked enthusiasm because she didn't like how he forced the conversation, "Yeah, I was two years behind you in high school."

The blank look on his face confirmed what she suspected: he didn't remember her name, only her face.

"I'm River," she finally said.

"That's right. River," he said while looking her up and down. He noticed that her hair was short just like her stature. She wasn't his type, but she was sexy in her own way, and the fact that she seemed nonplussed by him piqued his interest. "It's good to see you again," he said, with a look in his eyes that made most women swoon.

She stepped around him and threw, "You too," over her shoulder. His thick eyebrows went up as he turned to watch her walk away. He wasn't used to being brushed off like that, but now the chase was on. He could use a challenge, and he knew he'd see her around town.

She thought about Quinn on the drive home and reasoned that unless he had radically changed since high school, she wouldn't date him if he were the last man in town. Being one of the larger guys at school was an asset to him and a liability to others. He threw every ounce of his weight around. Both years that they attended high school together she watched him bully the few black kids that attended Stillwater High. Almost every day she saw him trip James, or slap Darin upside the head and call him 'dumbass.' She could only imagine what he did to them when she wasn't looking.

When River got home, she barely had time to change her clothes and brush her teeth before Sarah and Holly knocked on the front door. She glanced at herself in the mirror by the door, smoothing down her hair and shirt before opening it. Sarah and Holly rushed in with hugs and well wishes for her mama. River hadn't seen them for a couple of years, and even then, only briefly at Stillwater's annual Christmas On Main Street event. Holly and Sarah had never lived outside of Stillwater, and in this moment, River was struck, almost like an outsider, by how differently country girls put themselves together than did city women. She had gotten used to the more sleek, tailored look of city dwellers. Sarah's natural beauty couldn't be covered by the Wranglers and tennis shoes she wore or her boyfriend's camouflage cap over her brown hair, ponytail and all. Holly's clothing reflected her animated personality; sequined jean pockets, a bright floral shirt, and a familiar frizz in her blond hair that refused to relax with time.   They'd brought beer and fudge, which she invited them to set on the island.

"Chocolate and beer make the best of friends," Holly said.

River chuckled and asked, "Where's Jules?"

"She's comin'," said Sarah, "She's puttin' Drew to bed. Can you believe that boy is already two? I feel like he was a ball-in-a-belly just yesterday."

Sarah pulled the fudge toward her and took a chunk, "Yeah, when Jules said she was pregnant we wondered if we'd ever see her again. But she's goin' out now that she ain't breastfeedin' no more."

Holly grabbed the bottle opener River had placed on the wood slab, popped the tops off three beers and didn't waste any time spreading the local gossip. "Oh, River! Did you hear 'bout Jules' brother?" Holly asked with intrigue in her voice.

"No. But I noticed that he wasn't wearing his wedding ring at the store today." River tipped back her beer.

"Oh, yeah! He's working for your mama..." Holly stopped suddenly. She didn't know how to talk about River's mom. "Well, Ellie was cheatin' on him for a good year 'n Luke ended up catchin' her red-handed with Jeremy!" Holly looked amused.

River's eyes opened wider.

Sarah cut in, "Luke broke his nose before he could get out of the house. He managed to grab his pants on the way out." Both women were laughing so hard Sarah had a hard time finishing her sentence. "But he left his boots behind."

River gave a courtesy chuckle, but she felt really bad for Luke. That sounded like a nightmare!

When their laughter died down, Holly added, "and Luke tried to kill himself a couple months later."

"He did not try killin' himself," Sarah corrected.

"Then why'd Kev take all his guns and store 'em at his house?"

"He just said somethin' that…"

"ANYWAY!" Holly interrupted.

Sarah took a swig of her beer as a placeholder for the sentence that was cut short.

Holly continued, "Well, Luke drank 'imself silly for months and slept around with a bunch of college chicks. He was a fuckin' wreck!"

Sarah jumped in, "And it's weird. Like overnight, he was back to normal. Like Ellie never left or somethin'."

"I figured he met someone, but doesn't look that way." Holly added before putting a piece of fudge in her mouth.

"So, where'd Ellie go?" River asked.

"She ran off with Jeremy. He got a good job in Arkansas, or somethin'. OH! And also," Holly's voice shifted to sound compassionate, "a year before Ellie started cheatin' she miscarried Luke's baby girl." Her voice got quieter, "She gave birth to a stillborn like a few weeks before the due date."

Sarah nodded with pity on her face.

River swallowed.

"Luke had already built her a crib 'n everything."

Holly practically whispered, "They even had a funeral."

River's mouth dropped slightly open and her face lost a bit of color. *What a living hell*, she thought. To look Luke in the eyes after knowing this much about his personal tragedies would feel awkward, she feared.

There was a knock on the door and Jules walked in. *Thank God!* River thought, taking a deep breath. They couldn't talk about Luke now that his sister was there. Jules playfully tossed some chips on the island even though she could feel the sober, hushed atmosphere. It was obvious to her they were talking about Luke, but that was to be expected, so she customarily played it off. Holly quickly threw out a new subject, and the three of them gave River the rest of the town's gossip as they tipped back one beer after another. It was nice to think about other people's problems and forget about her own, even for a moment. But eventually she would have to give them what they came for, and the beer certainly assisted her in providing them with information about how she was handling Loretta's accident. Her balance was off by the time she popped open the third beer and clinked bottle necks with them saying, "To beer!"

"To beer!" they cheered.

CHAPTER NINE

The unusual amount of beer she'd indulged in the night before caused an unrelenting throb in her temples. Accomplishing ordinary tasks seemed impossible. She covered her eyes with the corner of her blanket, willing her empty fridge to fill itself.

A familiar sound of the antique door-knock hitting weathered wood startled her. She flung herself out of bed and hissed when the throb in her temples became a pounding. There was no need to get dressed. She hadn't undressed before falling into bed the night before. She looked at herself in the mirror and quickly wiped the sleep from her eyes while considering who would be stopping by on a Saturday morning. Jules maybe?

The opening front door revealed a handful of vaguely recognizable older ladies who were members of the Stillwater Chapel. As a youth, River didn't attend church regularly but she showed up occasionally with the Thompson family after a Saturday night sleepover. The ladies carried armfuls of food containers and bags. She welcomed them in such a way as not to reveal that she still felt tipsy and that she had crawled out of bed just for them.

Most of the women seemed slightly familiar to River, but Mrs. Miller was impossible to forget. She was a cheerful woman who had dominated every conversation she'd ever engaged in. Her chubby arms carried an impressive number of containers which she stacked onto the kitchen island. The other ladies followed suit, unloading their own containers of food.

Mrs. Miller began explaining their strange presence in her most motherly-sounding voice, "When we heard about what happened to your precious li'l mama we just had to do somethin'. We Monday-night-bible-study ladies put our bibles down and picked up our aprons. We whipped up some meals for ya', darlin'! No need for you to be cookin' right now."

Mrs. Miller's conversations always devolved into church politics disguised by the sanctimony of true concern, naturally. The casserole she was holding reminded Mrs. Miller of the last potluck she'd attended where she'd learned it was Pastor Jackson that leveraged his influence to move the decades-long Monday night bible-study to Tuesday nights. River wasn't sure where the conversation was going or if she wanted to follow along but she was happy she wouldn't have to participate in it, given Mrs. Miller's unceasing loquaciousness. At some point during the one-sided conversation, two of the ladies opened River's fridge to find a lonely carton of eggs. They exchanged knowing glances as they filled the vacuous space with containers.

Eventually Mrs. Miller remembered why she was talking to River and then explained the contents of each container and how to prepare them. It certainly wasn't the jolly woman's speech, but the warmth emanating from her soul forced River to stifle back tears. The fact that so many folks around town were supporting her during this awful tragedy reminded her of the benefits of small-town life. It was all River could do to keep the tears from falling as she expressed her heartfelt gratitude for their act of kindness. The ball in her throat kept tightening until she closed the door behind them and let the tears fall freely. She couldn't think of another moment in her life that near-strangers took so much time to consider what she might need. She pictured the ladies strategizing meals and then cooking up a storm for many hours, hours that translated into time River could sit by her mother's side. It struck her that city-life lacked the same kind of dutiful watchfulness or social obligation to minister to a neighbor's need.

She hoped the drive to the hospital provided enough time for the puffed flesh around her eyes to recede. Walking into her mother's room always made her feel powerless and small, like an infant who can't even lift its own head. There was nothing she could do to help her mother heal. She couldn't even figure out where her consciousness had gone, let alone how to bring it back. All she could do was be present. And so, she was.

It was both comforting and disconcerting to see that some of the bandages had been removed from Loretta's face, revealing a long row of stitches. River sat curled up with a book for a couple hours before the doctor came in to give her an update. It was a relief to hear him say that Loretta's body showed signs of recovering.

The next morning, she decided to attend church as an expression of gratitude to the ladies who had filled her freezer and her soul. The Stillwater Chapel sat in the heart of town, just a couple blocks from Main Street. Its brick and mortar exterior, bright white door and steepled cross harkened back to a simpler time before people questioned whether God exists. The congregation was a sea of color in the chapel's plain interior. River wondered if these folks ever question whether God really does exist. The rows of stained-glass windows running along the sides of the church certainly inspired a person to hope he did.

The few times she'd attended church as a youth, she felt awkward during the singing part. So, she purposefully arrived twenty minutes late to take a seat in the back before the preaching began. To her surprise, she saw Thelma Woodson—one of the few black folks who attended. Thelma was in her 80s, and River was pretty sure she wore a wig because her hair always looked exactly the same. When Thelma saw River, she patted the open seat, signaling her to sit.

"Hello, Ms. Thelma," she whispered.

As a youth, Thelma told River to call her by her first name, but Loretta would have none of that. She required River to use titles out of respect, so River called her Ms. Thelma.

"Bless your little soul, baby, I'm prayin' for your mama," Thelma said in a hushed voice.

"Thank you." River whispered. She was sincerely grateful to have Thelma's prayer going up for her mama. She figured if God did exist, he'd listen to her. Thelma had endured more than a person should have to and still lived the life of a saint. River always felt guilty when she saw her. Stillwater's darkest moment in recent history happened right before River was born—the murder of Ms. Thelma's son. At the tender age of 19, he was found with a note pinned to his chest with a hunting knife. The blood-soaked note had one word on it and it started with an "N." Ms. Thelma confounded River in two ways. She could never understand why Thelma still talked to white people after such a personal and horrific event. And, what's more, how Thelma could always keep that beautiful smile on her face. She couldn't comprehend how either could be so, but she knew one thing. She admired that woman's strength.

As the congregation began the final song, Thelma held the hymnal in front of River so she could sing along. River mouthed the words. She enjoyed listening to the vibrating bass of the men's voices as they solely sang the last line of every stanza.

> I've got peace like a river,
> I've got peace like a river,
> I've got peace like a river, in my soul.
> (men) In my soul.

> I've got joy like a fountain,
> I've got joy like a fountain,
> I've got joy like a fountain, in my soul.
> (men) In my soul.

> I've got love like an ocean,
> I've got love like an ocean,
> I've got love like an ocean in my soul.
> (men) In my soul.

After they finished singing and took their seats, River sat pondering the lyrics of the song, wondering why peace would be compared to a river. Joy like a fountain made sense to her, it comes bubbling up and overflows. And love like an ocean? Oceans are vast, they are deep, and the waves are constant. That made sense, she thought. But, why peace like a river? Rivers change their path after flooding, the water is always moving, and there's nothing constant or stable about them. So, why compare peace to a river? Thelma interrupted her thoughts by holding a bible over her lap and pointing to the scripture they were about to read.

The congregation read aloud together:

> Genesis 2:5-7
> Now no shrub had yet appeared on the earth and no plant had yet sprung up, for the Lord God had not sent rain on the earth and there was no one to work the ground, but streams came up from the earth and watered the whole surface of the ground. Then the Lord God formed a man from the dust of the ground and breathed into his nostrils the breath of life, and the man became a living being.

River couldn't imagine believing that this story was a literal historical event as did the congregants around her. *Such an antiquated idea*, she thought. Yet, she wanted to find a way to appreciate the origin story of the good people she knew sitting in the pews. Classes in psychology and sociology had provided her a framework for analyzing the significance that myths held for people as archetypal narratives. She knew they informed people on deeper cognitive levels.

The preacher said, "What does it mean that man was not a living being until God breathed into him? The Hebrew word used for 'breathed' in this passage is 'rauch' which can also be translated 'wind' or 'spirit'. The scripture says that people were physically alive, like any other animal or plant, but until God breathed life into them, they weren't really alive, not spiritually anyway."

River thought of this as a meta-narrative that addressed two questions science still couldn't answer: What is consciousness, exactly? And, how did humans become aware that they're alive and that they will die? The more she thought about it, the more she could see the beauty in this myth—a single source of consciousness transferring awareness to physical matter. This would make sense to archaic people as the most logical way that humans became aware of being alive. Interestingly, she observed, science hadn't offered a better answer yet, though she was sure that it would, eventually.

She wondered where her mother's consciousness went— her brain was alive but her awareness was nowhere to be found. A terrifying thought slipped to the surface of River's mind. *Mama isn't aware of being alive.* Loretta's consciousness was missing. *If she's not in her body, then where is she?* The existential weight of this question came pressing down on every fiber of her being and she could barely breathe. It took all of her strength to shift her mind to think about something else, anything else.

She endured the remainder of the sermon by mapping out how she would busy herself that afternoon before the hustle and bustle began at the Land and Cattle Co. the next morning. After church, Thelma invited River to come to her house for lunch one Saturday afternoon. They made plans for a few weeks out when River felt more settled.

CHAPTER TEN

It was the second night in a week that Carl lay sleeping in his recliner after warming his favorite barstool at The Corral. Linn didn't know how many more nights this would happen that week. She prayed she wouldn't be around to find out. Her hands shook as she dumped the cash-filled tampon dispensers into her canvas duffle bag, leaving the empty box on the cold linoleum floor. She slid the bag over her shoulder and crept out of the bathroom, down the hall and toward the front room where Carl slept. Her heart pounded behind her ribs as she wiped the sweat off her brow with icy fingers. If Carl woke up she would be a dead woman, and she knew it. The last time she tried leaving him he had beaten her so badly that she had been hospitalized for a week; that was almost 10 years ago.

Before Linn even got home from the hospital Carl had gotten a dog, which he trained to bark loudly whenever she left the house. She'd leave the house on his terms alone. He named the dog "Barkley" to emphasize its purpose and also to mock her prison-like existence. But Barkley had been dead for months now and Carl hadn't bought a new dog, preferring instead to drink his money away. His constant state of drunkenness fleeced his need to contain Linn, but it also fueled his temper. She noticed three months ago that the blows he delivered had gotten more severe and more frequent. She believed what he said when he held a gun to her head not long before--that he was going to kill them both. It wasn't the first time he'd held a gun to her head, but it was different that time. He had threatened to pull the trigger just to see the fear in her eyes. But the mood shifted. He stared off into space, as if he were considering actually doing it. Something needed to change, this time for good.

The morning after the incident she found an excuse to go to the library. She appealed to the tiny shred of hope he retained for their farm's survival, asking him if she could find a book about tractor mechanics so they could try fixing their failed machinery and get the farm up and running again. He hesitantly agreed to it, so she went straight there without detour. He'd convinced her years ago that he had spies all over town reporting back to him her activity.

A skinny librarian directed her to the section she needed, and Linn was relieved to have found a book that might help, if only to avoid questions that could expose the real reason she went there. The woman behind the counter took pity on her by overlooking Linn's library fees, as everyone knew she was Carl's wife. Letting her check out a book was the least they could do to bring some joy to her life.

Linn didn't know which one of the librarians Carl had secured as a spy, so she didn't risk asking the woman behind the counter to help her find the phone number that she needed. Instead, she went to a computer whose screen faced a wall and kept looking up to see who was watching her as she searched. When she secured it, she asked the librarian for one last favor, the use of a phone. The woman pushed her green glasses up the ridge of her nose and brought Linn to the back room for privacy sake, a gesture that only made Linn more paranoid, wondering if they were recording her. But, the longer she spoke to the woman on the other end of the phone the saner she felt, and she knew that this was the most important call she'd ever make. Now that Barkley was dead and she had no kids to care for, leaving Carl was then or never.

He still laid slumped to one side as Linn walked quietly into the room where he slept; she paused when she got to their gun safe which was almost as tall as she. Linn stood mesmerized, picturing herself opening it, loading his favorite rifle, holding the cold barrel against his chest and waiting for his eyes to open before pulling the trigger. There was no way to undo all of the horror and damage he'd inflicted on her and the kids, but she could eliminate the source. It was too risky, she decided. He'd probably wake up to the beeping of the safe keypad. But her eyes remained fixed on the forest green steel. What if she took all of his precious guns with her, just to spite him? She smiled at the thought of it. But the corners of her mouth dropped when she realized this also was too risky. "Stick to the plan, no matter what," the woman on the other end of the phone had told her that day at the library. The woman warned her earnestly to stick to the plan or she would risk losing her chance to escape. Linn only had $108 but it was enough to drive six hours north to a shelter in Iowa, a state to which she had never been, a state where she didn't know a soul, and a state in which Carl would never think to look for her. That night would be the night she left him. The shelter in Iowa was expecting to see her the next morning, after she drove straight through the night from Stillwater, Oklahoma.

A jolting snore from Carl broke Linn's hypnotic stare, compelling her toward the door where she picked up the ring of keys, making sure not one of the small metal pieces touched the other. No ferociously barking dog met her there. She wasn't used to the haunting silence when the door opened. The adrenaline running through her veins made everything feel dream-like as she walked through the door and made it safely into the truck. Her cold, shaking hands made it hard to get the key into the ignition, but when she did, she pulled away from the farmhouse like it was on fire. She looked in the rear-view mirror. There wasn't even a flicker of the porch light, just the old, dark house shrinking further into the distance.

She felt a rush of hope wash through her realizing she might successfully escape him. If she could drive through the night to a place Carl wouldn't expect, maybe she could start a new life, even at the ripe age of 48. She hadn't told a single person about her plan, not even her grown children. And she was pretty sure no one saw her leave town.

Carl wasn't sure what time it was when he woke up. The smell of coffee didn't fill the air like it should have. He called out for Linn, but there was no reply so he made his way to the back window to see if she was collecting eggs. There was no sign of her, inside or outside of the house. When he saw that the truck was gone, he momentarily let himself believe that Linn had only been foolish enough to go to the grocery store without asking him, but deep down he knew. She'd finally done it; she'd left him. His alcohol tinged breath hurled out a stream of curses at God as he sent the front door swinging on its hinges. His large arms hurled the rocking chairs off the porch. Their cell phones had been out of service for months now, so he couldn't call her, as if she'd pick up. But he'd find her. And he'd make her pay for this! He grit his teeth as he pictured what he'd do to her when he finally got his hands on her. One thing was certain, the day he found her would be the day they both died.

He drove around town for three hours with rage in his heart and a loaded handgun in his passenger seat. She wasn't at the grocery store, the library or the corner market.

He slowed as he passed the Land & Cattle Co., but it wasn't open yet, so he kept driving.

CHAPTER ELEVEN

The first week of running her mom's store introduced River to a kind of monotony that threatened to claim her foreseeable future. She spent evenings talking to her unconscious mother, with the almost futile hope that Loretta could be prompted back into consciousness by the sound of her daughter's voice.

She arrived at the store early Friday morning, eager to bring the week to an end. As she eased her old Jeep to the curb out front of the store, she saw Luke opening the door for some farmers who were already waiting for it to open. To River, they were a blur of Carhartts and beer bellies.

As she passed by them, she heard the shortest man say, "So I threw my pants at her 'n said, 'Try those on for size." She threw 'em back 'n said, 'I can't fit in those!' 'n I said 'Damn right you can't! Don't forget who wears the pants 'round here'!" The men roared with laughter. Luke chuckled along with them, until River shot visual daggers at him.

He answered her silent rebuke. "Oh, come on, River. That was funny! 'Specially cuz everyone knows his wife wears the pants."

She rolled her eyes at the old-fashioned notion that pants had something to do with being in charge. "Have I reached the seventh level of Hell yet?"

"Nope." He replied without hesitation.

She pictured her mother's motionless body atrophying in the ICU. The Boston Globe flashed through her mind. She pictured Brian's face.

"How do you know?" Each word hit the air with a punch of resentment.

He leaned on the counter in an ape-like manner and his face hardened. "'Cuz when you get there you won't need to ask."

An image of Luke standing over his infant's grave flashed through her mind and her eyes darted away from him. She grabbed the inventory list off the counter and found an excuse to review it early.

She was looking at but wasn't seeing the stapled stack of sheets in her hands while moving to the isle furthest from men who seemed to be one step up from Neanderthal. A heavy weight settled over her shoulders, and a question she'd successfully forced into her subconscious finally gained traction in her mind. Would she end up like her mom, wasting away in Stillwater Oklahoma, running a farm store? As a child she'd admired her mother's hard work and business-savvy ways. But when she moved to Boston her mother's life seemed small and insignificant despite the fact that Loretta was happy. She was thankful the store's weekend closure turned Fridays into the busiest day of the week. The rush would inevitably make the weekend arrive faster.

Sure enough, the evening sun shot through the windows sooner than she'd expected, but relief didn't come along with it. As she locked the door behind the last customer, she imagined walking into Loretta's farmhouse and being greeted by the spacious void that her mother's boisterous laughter used to fill. A distinct loneliness shot through her veins. She wondered if she would cry before she could leave the store.

Luke pulled her from her thoughts saying he was going out with a bunch of friends that night and wondered if she wanted to come. He added that Jules and her husband would be there, to make sure River knew his intention was not to get her out on a date. She wondered if he could sense her loneliness which made her self-conscious, but, nevertheless, she was grateful to be invited out.

"Actually, I could use a drink. Maybe a couple." She tapered off at the end. Luke offered to drive since it seemed she planned on drinking significantly, but she declined and arranged for Holly to pick her up instead.

She didn't remember the next fifteen minutes of driving home and walking through the door. She was thinking about where they were going. Wild Willy was uncharted territory for her as she would have been too young to enter last time she lived in Stillwater. This saloon's claim to fame was that it was the first place Garth Brooks had ever performed publicly. And Wild Willy made sure no one ever forgot that.

Her mood had lifted somewhat knowing that she had a crowd to disappear into, and alcohol to numb the pain. Only when she was tossing clothing over her shoulder, looking for something to wear did it occurred to her that she hadn't felt the empty greeting that lonely house had promised.

She decided that every shirt and jeans she pulled from her drawer would make her look like a pompous yankee or a city hipster. She would surely stand out. Then it struck her--- she and Loretta wore the same pant-size---so she wiggled the drawer open on her mom's antique dresser, looking for something appropriate. Grabbing a pair of Wranglers, her face twisted in disgust. She chucked them on the floor. But just beneath them were frayed Daisy Duke's. She slid them on and turned around to look at her butt in the mirror. They covered her cheeks entirely, though barely.

Her childhood closet still had some cowboy boots she'd intentionally left behind when she went off to college. She pulled out a pair that had turquoise flourishes embroidered down the sides and slid them up to her calves. Her outfit brought back memories of the last concert she had attended as a teenager. She imagined what Olivia and her roommate in Boston would say if they could see her right then. It made her smile, imagining them laughing at her. Olivia had a loud "BAH, HA, HA!" kind of laugh that got higher pitched the longer it lasted. But Tammi had the classic silent laugh and she covered her mouth the whole time. For a moment, it felt like they were right there with her. "Giddyup!" River said in her best Oklahoma accent.

Holly and Sarah rolled up the dirt drive in a beat-up truck caked in dried mud up past the splash guards. With the slam of the door, the three of them kicked up dust as they tore down the driveway, windows down, Creedence Clearwater Revival up. Even though she felt like she was in high school again, she had no intention of getting drunk, but, good Lord, there were nights she just needed a stiff one and tonight was one of those nights.

They entered the saloon under an illuminated sign shaped like a mustache hanging on red brick. Just inside on the right was the small stage where a local artist played country music, the real stuff—Red Dirt Country. An empty cobblestone fireplace directly ahead featured a 10-point set of antlers above the hearth. They joined Luke, Jules and her husband, Kevin, at the bar. The gang scanned the specialty drink menu and agreed they should try something called "Shots on a Ski" where the bartender lines up a bunch of shot glasses on a snow ski and everyone tips it back, each person shooting their whiskey at the same time. The bartender poured whiskey into shot glasses with striking accuracy, splashing only one drop outside of one glass. They counted down and tipped it back, getting most of the potent liquid in their mouths and laughing as they wiped the rest of it off their faces.

The old friends had only begun to catch up before River ordered another drink. A warm hand resting on her hip surprised her. Expecting to see one of her girlfriends she looked over her shoulder but instead found Quinn. She removed his hand with hers as she turned around on the barstool. He stood closer than she would have invited him to. She crossed her arms in front of her chest unconsciously. She noticed how he put his thumbs in his jean pockets conveniently outlining what she figured was his favorite body part. The man knew how to put himself together, she had to admit, but she had no interest in him. The fruity drink the bartender slid in her direction released a bit of tension in her shoulders so she kept it in hand.

His tall frame towered over her even though she was taller than normal when sitting on a barstool. Quinn made small talk about the band playing on the stage and the best drinks at the bar while she racked her brain for a way to get out of the conversation. He got her attention when he said, "You grew up 'round here. Ever go to rodeos?"

She shook her head and took a big drink wondering where this conversation could possibly be going. *Do I look like a rodeo-chick?* she thought.

He explained the horse-riding sport in some detail, while she scanned the room trying to make eye-contact with someone else. Anyone else.

But he got her attention again when he said, "Not many girls know how to ride a bronc." The tone in his voice and a look in his eyes implied a double meaning. "You ever ride' a bronc, darlin'?" he asked with a certain look in his eyes.

She was 99% sure she was walking into the worst pick-up line ever, but she eventually shook her head anyway.

"I could show ya how," he said as a grin spread across his face.

She spun back toward the bar, relieved to have an excuse to leave the conversation. "Thanks for making this easy."

He chuckled.

"Not interested!" she added, for good measure and slid her empty shot glass toward the bartender who filled it up.

"I'll wear you down."

She tipped back the shot and shivered from the burn that moved down her throat. "Don't bother," she said, keeping her back to him, "Ain't gonna happen." Her Okie accent kicked in along with the whisky and strong resolve. The way Quinn hit on her made it clear that he relied on superior looks to get women in bed and not his technique. She figured he would lack just as much technique once he got them there.

"You sure about that, are ya?" he challenged.

"Yes, I am." She waved the back of her hand at him as if to say, "move along."

Until then, there wasn't a woman in town who had shut him down so fast or so definitively, which only solidified his resolve to pursue her. She was a challenge he didn't plan on giving up. A seed of contempt sprouted inside him and he decided the harder she pushed, the harder he'd pull.

At the other end of the bar River heard Holly suggest that the group go to a bar down the street because it had a dance floor. River cast her vote to go somewhere else. Anywhere else. Outlaws won the vote so the group made their way down the worn-out sidewalk lined with bars and diners. Luke held the door open for the women as they entered the wood-planked building below the western-style sign out front. The gang pulled up to the bar and even though River had started to feel good she ordered another shot of whiskey, then turned to watch the dance floor. Her vision followed slightly after her eyes.

Stillwater kids learn the two-step and horseshoe shuffle at school dances before the teachers turn them loose on the dance floor. The kids were obligated to do a few partner dances before they could freestyle dance. It was an attempt to pass on the tradition from one generation to the next. It worked. When the kids partner-danced they could touch each other, even if only hand-in-hand and arm-over-arm. River enjoyed partner dancing as a kid, but she saw it differently now. She yelled over the music, "Partner dances are so sexist. The guys are always the leaders and women are expected to follow. It's so antiquated."

"Damn River!" Sarah yelled, "You here to have some fun or teach a class?"

Luke could tell she was the politically-correct type and it would be easy to ruffle her feathers. Teasing liberals was one of his favorite pastimes, so he stepped into her personal space and said, "Until the feminist utopia arrives, you wanna shake those Daisy Dukes with me, baby?" The look on her face made him laugh out loud.

She put her hand on his chest and pushed him as far away as she could. "If you promise to never call me 'baby' again."

"You got it, kid!" He laughed again.

She grunted and rolled her eyes. Another shot of whiskey seemed necessary to tolerate dancing with Luke, so she tipped it back. Her reactions only encouraged him, so he held his hand palm-up to guide her to the dance floor like a good sexist would. Her bare thighs stuck to the leather barstool as she hopped down from it and took his hand. It took her a few attempts to move her feet in time to the two-step, but it was an easy dance to pick up again. Maybe it was the potent liquid running through her veins, but River thought Luke was a particularly good dance-lead. He never threw her off balance when he spun her around. And when she did step off-base for lack of practice (or maybe it was the whiskey) he adjusted his lead perfectly to compensate for it. He made it easy to pick the sport up again, even reminding her how to do some of the steps she'd forgotten.

When the song ended River felt dizzy from spinning around and veered right as she went back to the bar where she ordered another drink. Luke leaned on the bar right next to her and asked, "You sure that's a good idea?"

Her well-trained feminist brain told her that not only did he call her 'kid' but now he was parenting her. "You tryin' to tell me what to do, Luke Thompson?" she snapped as she tipped back the glass in front of her.

"Suit yourself, kid," he said pushing away from the bar and walking in the opposite direction. He left her alone but he kept an eye on her. I mean, how many shots of whiskey could a small girl handle? And as sure as gravity, the whiskey did its job within minutes, she was officially stumbling around. Luke collected her and told the group he was taking her home to sleep it off. She no longer had a feminist brain to reason with so she let him. Luke put his hand on the small of her back to keep her from veering off the sidewalk as they made their way to his truck, which was parked across from Willys. Outside of the bar Quinn blew smoke through narrow lips as he watched Luke handle drunken River. When Luke successfully guided her to his truck, she swatted his hand away saying, "I can find my own way home."

"Sure, ya can." He slammed the passenger door of his double-cab truck after getting her inside and walked around to the driver's side. "Buckle up," he commanded.

"You buckle up!" she snapped.

He looked at her under raised his eyebrows, wondering what devil possessed this woman besides whiskey. He leaned over her lap, grabbed her seatbelt and buckled her in. She reminded him that she could find her own way home.

As he backed out of the parking space she slurred, "I don't need no sexy Neanderthal helping me do nothin'."

A smile spread across his face as he drove down Main Street. He said, matter of fact, "You think I'm sexy."

"No, I don't!"

"You just said I'm a sexy Neanderthal."

"You are a Neanderthal!"

"Thank you! I take that as a compliment."

She made a loud guttural sound, "Ugggghhh! You would!"

He laughed, loving that he could get her all riled up, even when she was drunk.

River added, "Such a white-male thing to say."

"Whoa, whoa, hey! No need for hate speech!" he looked at her, then back at the road.

"That's not hate speech!" She spun her head in his direction, her vision slowly followed.

"Okay, then. How 'bout changin' the sex 'n color 'n sayin' that again. See how that hits your ears!" She made another loud sound, then turned the radio up and tried singing the song the rest of the ride home. He noticed she wasn't much of a singer.

They drove down the long road to the farmhouse where he killed the engine. He was reaching for his door handle when she said, "Why aren't you flirtin' with me? Don't you want to flirt with me?"

He looked down at her thighs which were popping out of her shorts. He definitely thought they deserved to be flirted with but there was no way in hell he was going to touch her. That speaker in high school really messed with his head when she said sex with a drunk woman was rape every single time, even if she throws herself at you. Drinking with women always made him nervous for that very reason. He never knew how many drinks turned consensual sex into rape. I mean, how was he supposed to know if a woman was drunk or tipsy? He thought a good test might be spinning her around on her barstool to see if she flirts the same way with the guy on the other side. He hadn't tried that yet. But drinking with women wasn't just nerve-wracking, it was frustrating because the more women drank, the more they did throw themselves at him. Sometimes they even asked for it. Literally. With words! The only time he had sex with a drunk woman was when he was driving her home and she took off all her clothes and went straight for his goods before he'd even parked. What was he supposed to do? Plus, he reasoned, he was intoxicated too, so maybe he could claim that she raped him, if he ever needed to make such a ridiculous claim about consensual sex. But he was pretty sure the rule about drunk-sex only applied to women, which he didn't think was fair. But, after that night a haunting fear always lingered in the back of his head that one day he might be accused of rape.

"You're drunk," he finally said. As he came around the truck, he could hear her arguing through the open window.

"I'm not drunk!"

He opened her door, picked her up and carried her toward the front porch.

"I'm not drunk," she repeated.

"Then why am I carrying you like a damn child?"

"What?" She looked around at her situation as if seeing it for the first time. "Put me down!"

"Gladly!" He stood her up by the front door, opened it, reached around the inside, locked it, gave her a little shove inside, and then closed the door between them. He shook his head on his way back to his truck thinking, *feminist!*

The night was still young so he made his way back to Outlaws. When he got there, Holly made it clear that she was happy to see him come back. They ended up dancing together the rest of the night. He always liked dancing with Holly because she was professionally trained in all kinds of dance. She could follow his hand and shoulder leads like a pro, which meant he could practice more advanced dance moves. And she could spin like a twister, sometimes more than three rotations, and then land right on-base. But he paid a price. He had to peel her arms off his chest in between songs. It was clear he could have her if he wanted her. But he didn't. Well, not all of her anyway. He couldn't deny she had curves like a back-road and wore Daisy Dukes like a pro, but he didn't like anything else about her. It annoyed him that she always had something to say about somebody else's business, even when she didn't know anything about it. Luke decided that if Holly believed half of what she said, he'd be willing to believe the other half. But most of the time he didn't know what she was trying to say. If she wasn't being vague, she was being oblique. And gone were the days he would get himself tangled up with a woman who needed interpretation.

Luke decided to call it a night when the crowd began to thin. Watching him head for the door, Holly gave it her best shot and invited him to her place making sure to tell him other people might be coming over as well. He was pretty sure he could interpret this. No one else would be there. He declined. Sleeping with her would mean half the town would find out within 24 hours. Then he'd be stuck with her! Too much drama. Too high maintenance. Not worth it!

BREATHING IN WATER

CHAPTER TWELVE

The stabbing throb in her head made waking up to sunlight unwelcome. The water and pain-killer River gulped down provided no immediate relief. She went back to bed and blocked out the assaulting daylight by sealing the covers over her head. It was past noon by the time she revived and ate breakfast. But not even coffee made her feel alive again.

Well into the afternoon, she made her way to Loretta where her one-sided conversation took a confessional tone. River admitted how humiliated she was to have gotten drunk the night before. And, so quickly! She couldn't remember the details of the evening, but she knew two things. Luke drove her home. And she probably acted like an idiot. That worried her. She blushed at the strangeness of her subconscious at a vague recollection of a dream where Luke carried her in his arms like a child. A bit of guilt washed over her when she realized she was glad her mother likely couldn't hear what she was saying.

She settled into an armchair and pulled out a white laptop, which felt lighter than she remembered it being. It was time to repay her roommate for the flight. It had been a week since she'd checked her email. She told herself she'd transfer funds before getting distracted with other things. But when she opened her computer, something more important immediately grabbed her attention--an email from Sam Harkens. Despair pulsed through her veins. She knew what the email would say before reading it. The second she saw Loretta in the ICU she knew her internship was over before it had even begun.

Hello River,

I hope your family situation has been resolved.

We are eager to have you begin the internship. As I said in my last email, you have a two-week delay for beginning your position at The Globe. This ends Monday. You will either need to show up for the job Monday or resign your post at that time.

Best,
Sam

River looked up at her mother's limp body connected to machines. Her face contorted as the tears began to fall. However, this time she wasn't crying for her mom. She'd never worked so hard to get something, and she'd never wanted something more than this internship. Her tears hit her fingers as they moved across the keyboard to resign her position. Would she ever get an opportunity like this again? There was no way of knowing. Her Master's program came to mind. Would she have to take a leave of absence? If Loretta woke up right then, she would need physical therapy for months, but she might be independent by fall, right? River knew this was extremely unlikely but she couldn't bring herself to pause her entire life all at once. After sending her resignation and transferring funds she curled up in the stiff armchair and managed to sleep the afternoon away.

❖

Seeing Luke that Monday morning made River's stomach unsettled. She strategically avoided speaking to him for that reason. He made eye-contact a few times but waited for her to speak first, curious what she'd say. Discussing the missing products from last week's shipment seemed like a natural way to break the silence. She led with that. Eventually she inserted, "Hey, thanks for driving me home Friday night."

He paused and smirked before saying, "Sexy Neanderthals are helpful like that."

Heat radiated from her cheeks as she remembered what she'd said. "I was really drunk, Luke" she sputtered.

"Oh, ya were? Hadn't noticed."

Luke having the upper-hand in this conversation was unnerving to her.

He winked.

Oh, dear god, she thought, wondering what else she couldn't remember saying that night. Her back pocket vibrated. She grabbed her phone, relieved for the distraction. Olivia's smiling face appeared on the screen. "Liv!" she answered.

"Hey woman! I miss you! How's your mom?"

River paused, not sure how to answer. "Well, she's stabilized. But she hasn't woken up yet." They caught up a bit before Olivia told her the big news. Next week she'd be driving across the country to see family in California and planned on taking the southern route, stopping by Stillwater. River's heart jumped. She could use a friend, especially the feminist type.

River conveyed her excitement and asked if she was traveling alone, curious if she'd be hosting more than just

Olivia. She was relieved but put off when Olivia said, "Just me. I'm taking on the patriarchy single-handedly!" In context, it seemed Olivia was referring specifically to the south as "the patriarchy." In Boston, River noticed how northerners liked to assume that the south was more chauvinistic than the rest of the country, which was not her experience. In fact, she thought southern men showed some respect that northerners didn't by saying, "yes, ma'am" and by calling them "Ms. So-n-So."

When she hung up, she helped Luke unpack a new shipment of supplies, but kept her eye on the register where she noticed some unusual activity. Instead of taking payment, Skippy was recording someone's merchandise on Loretta's "List of Debtors." It was Carl Stenton. He looked even more disheveled than her younger self remembered him being. His farmer overalls made him a walking cliché. Carl had been on the debtors-list for many years, and usually settled his debt after harvest, except for last year. She wondered where his wife was. People were saying he wouldn't let her leave the farm. The abuse was no secret. The whole town knew about it, and it boiled River's blood to hear people say Linn deserved what she got for staying with him. The darker rumor around town was that Carl had already killed her and she was buried somewhere on their property. She imagined Olivia meeting Carl and having all of her stereotypes of the south confirmed.

It was as if Carl felt her eyes on his back. His head slowly turned his head over his shoulder, halting her stare. Her eyes shot back to the box in front of her. Luke stopped checking items off the packing-slip to watch her clumsily run the box cutter over the packing tape. It was obvious she was still out of her element. He couldn't help noticing her curves, the way she was bent. After some fidgeting with the packing tape, the box popped open, with a waft of new leather revealing cowboy accessories. She pulled out a belt with a large buckle and a silver buckle bolo necktie. Her face crinkled thinking of how any man could wear a long, skinny piece of braided leather with a metal, adjustable clasp and call that attractive. Her face crinkled. When it came to cowboy-wear, River didn't mind the boots and hats but she particularly disliked the neckties and belt buckles. Especially the buckles. Belts are supposed to hold pants up, not weigh them down.

She ran her fingers over the metal relief outlining the state of Oklahoma and a bronco kicking up his back legs. "These are hideous." She held one up for Luke to see, "I hate them!"

"That's 'cause you don't know what their good for."

She raised one eyebrow, "What could these possibly be good for?"

He paused before saying, "I'll show you someday."

She looked at his smirking face from the corner of her eye. "Whatever you say, Luke."

"Damn straight!"

It seemed like he always had to have the last word. She wouldn't let him. "Just... finish what you started, Luke."

"Yes, Ma'am!" he said obediently, maybe even flirtatiously.

She did a double-take looking at him, but he'd gone back to checking items off the packing slip. If there were something left to say she would have said it.

Some customers stopped nearby to update each other on their kids who had graduated and moved out of Stillwater. Eventually, one of the women said to the other, "Remember that diet I told you about? I've lost twenty pounds on it!"

Her husband was looking at her butt when he said, "Honey, I think I found it."

The man was roaring with laughter when his wife turned and punched his arm hard enough to make him wince.

Luke jumped in, "Ma'am, he was just talkin' about that tractor tire 'round his waist." Everyone laughed, including her husband.

River let out a little chuckle at Luke's comment after silencing the feminist voice in her head telling her to be offended for the wife. She decided that if she took everything she heard seriously she wouldn't survive the summer, or however long it took for her mom to recover. Her new goal was blending in unless it compromised her soul. Belt buckles made the soul-compromising short-list. That was one thing that would never change.

Later, the noon sun beat down on her shoulders as she ran across Main Street to grab a pulled pork sandwich and some cornbread. Boston had converted her to a lifestyle of healthy eating but sometimes she just needed some comfort food. On her way back, a bumper sticker on the back of Luke's truck stopped her in her tracks. It said, "Trump: Make America Great Again." She shook her head, but she couldn't shake the disgust she felt.

The summer warmth begged to be enjoyed, so she brought her lunch out behind the store where there was a small table set up for employees. Luke was breaking down cardboard boxes by the dumpster. She didn't want to talk about Trump, but the fresh disgust compelled her to say, "So, I have you to thank for Donald H. Christ?"

It took him a second to figure out what she was talking about, but when he did, he said, "You're welcome! Trump's bustin' up DC," he stomped his shoe through the bottom of a box to flatten it before throwing it in the dumpster.

"I totally agree! The Oval Office won't be the same when he's done with it. And, that's not a good thing!" She arranged her food on the table.

"At least Hillary Incorporated ain't in there sleepin' with big business."

River noticed the disrespect he showed by calling Clinton by her first name. "You're right, Donald's not connected to big business AT ALL!" She let out a small huff. "At least Clinton can hold her tongue." She unwrapped her sandwich.

"I'm more concerned with what comes outta Trump's policies than his mouth. I know he's a dick—actually that's what I like about him! He ain't afraid to bomb the hell out of ISIS, or tell Mexico we're buildin' a wall, or man-up to North Korea."

She slapped her forehead, leaned her elbow on the table and said under her breath, "Oh my God, don't remind me. I have enough to worry about." She sat up and said, "You know, that's exactly what makes liberals think conservatives are racists!"

"Guess how many shits I give what liberals think?" he held up his hand in a circle then stomped another box flat while saying, "I like knowin' my president ain't afraid to take on bullies."

"Trump is a bully!" she snapped. "He's a raving-mad lunatic! God, I still can't believe he's running the country!"

"Sounds like you got a case of TDS."

"WHAT?" She sounded authentically confused.

He moved on. "Nah, Trump ain't a bully. You know what Trump is?" Luke looked at her. "He's my big, fat middle finger to the Left." He threw a pile of cardboard into the dumpster. When he looked back at River, she was holding up both of her middle fingers. "Is that an offer?" He laughed.

She rolled her eyes before taking a bite. "Don't be a cliché, Luke."

"What cliché?"

"A white-man."

"There you go again, judgin' people's color 'n sex." He made a tisk-tisk sound with his mouth. "You should be ashamed of yourself. Haven't you heard? People aren't supposed to do that anymore. What would your liberal friends say?" He chuckled.

She wanted to reply but her mouth was full.

"Guess what's not a cliché?" he added. "Gettin' a college degree without pledgin' allegiance to the liberal flag. I'm tryin' to remember what that looks like. It's not the one with the rainbow on it. Oh yeah, it's the one with a hammer 'n sickle, right?" He looked at her from the corner of his eye.

His teasing was almost completely intolerable to her. The look on her face revealed her mind. The little respect she held for him was dissolving. She could reason why people voted conservative in general, they think small government and a big military solves everything—she disagreed. But, how could Luke, or anyone for that matter, proudly vote for a man who obviously judges people by their race and sex... and then she heard it. Luke had just accused her of doing that. She quickly shook the thought out of her mind. There was no way in hell she was anything like Trump. Plus, Luke was obviously ignorant to all of the privileges that came along with being him. She would educate him.

"Being a man, especially a white one, comes with a whole package of privileges that other people don't get, Luke."

"Oh, is that right?" He paused trying to think of a clever response to a statement he'd heard one too many times in college. "Hey, if I ain't around when that package arrives, would you sign for me?" he laughed from his gut, impressed with his ability to joke about a sentiment he found so repulsive.

She rolled her eyes at his willful ignorance and decided not to waste another minute of her off-the-clock time engaging with someone like him.

When he saw her packing up her food he was no longer amused. Her judgement of him was palpable, so he added,

"Yeah, probably best to assume people like me don't earn what they have. My type don't deserve respect." He threw the last stack of cardboard in the dumpster harder than he needed to as she walked inside.

❖

That Thursday was payday and River needed to figure out how to do payroll for the first time. She told Luke and Skippy it might take longer than normal to get paid. Luke offered to help as he'd seen Loretta run through payroll once before. She accepted the offer. That evening he showed up at the farmhouse after dinner.

Not having air conditioning, hot summer air had invaded the space entirely. Beads of sweat formed on their brows and River was thirsty. She thought it was immature of Luke to look at her breasts when she said, "I'm so hot," even though he probably didn't even realize that he did. "Do you want some lemonade?" she said flatly.

Luke nodded and smacked her butt as she stood up.

"What the hell is your problem!" she yelled stepping away from the table.

"What the hell is your problem?" he replied, even though he realized what he just did was a really stupid. He wasn't sure why he did it, actually. Maybe he wasn't thinking clearly in the humid heat. Or maybe he was trying to ruffle her feathers. Well, it worked!

"YOU CAN'T JUST SMACK MY ASS!" she protested even louder.

He tried to play it off by saying, "Well, I just did… so technically I can." He meant it to sound funny but after he said it, he realized the statement sounded predatory. In fact, other than touching her again, that was the only way he could've made the situation worse.

"NEVER touch my ass again without my permission!" she yelled. Her neck turned dark red.

The play left his voice, "You got it."

River fumed an angry breath, "You know, guys like you think you own women's bodies, like you can just touch them whenever the hell you want!"

It pissed him off to hear her say 'guys like you' as if he were some kind of rapist, but he knew he didn't have a leg to stand on in this conversation, so he stayed silent. He tipped his head to one side hoping the conversation was over.

She turned to go to the kitchen but then turned around again and said, "You know, plenty of people would call what you just did 'assault'."

His eyes darkened as his brow furrowed. "Would you call that 'assault' if Penny Stone were here?" He couldn't help raising his voice at the suggestion that he'd assaulted her.

Penny's bloodied, terrified face appeared in River's mind. She stared right through Luke, as images of that devastating night flashed through her mind. Every fiber of her body recalled the terror of the moment she found her friend beaten and afraid. River swallowed.

"What the hell'd they teach you at Harvard? Damn, River! Do you think I'd actually hurt you like that?"

She realized she wouldn't call what Luke did 'assault' in front of Penny. And she didn't think Luke was capable of something like that, either. It was only a slight movement, but she shook her head no.

Luke ran his hand through his hair and then down his face. He couldn't believe she'd accused him of assault when she knew damn well he was just messing with her. "Some words should be reserved for people who actually need 'em. There's a difference between a jerk and a predator, for fuck-sake!"

Penny's terrified face still lingered in River's mind. She knew Luke was wrong about touching her, but she knew he was right about not calling what he did 'assault'. This realization effectively silenced her. She decided, for Penny's sake, she would never cheapen that word again. Had Luke actually convinced her about this in a few short sentences? He had. But there was no way in hell she would concede a point to a guy who just smacked her ass without permission. She gave up no territory. Her sustained silence grew into a third party in that room, and it was two against one.

Luke's eyes scanned the clock on the wall, "I should go."

"Good idea," she said with more disdain than she'd intended.

Luke shook his head and palmed his hat sitting on a chair next to him. He made his way to the door but before walking out he turned around, and said, "I didn't mean to piss you off, River. I'm sorry." She acknowledged his apology with the slightest nod of her head, but said nothing as he walked out.

After he left, she thought about the situation for a while. As a feminist, she'd learned that words should to be used strategically. But in this moment, she absorbed a new idea: if words are to maintain potency, they needed to be used correctly. She couldn't believe she'd learned this from someone like Luke, especially after what he'd done.

What did he do? If it wasn't assault, what was it? She thought honestly about this. His touch was unwanted and it pissed her off, but it didn't hurt or scare her. "Assault" didn't come close to describing what he'd done. "Harassment" had a sort of ongoing or intimidating sound to it. She considered the word "abuse," but that sounded too intense for something that did no permanent emotional or physical damage. The only word she could find to adequately describe his smack on the butt was "violating."

Actually, "degrading" was more accurate because it made her feel like a child. She hated that these were the strongest words she could find to describe this experience because she was still really mad.

When some people sought God in times of trouble, River sought truth. And if she found it, she held onto it like an anchor in the storm. Truth was something she could organize her life around.

And so, she did.

CHAPTER THIRTEEN

Carl's fingers gripped tight his leather-handled switchblade as he ran a steel rod across the blade. The sound of grinding metal filled the otherwise empty air. A dim lamp illuminated Carl's lap but little else, certainly not his mind. His thoughts were dark. Vengeful. He thought about what he'd do to Linn when he found her, as he took a swig of Jack Daniels. She had it coming. For leaving him. For taking his truck. For making him search for her. He imagined the terror in her eyes when she realized this was finally the end. He meant business this time.

Even though Linn's absence enraged Carl, it also invigorated him to hunt her down like the prey that she was. He hadn't had this much purpose in life for a long time, even though that purpose wouldn't last long once he found her. He'd watched his oldest daughter's house for weeks, looking for any sign that Linn was inside. Kelly even let him look through her house just to get him off her porch and out of her life again. He took another gulp from the tinted bottle and slammed it down on the side-table. She wasn't camping at the lake where they had taken their kids when they were small. He'd already checked there and every other location in and around town that he could imagine her being, and even places that he couldn't. He had successfully isolated her from her friends decades ago but he still stalked their houses, just in case she'd reconnected without him knowing. No one had seen her around town at all, or so they said. He needed to sell some things to afford the trip he was planning to Texas where he would stalk her cousin's house and an old friend. Carl was single-minded, determined that he'd find her. He couldn't let Linn get the upper hand. Her place was with him. Even her gravestone would stand next to his.

The next morning, when River arrived at work, Luke was already there and had set the shop signs out front on the sidewalk. An Americano sat steaming on the counter with her name scribbled on the side of it. She didn't thank Luke, but she also didn't mention what happened the night before. Neither did he. Each of them had clearly outlined a boundary they didn't want crossed, and each had silently agreed to observe it.

River was relieved when Luke left the store for lunch, but her relief was short-lived when Quinn walked in. When Quinn noticed her, he mapped out a strategy for getting on her good side. The last time they spoke he'd learned that his sex-appeal held no sway, so he decided to turn on his country-boy charm. As he approached the register, he tipped his hat and said, "Miss River Novak. That's right, you're Loretta's girl, aren't ya."

College had trained her to be offended at being called Miss, which drew attention to her marital status or lack thereof. And also, being called a 'girl'. After all, people don't call grown men 'boys.' She wanted to correct him but the only way she could imagine getting her point across would be to say, 'I'm hardly a girl anymore.' But she was certain he would think she was flirting if she said that, so she just nodded and begrudgingly rang up his items.

"Well, now I know where to find ya," he said leaning on the counter.

"I'll let you know if I get lost." Her words fell flat.

He chuckled and pointed at her. He felt the distance she'd created with that statement. Each new interaction with her confirmed his realization that the prospect of getting River in bed was not good. But Quinn never backed down from a challenge. In fact, the longer the chase the more satisfying the conquest would be. And, it wouldn't just satisfy him physically. The more independence River showed, the more he wanted to crush it. He had little sympathy for women with attitudes. It was a sore-spot for him. He hid his growing contempt with a flirtatious smile and eye-contact, while tipping his hat and saying, "Miss Novak."

She nodded.

By the end of the week, the weighted air between Luke and River had lightened; they'd returned to meaningless bantering. River left work early Friday afternoon to be present when Loretta was moved out of intensive care and into a recovery ward. It had been almost four weeks since the accident. This transition gave River unmerited hope that her mother would soon awaken. River's conscious thoughts still refused to acknowledge that Loretta no longer looked like her mother, that her brain had been so severely damaged the likelihood of Loretta regaining her former memory was negligible. River was desperate for something to hope for in the void of waiting.

So, she hoped.

When the doctors and nurses left the room, River encouraged her mother to wake up and take a look around her new environment. She sat quietly for a while taking in the new surroundings but noticed the air was still filled with the nag of beeping machinery. They seemed to mock her will to hope. They threatened to unravel it. She shifted her focus along with her body. "Mama, I'm starting to see why you never got married. I wonder what the hell men are thinking, sometimes." She talked a while on this topic and then, just in case Loretta could hear and was wondering, she gave her mom an update on the store.

On River's way out of the hospital, Jules caught her in the hallway. Jules invited her to join a Tuesday night get-together at Penny's house every other week. River gladly accepted. She hadn't had the chance to connect with Penny yet, and she could use some female company.

As Penny opened her door, River was reminded of her old friend's intense enthusiasm, which her mass of swaying red curls piled atop her head only emphasized. Penny squealed at River with delight, bending to bridge the five-inch gap between them. She grabbed River around the neck, pulling her in for a tight hug. River hugged her back the best she could with her hands full of lemonade and strawberries.

"River! It's so good to see you, honey! Come on in. My baby-boy's still getting settled for the night. He had a rough day at school, you know? Kids these days are so awful. So, he's dragging his feet gettin' into bed but he'll get there." River nodded as she looked around. She saw no boy. The place looked well lived in. It wasn't dirty but it seemed as though items had been pushed to the edges of the room in a hurry. River made her way to the kitchen table where a stack of papers sat at one end. Jules knocked only briefly before walking in.

"Come on in!" Penny yelled, while collecting glasses for the lemonade.

"Phew!" Jules huffed as she sat next to River, "Good lord, what a night! We're moving Drew from his crib to a toddler bed 'n it ain't goin' well! Doesn't matter what we do, that little bugger won't stay in his damn bed!"

"Oh, Lord, I know!" Penny said, joining them at the table. "Took Stevie the good part of a year to get out of my bed and into his own! I'd put him in his own bed and by morning he was back in mine. Dang, I still find him in my bed sometimes and he's EIGHT!" Penny's curls shook back and forth along with her head.

"I can see why parents beat their kids," Jules added with exhausted laughter. "Course, we didn't do that, but I can see why people do. We held Drew down in his bed for, like, fifteen minutes so he gets the idea he needed to stay there, you know? But the second we'd leave the room, lil' bugger's up again!"

A boy walked into the room, his tight-fitting pajamas emphasized his skinny arms and legs. River hadn't seen Penny's son since he was a toddler. She thought he must have gotten his dark hair from his dad.

"Hey, baby-cakes! Say hello to mama's friend Ms. River."

"Hi, Ms. River," he whispered.

"You can call me River."

"MS. River!" Penny corrected. Stevie nodded. "Say goodnight 'n get in bed. I'll be in soon."

His eyes watched his feet walk down the hall.

"He's having a rough time at school," Penny explained. "When he got outta the bath tonight I saw bruises all over his ribs 'n I said, 'What on God's-green-earth happened to you?' He says kids are hittin' him at school! Isn't that the livin' end?" Penny exclaimed.

Jules motherly sympathy came through in her voice. "Poor, baby!"

"Luckily, there's only a couple days left of school. But I called the principal 'n he says kids don't get supervised at recess 'cause teachers are eatin' their lunch. I told him, 'Y'all need to get those stay-at-home moms to stay-at-school 'n do somethin' useful with their time'!" Penny huffed and then excused herself when Stevie's voice rang down the hall.

Jules said, "I'd smack those kids right across the face if I saw 'em doing that to my boy."

River's eyebrows rose. "I think hitting a kid is overreacting a bit, don't you?"

"No, I don't! You'll understand when you have kids of your own someday, Riv. It's a mama-thing."

Penny came back in and poured lemonade for them. The women continued their conversation about mothering. River found that she had little to say on the topic but she participated whenever she could, referencing some nanny work she had done during summers as an undergraduate student. The fact that her peers where actually mothers struck her. She was glad she didn't have to deal with that responsibility at age 23. But then it struck her that she had the huge responsibility of running her mother's business with no training at all, which felt like a "baby" of sorts, fragile and overwhelming. River was brought out of her contemplative state when Jules said, "Kev and I are trying to get pregnant again."

Penny squealed and clapped.

"That's exciting," River said.

"Sorry Riv! Here we are talking about mama-stuff this whole time."

River reached for a strawberry, "That's okay. I might be a mom someday. I'm gettin' the scoop ahead of time." She was glad Jules noticed actually. The conversation was getting duller every minute.

Penny changed the subject, asking River about "big-city life."

"Well, right now I'm just trying to figure out what I should do about the place I rent in Boston. I mean, I'll probably be in Stillwater through the fall, even if my mama wakes up tomorrow." She didn't like hearing herself say that. Somehow, speaking the truth made her circumstances feel permanent. She finished her thought anyway, "My mom will need physical therapy for a long time, and she'll have to adjust to using one arm when she wakes up." River stared right through the strawberry in her hand while picking off the stem. She told them about the internship she'd had to turn down because of the accident, then swallowed the ball that had formed in her throat.

"Wow!" Penny exclaimed. "I just got my GED, and I thought that was an accomplishment." In the context of Penny's life this was a huge accomplishment and River knew it.

River perked up, relieved to shift the focus away from her. "Penny that is a big deal! You should be proud of yourself for getting that done."

"I am proud. But it's nothin' to write home about, ya know? Maybe if I finished college, or started college even, it would be."

"Are you interested in college?"

"I thought about it. I'd like bein' a veterinarian. But college is overwhelming to figure out--even just how to sign up and get into classes. No one's there tellin' you how it's done. It's just confusing."

"I'll walk you through it, Pen."

"Yeah, but I also work in the day and I'm with Stevie at night, you know? I'm his mom and his dad. He needs me."

River suspected there was something more to Penny's dismissal of the idea. Maybe she was nervous about being on campus because she'd been attacked by a college student. "What about taking classes online?" River suggested. "You can take classes from home after Stevie goes to bed."

Penny's face lit up. She had never heard of doing college at home before. She wanted to try it. River determined to walk her through the process. There was something redemptive about this for River. She and Penny were both top of their class in high school, until Penny became a mother at age seventeen. She'd always wondered what Penny would have done with her life if it weren't for that fateful night that changed everything.

CHAPTER FOURTEEN

River leaned over her table that morning transfixed by her computer screen. Her finger scrolled, looking through the list of The Globe's summer interns. There he was. The Suit. She bemoaned the fact that she wouldn't be sitting next to this eye-candy all summer long. It looked like Akemi Ozaki would have that privilege. River decided Akemi was pretty but was probably a snotty bitch. She slapped her forehead frustrated with how hateful she could feel about someone she didn't even know. She let out an audible groan and slid her forehead down her arm.

Her computer slammed shut and she pushed away from the wood-beam table to warm her coffee. She stared through the microwave asking herself a question she already knew the answer to. How did I end up working at the fucking cattle store after a Harvard degree? She felt antsy. The store was under control at this point, kind of. It had a rhythm anyway. She imagined herself writing a piece for a local news source on the side. I mean, why waste the entire summer standing behind a register? She stood up a little straighter. The microwave beeped and stopped, but her gaze stayed fixed on the wall as she pulled the hot mug out.

She came back to the table with new energy and pushed aside the stack of college materials she'd collected for Penny. She opened her computer again and typed in the search bar, "Oklahoma, jobs, freelance journalism."

❖

That afternoon Olivia pulled up to the farmhouse in a sea-green sedan and River went out to meet her. When they embraced Olivia mentioned how middle-of-nowhere she lived. River thought of Stillwater that way for years while living in Boston. But over the past few weeks the farmhouse felt less like the middle-of-nowhere to River and more like the center-of-everywhere.

They settled at the dining table and River asked, "So how's your trip going?"

"Good! So far, I've been through Pennsylvania, Maryland, West Virginia, Virginia, Tennessee, Arkansas and, now, Oklahoma. I stayed in Memphis last night, it's a surprisingly progressive city."

"What makes it progressive?" River asked, authentically curious, since Tennessee hadn't voted for a Democrat in over twenty years.

"I just got that vibe from people, ya know? I just didn't expect that in the south. But it's weird, everywhere I turn men are calling me "ma'am." I'm like, 'Dude! We're the same age! Why are you calling me ma'am?'" Olivia let out a high-pitched laugh.

River became keenly aware of something that she'd never noticed before, even though it had been always before her. She and Olivia shared a habit of assigning negative intentions to everything men did and said. It felt as though she was going off-script by disrupting the pattern. "It's a southern thing, Liv, not a commentary on your age. Just take it as they mean it. Respect."

Olivia took a drink of her sweet-tea in place of a reply but she swallowed fast, "OH! Guess who ended up being my roommate."

"I know someone in New York besides you?"

"Xandi!" Olivia's speech slowed. "Xandi's dad kicked zim out when zie came out as non-binary." She stared past River when putting the sentence together, almost like there was an invisible text she was reading from.

River ignored the effort her friend made.

"And, I was like, 'Xandi! I desperately need a roommate! Move to New York,' so it worked out perfectly."

"Wow, that's great! At least you won't have to weed through anymore weirdos. Did his dad finally stopped talking to him?"

"Zie, zim, zer. Those are zie's pronouns." An air of moral superiority came through in Olivia's voice, making her correction of River feel that much more chastising.

Over the last few weeks of enduring overwhelming tragedy, River had lost patience for other people's problems, and she didn't mind saying so. But even she was surprised when she heard herself say, "Yeah, I'm probably not gonna say that."

Olivia's eyes shot wide open. "Oh my God, River! Why not?"

River hadn't planned on saying that and immediately regretted it. Now she was obligated to explain herself and she wasn't sure how to. So, for lack of a planned reply, she said what seemed true. "Because, those aren't real words, okay? If he transitioned to female, I'd be happy to call him 'she,' but this is ridiculous, Liv. The next person is going to ask me say 'vie, ver, verself' and there will be no end to the madness. I'll have to refer to a notepad just to speak right."

Olivia didn't even consider what River had said. Her friend was in danger of becoming legitimate bigot. She had to correct her. "You'll acknowledge trans people but not non-binary people, is that what you're saying?"

River paused. "No. I don't know." She paused, "I-I haven't worked it out yet, okay? I'm just not going to say that," River's resolve increased with the push-back. She avoided Olivia's dramatic expression by looking at the cupboard that was open in the kitchen.

Olivia never broke her gaze at River. "You're denying Xandi's humanity when you disregard his pronouns." She stopped suddenly, "I mean, zie's pronouns."

River gave Olivia a face that said, "See what I mean?" "I'm not denying Xandi's humanity. I'm denying his demand that I talk like a Dr. Seuss character."

"Maybe you don't take him seriously... I mean, ZIM seriously, but I do!"

The corners of River's mouth went up slightly at the effort her friend was putting into speaking. "Look, if Xandi were standing right here when I was talking about him maybe I'd put in some effort, okay? I have no problem with his journey or calling him some new name. Hell, I'd call him 'Fork' if he wanted."

Olivia rolled her eyes.

"But I don't like people telling me how to talk, especially when they're not even around to appreciate it!"

Olivia threw her hands up a little and let out a huff, "This is just typical of non-binary people's experience. They get erased from the world. They feel invisible."

River could no longer take the chastisement. She didn't appreciate being bullied into doing something she didn't want to do. Her voice raised a little, "You know what's gonna make them ACTUALLY invisible? No one talking about them AT ALL because it's so damn hard to put a sentence together! I mean! I started this conversation curious about Xandi, but all we've done is argue about grammar! Now I don't even give a damn!" River let out an angry huff. She didn't like being treated like a hater. She figured Olivia knew she was a good person. She was as liberal as the next person.

"So, what you're saying is, you would rather silence a minority voice than put a little effort into your own privileged speech?"

"Oh, my God, Olivia! What is this? The inquisition? What ever happened to live-and-let-live? I'm happy to let people do their thing and I'd appreciate it if you'd let me do mine!" The volume of River's voice effectively ended the interrogation.

Both women's cheeks had turned a shade or two darker. Neither of them would budge. The conversation was over. Olivia shook her head, *apparently, you can take the girl out of Oklahoma, but you can't take Oklahoma out of the girl*.

River got the distinct feeling she was being judged as "conservative" just because she wouldn't follow her friend to crazy-town on this issue. Both women filled the awkward silence by acting like they were thirsty. Their ice had melted in the heat of debate. River was surprised when the tepid tea hit her lips. The silence gave them time to calm down but after River refilled their ice the silence was awkward. They both racked their brains for a new topic.

Olivia pierced the silence first, "Oh, yeah! I brought a Black and White cookie for us to share."

River was relieved for the topic change. She perked up a bit. "Oh, I haven't had one of those since I visited you in New York. Remember when that homeless guy that tried to sell us his half-eaten Black and White cookie?"

They both forced a laugh as Olivia went into the kitchen. As Olivia pulled a plate out of the cupboard, River noticed she had a couple of new tattoos. A colorful one stretching up her neck into a flourish, and a black one nestled in between some others on her arm.

"Is there something you haven't told me?"

"What?" Olivia sounded surprised.

"The satanic star on your arm!"

"That's not a satanic star!" Olivia laughed. "It's a Pagan symbol." When Olivia brought her arms down from the cupboard the symbol had flipped right-side-up.

River nodded, seeing it now. She smiled at the silliness of promoting two different religions depending on which way your arm was angled.

Olivia set the large two-toned cookie between them. "Speaking of Paganism, I successfully induced an OBE during transcendental meditation."

"You, did what?"

"I had an out-of-body experience."

River paused before saying, "Honestly, Liv, that sounds creepy." She broke off part of the cookie and took a bite.

"It was a little creepy, actually." Olivia bit into a piece of the cookie, "But it's really amazing to leave your body and move around outside of it. I mean, you're totally conscious and aware but you're disembodied. Like, literally out of your body."

River assumed this was some kind of trick of the imagination. She wasn't convinced it was possible for peoples' consciousness to leave their body. She wasn't even sure that she believed in human consciousness being something other than the brain. Thoughts about her mother's condition tried surfacing but she successfully suppressed them. "What is consciousness anyway?" River asked, "I mean, is it even something other than a human's brain. It seems like scientists would have measured it by now, if it were."

"You'd understand if you were a spiritual person." Olivia always sounded condescending, even when she wasn't trying to be. "When you enter an altered state of consciousness, you're less aware of physical stuff and you go to another realm."

River's eyebrows shot up. She wondered if Olivia knew just how ridiculous she sounded. Almost like she never attended an ivy-league university.

"I came in contact with some dark energies out there, actually. It freaked me out and I wanted to get back into my body. But it's not as easy as it sounds."

River was feeling uneasy.

"The night after I induced OBE for the first time, I had night paralysis and it's been happening to me regularly ever since."

River wasn't sure she wanted to know the answer but she found herself asking, "What's night paralysis?"

"When you wake up at night unable to move." Olivia knew she was pushing the limit of what her highly rational friend was willing to believe, but she felt compelled to tell someone about this experience. Olivia paused before saying, "When I was out of my body, I saw these floating red eyes. Then a few days later, when I had night paralysis, I saw those same red eyes floating the end of my bed." She looked up at River in search of reassurance from her friend that everything would be okay. "It's like that realm and this one merged, or something."

River swallowed. She was officially freaked out. In an attempt to bring the conversation back to reality she said "But, seriously, Liv. What is consciousness anyway? Maybe it isn't just our brain." Loretta surfaced in River's mind. She was haunted by the realization that her mother's brain pulsed with blood but not with thought.

It became clear to Olivia that her friend wouldn't be able to discuss alternative realms so she joined River in hers. "It's awareness. The soul. The part of you that lives on after you die. You saw 21 Grams, right?"

River pushed the cookie plate away, no longer interested in food. "No, but I know the movie you're talking about. It's based on research done weighing people when they died to see if they lost weight, or something like that. They were trying to measure the soul. I guess some of the research concluded that people lost weight at the moment of death. But the research isn't conclusive, you know? The results aren't able to be reproduced enough. There's no proof the soul is real."

Olivia still craved a more ethereal conversation. "What is reality anyway?"

"The physical world. The measurable one."

Olivia broke off another piece of the cookie. "Are you sure? How do you know that all of this isn't a dream? And, is it your dream or mine?" She took a bite of the cookie and wiggled her eyebrows, as if she hadn't just parroted a tired idea, as if she weren't being the epitome of cliché.

"Oh, Liv." River was getting exhausted by her friend's idiomatic eccentricity. "Once you question reality then nihilism sets in."

"What's wrong with that?"

"Well. Once you decide that nothing matters then what's the point of life itself? Frankly, I think nihilism is just an excuse to stop taking responsibility for yourself and the world. Nihilists say, 'Nothing's real,' but they act like things are real. They scream like the rest of us when they hit their thumb with a hammer. Everyone knows pain is real. Even nihilists."

Olivia chuckled a little. She could appreciate this logic. "Okay. So, what's the antidote for suffering if we can't escape being conscious of pain."

"People escape it all the time. Drugs, alcohol, not growing up, suicide..."

"What if... instead of trying to escape being conscious, the antidote is achieving a heightened state of it? I mean, isn't that the goal of Buddhism and eastern religions?"

This made River think about research done on meditation and prayer. She remembered reading, there is evidence that people who pray enjoy increased psychological well-being. But the real question is, does prayer actually work? Does prayer achieve an altered outcome to any given situation? There was no way of knowing, she concluded. You can't measure potential future outcomes. But still, River wondered for a brief second if prayer could summon her mother's thoughts back into her body.

Olivia watched River's demeanor change suddenly. River could no longer suppress honest thoughts about her mother's condition. She could see, for the first time, what everyone else could see, the futility of her mother's condition. Her mind's eye could see Loretta's mangled and atrophying body hooked up to machines, which were doing the work of keeping her alive. River's grief became palpable as she stared past Olivia. Olivia stayed quiet, waiting for her to speak.

"Sometimes I wonder where my mama's consciousness went, you know? Her brain is alive but she's not there. She's just gone. There's no evidence of her being in a dreamlike state either. She doesn't respond to pain." River swallowed down the ball in her throat. Images of the doctor poking her mother with needles and her brainwaves not changing flashed through River's mind. She recalled her earlier statement, 'Everyone knows pain is real.' She let out a huff of air. "I guess pain isn't real for my mama. Nothing is." She let a tear roll down her cheek. "I mean… what's the difference between death and the state my mama's in, ya know?"

Olivia took both of River's hands and looked her in the eyes, "She'll come back, Riv. She's just waiting for the right time."

River nodded. She liked hearing this, even though she knew Olivia couldn't verify that her statement was true.

And for River, truth mattered.

CHAPTER FIFTEEN

It was a hot summer day in July, the fourth. Tradition inspired Stillwater folks to migrate east to Canton Lake for the annual fireworks display, a celebration of the country's independence and pride. River suggested she and Olivia join the rest of the town at the lake. Olivia said she didn't celebrate the Fourth of July because, as far as she was concerned, the U.S. was an illegitimate nation. It was established by genocide and colonization. River felt a tinge of guilt when she thought, *show me a country that wasn't.* However, Olivia reasoned, a picnic by the lake sounded like a fun way to spend the hot summer day, so the two of them made their way to the lake.

The lakeshore was a blur of red, white, and blue where a couple hundred people colonized the shore with picnic baskets, coolers and sunblock, enjoying the water before sunset and fireworks. Diapered toddlers ran across picnic blankets, people played corn-hole and children splashed in the lake. Olivia and River joined a group of friends already camped out: Jules, Kevin, Luke, Penny and her boy Stevie, as well as a few other people River didn't know. They claimed some territory by spreading blankets and enjoying the watermelon they'd packed. The cold fruit refreshed them as the sun warmed their shoulders like an old friend.

Olivia elbowed River and pointed at Quinn. He was standing nearby posed like a supermodel, wearing only his shorts and his abs. A chunk of his hair fell over his brow.

Olivia said, "I'd let that guy man-spread all over me."

Watermelon shot out of River's mouth and she unsuccessfully tried catching it. The volume of her laughter surprised even she. Quinn looked over. She could definitely appreciate him from a distance. But once her laughter died down, she felt compelled to say, "That guy's a dick!"

"Exactly!"

They laughed again.

River knew she was poking at a sore spot when she said, "Remember when you tried being a lesbian?"

"I don't want to talk about it." Olivia always said this when River brought it up.

Her eccentric friend had an affinity for novelty, but this was one experiment River wouldn't let her forget. "You said feminists shouldn't sleep with men because it perpetuates the patriarchy."

"I said, I don't want to talk about it." Olivia's tone had sobered.

"Just sayin'. I've never denied that I like to be man-handled."

"Would you just shut up and let me enjoy the view?"

River laughed. "Knock yourself out." She looked around for the drinks they packed but then realized she'd left them in the back of her Jeep. When she got to the parking lot, she pulled the cooler out of her Jeep and set it on the gravel. She pushed the seats back into position and turned around to find Quinn towering over her.

"Oh my god, you scared me! What do you want?" she somewhat yelled.

"Sorry, darlin'. Let me get that for ya."

He reached for the cooler but she grabbed it first. "I got it." She tried stepping around him but he stepped in front of her.

"What the hell is your problem?" she yelled.

"I just wanna chat. Catch up."

"Catch up on what? The rodeo?" She decided she's had enough with Quinn's physical jockeying. Her voice took a threatening tone. "Next time you want to talk to me use your words. Not your body!" She stepped around the other side of him and heaved the cooler to the shore by herself. That's when Quinn admitted he would not conquer that woman. She won. And he didn't like her tone. His jaw twitched when he imagined himself taking her shoulders and shaking her tiny frame.

The sand adjusted beneath her as she settled on the plaid blanket in between Penny and Olivia. Nearby, someone's truck had huge speakers on top, blasting out country music loud enough for everyone on the shore to hear. The DJ said a few words before Carrie Underwood began singing the national anthem. Suddenly, all the men removed their hats. Some people put one hand over their heart. But everyone stood. Everyone, that is, except Olivia. River wasn't overly patriotic, but she always stood for the anthem. It was tradition. And she saw no need to protest that. Other than toddlers and infants, Olivia was the only one sitting down. River's heart picked up pace as eyes looked their way. She knew she was being judged for associating with someone like Olivia.

Whether Olivia admitted it or not, she was telling the folks around her, 'I don't give a shit about your dead relatives who died for this country.' River was ashamed for the disrespect Olivia was showing her hometown folks. The visual daggers were hitting their mark. Luke was among the assailants. He didn't take his eyes off Olivia throughout the entire song. When the anthem ended, he walked straight over to Olivia, put his cap back on his head, and sat down next to her.

Oh, shit, River thought. *Here we go.*

"What country are you from?" he asked.

"Here. The U.S." She sounded surprised.

"What country are you movin' to?"

"Nowhere? Why?" Olivia's eyes asked River if he was crazy.

"Looks to me like you hate bein' here, so I's just wonderin' where you'd rather be."

She finally realized he was chastising her for not standing for the anthem. "I don't feel obligated to celebrate empires and capitalism."

Shit! Shit! Shit! River thought. She decided to stay out of the conversation entirely. She knew this would go nowhere fast.

"You don't celebrate it; you just support it. I see."

"I don't support it at all when I see it!" Olivia had her usual air of superiority.

"You see that, dontcha?" He pointed to the iPhone in her hand. "Made and sold by a capitalist. Looks to me like you're doing just fine supportin' it."

Olivia gave River a quick eye-roll.

"Where do you live?"

"I live in New York City. Before that Boston. That's where I met River," she put a hand on River's arm and smiled. "Before that California."

"Ah! Big city bastions of liberalism. Figures!"

She decided not to take the bait on liberalism. Talking politics with a pissed-off white man wasn't how she had planned on spending her sunny day. She didn't normally announce her humble beginnings, but she knew it would give her some street-cred in this conversation. "I grew up in a small town, actually. It was very progressive for being so small. But unfortunately, it was very white."

"What's wrong with being white?"

Olivia shot eyes at River to demarcate the moment she'd hit the tip of the racist iceberg she was sure laid just beneath the surface. Luke's question got River wondering if there is something inherently wrong with a population being predominantly white, as Olivia had suggested, or predominantly any color for that matter. Japan, came to mind. River wondered if Japan, being mostly populated with Japanese people, meant that it was automatically filled with racists. She remembered a social psychology class she had taken in college where she learned about 'in-group favoritism'—the phenomenon of humans preferring the company of their own kind. If society is predominantly one ethnicity, she reasoned, it would be easy to favor the majority race, which certainly provides opportunity for racism to thrive. But their off-balance demographic doesn't mean people in those societies are therefore racist. Though the risk is always present if they aren't aware and diligent, she concluded.

"Having cultural diversity enriches society and makes you a more tolerant person." Olivia schooled.

"Does it, now?" Luke asked slowly, as if to question her tolerance for him.

"Small towns are quaint but they lack culture."

Luke thought about the Red Dirt music he loved so much, which sprang up right there in Stillwater. "Where you find people, you'll find culture, darlin'."

"Don't call me that! And, you know what I mean."

"I DO know what you mean, Olivia. You mean white folks ain't worth bein' around." Luke and River made eye contact briefly when he said Olivia's name. She didn't know that in Oklahoma calling someone 'darling' fosters intimacy, while using their first name, especially someone you don't know, is a gesture of disrespect. But Olivia was satisfied with what sounded like Luke's concession.

"Small towns are great but nothing compares to the diversity in big cities."

"Guess that depends on the kind of diversity you're lookin' for."

"KIND of diversity?" she asked, believing she was exposing more of Luke's racism.

"No two people think alike. Just because a town is filled with white folks don't mean it ain't diverse. Five white guys gonna have five opinions on the same topic. Guess some people just care more about skin color than I do."

Olivia opened her mouth to speak but nothing came out immediately. "A bunch of white people are gonna have similar ideas and culture."

"Kinda like you 'n me?"

Olivia paused at the truth, even though she refused to absorb it. She rubbed her neck and faced him more directly. "So, what you're saying is, white people don't need to be around people of color? We don't need to hear from black and brown people?"

"So, what you're sayin' is, black and brown people think with their skins?"

"I did NOT say that! I'm saying, multiculturalism makes society better and that's what small towns don't have."

He pointed at the array of colorful tattoos that concealed her white skin, "Looks like the city's marked its territory."

"I don't think like a colonizer!" Olivia was pleased with her quick reply.

He stood to leave the conversation, "Your tatts do. Better watch out. They're aimin' for your face!"

Maybe it was the nervous tension, but River almost burst into laughter at Luke's last comment, even though it was quite immature. She agreed about Olivia's tattoos. They were out of control.

Shock gripped Olivia. "Can you believe that guy?"

River nodded. "Yes. I can. That man's infuriating!" But River wasn't sure if they were talking about the same thing. She knew Luke was ignorant about the larger context of racial dynamics in the U.S., but she thought he brought a unique challenge to permitted discourse on the topic. And, the man really knew how to get under a person's skin, even when they weren't drawing attention to it.

The expression on Olivia's face suggested she had just discovered the hate-land of America. River was pretty sure this was why she was taking the southern route anyway, to gather evidence of "southern-white-male hate." So, she wasn't surprised to see Olivia as happy as a lark right after this conversation. She'd found what she was looking for.

Olivia and Penny struck up a conversation soon afterward about universities and degrees. Women's Studies came up just as River's attention was demanded by Jules.

"Hey, Riv! For old time sake!" she motioned River over to her truck where there were a couple of kayaks in the back. Jules was wearing traditional Independence Day garb--jean shorts, a white tee-shirt with an American flag on it, and her wavy brown hair pulled through a baseball cap. River wore shorts and a tee-shirt, too, but no flag. The flag was increasingly becoming a symbol of hate to Olivia and River didn't want to appear compromising to her liberal visitor. The women opened the tailgate and unloaded the kayaks.

"I'm so excited," River exclaimed, "I haven't done this since high school, that last summer we were at the lake house. Wow, six years ago!"

"I know! Remember? We'd spend hours out there and come back burnt to a crisp. Well, I'd be burned to a crisp. You'd just look Mexican." Jules laughed loudly.

"I remember your skin peeling off your legs like a snake after those sunburns. Gross." River shivered. They set the kayaks at the water's edge while they took off their shoes.

"I know! And you'd never help me peel it off either!" Jules complained.

It then occurred to River that Jules was kid-free. She looked around for Drew. He was running back and forth between Kevin and Luke, giggling uncontrollably, trying not to get caught by his dad or uncle. The women climbed into their kayaks and tried to avoid the splashing kids on inner tubes. They set off toward the winding edge of the lake near the reeds. The evening sun warmed their bare legs as they paddled out and talked about those summers at the lake house. They laughed about the night they followed the boys who had snuck out of the cabin just to end up watching them skinny-dip in the lake. Jules remembered being horrified because her brother was one of those naked boys flying off the rope swing in the light of the full moon. River blushed as she paddled into some reeds. She remembered that, too.

"Hey, look! It's a Spiny Soft-Shell turtle," River interrupted.

"Where?" Jules paddled closer.

"On that rock." River tried to get closer but the reeds were so thick she couldn't get all the way to it. River yelled, "I love those things. I remember writing a school paper on them in fifth grade and the teacher kept the paper as an example for future classes." The turtle decided River had gotten close enough and pushed off the rock into the rippling water.

"Where is it?" Jules called.

"It's gone."

Jules turned her kayak around and headed out of the reeds. River tried to move out of the reeds, too, but she had gotten in pretty deep. She tried using her paddle to push the reeds out of the way but the kayak was too long to budge. Her paddle was within reaching distance of the rock. She pushed against it, but instead of going backwards she went sideways and tipped herself right into the lake. Jules heard the splash and turned around to see River's head pop up from the lake like a drowned rat just before she started screaming like a stuck pig. Jules laughed so hard she couldn't even paddle over to help. There was a mass of reeds tickling River's legs and feet. Her panicking imagination saw a lake monster grabbing her feet and pulling her under. She didn't stop screaming until she got her kayak flipped back upright and moved out of the reeds. River finally climbed onto her kayak to realize that Jules had been laughing so hard for so long that she must have peed her pants.

There was nothing Jules could have done to help River, but River still complained, "Thanks a lot for your help, Jules!"

When she was finally able to speak, Jules said, "I'm sorry Riv, but that was so funny!" She laughed some more.

Humiliation washed over River when she looked toward the shore and saw the majority of people looking at her, among whom was Luke. *Oh my god*, she thought, *there will be no end to the teasing.*

When they got to the shore Jules was still laughing even though she was trying not to. River climbed out of the kayak in front of a crowd of smirking faces. The only way to handle this with any class was to take a bow. And so she did. Some people actually clapped, which only added to the humiliation. River pulled her wet shirt away from her chest and shook her head. She knew it was going to be a long, cold night when the sun went down.

Luke walked over with a big smug smile on his face and said, "I have an old tee-shirt in my truck if ya want it." As they walked to the parking lot, he tried coming up with the perfect line for teasing her, but as they neared, he became distracted by something just ahead.

CHAPTER SIXTEEN

Just beyond River's Jeep Luke could see Penny's son, Stevie, being punched in the stomach by a kid while two boys held his arms. Luke called ahead, "Hey! Hey! What's your problem, boy?" The boys let go of Stevie's arms and the aggressor had the look of someone who got caught. Luke approached the kids and aimed his words at the aggressor. "Only cowards hit a guy who can't hit him back. Looks to me like you're a coward. You a coward, boy?"

The kid looked down from Luke's towering frame. "No, sir."

"Well, next time you take a swing at Stevie, you'll make sure it's a fair fight, woncha?"

The slightly threatening tone in Luke's voice made the kid say, "Yes, sir" again. He waited until Luke nodded before walking away with his friends. Luke made sure Stevie was okay. Turned out it was Stevie's pride that took the biggest hit.

Surprise came through in River's voice, "Why are you encouraging this?"

"I ain't encouraging nothin' 'cept a fair fight for Stevie, here." He put his hand across Stevie's head and patted it.

"But you could've told those kids to leave him alone!" She shivered as a shady breeze blew past her dripping clothes.

"Boys are gonna talk with their fists 'n someone's gotta teach 'em what the rules are. A cheap shot's a cheap shot 'n there ain't no respect in that."

River shook her head. She didn't understand Luke's logic at all.

Luke focused on the boy. He knew Stevie didn't have a dad to teach him these things, so he did what needed to be done. "Look at me, son. I'm gonna show ya how to get this kid off your back. Put your fists up and look through 'em."

Stevie put his fists up by his eyes.

"Good. Legs apart 'n bend your knees. Bring your left foot 'n shoulder forward." Luke's foot tapped the boy's skinny leg, signaling which side was left. "Good. Your fists guard your face from takin' a hit. So, keep 'em at your brow unless they're swingin'. Never drop your guard."

Stevie did as he was told and nodded.

"Now, I'm gonna take a swing at you and your hand is gonna block it while your head dodges, okay?"

Stevie nodded. Luke swung his fist at the child's face in a controlled manner. River squeezed her eyes shut. Stevie put his fist in the way and moved his head.

"Good! Now if he hits ya, move your head back with the punch. That way it ain't a solid shot."

Stevie's dark hair flopped over one eye as he nodded.

"Now I'm gonna show ya how to throw a punch. A punch starts with your feet. You gotta step into it, put your weight in it, like this." Luke stepped forward and punched the air. Stevie imitated him. "Good. Now, you're lookin' for a dropped guard. If his face is open, take the shot, and make it solid." Luke stepped forward and punched the air again, this time with more force. Stevie did the same. His mini stature aped Luke's.

"Now punch my stomach and show me whatcha got." Stevie punched Luke in the stomach. Luke corrected, "Gotta keep your wrist straight 'n step into it, son. Try again." Stevie stepped forward and punched Luke again. "Much better. Again." Stevie stepped in and punched Luke with his left fist followed by his right, then left-right-left. River winced when Luke punched Stevie gently on the side of his face. The boy stopped swinging and looked up at his towering instructor. "You dropped your guard. After you swing, pull your fist back to your brow 'n guard your face. Got it?"

"Yes, sir."

"Otherwise, you're gonna take a hit. When you're swingin' with this fist where's the other supposed to be?" Luke showed him by putting his fist by his brow.

Stevie mimicked.

"You got it! Now try it again." He stepped forward and punched Luke in the stomach with his left hand, keeping his right hand at his face, then switched and punched left-right-left, keeping his opposite hand at his brow. Luke swung his fist gently toward the boy's face and hit his hand instead of his cheek. He smiled at the progress his little protégé was making. River thought Luke was having way too much fun teaching a small child how to fight.

"You got it!" Luke said enthusiastically. "Okay, now here's how you get a guy on the ground before he gets you there. When he steps in to take a swing, he's expectin' a wall, right? You wanna dodge his shot and use his movement forward against him. When he's comin' at ya, lean to the side and pull 'im forward so he falls off balance. He'll fall right over your leg 'n when he hits the ground you got the advantage, don't ya?"

"Yes, Sir." Stevie's demeanor had a new confidence.

"I'll show ya. Take a swing at me."

River considered protesting this but before she knew it, Stevie had swung at Luke's stomach. Luke turned sideways, grabbed the boy's shirt and pulled him forward. River covered her face, yet, peeked through her fingers to see Luke ensure that the boy didn't hit the ground too hard. "See that?

Now, I'm too big for you to try this on me so just remember. Lean to the side 'n pull him forward when he's comin' at ya, 'kay?"

"Okay." Stevie picked himself up off the ground.

"Practice your punches. Keep your guard up. Before ya know it, that boy won't have nothin' to do with you."

Stevie nodded enthusiastically.

"Now, let's hope you won't need to use those skills I just taught ya." He ruffled Stevie's overgrown hair. "Go on."

Stevie walked away but then turned around and said, "Thanks, Mr..." Stevie couldn't remember Luke's name.

"Luke."

"Thanks, Mr. Luke!"

"Anytime, Stevie."

The boy was so excited about his spontaneous fight-instructor that he practically skipped away.

River was actually impressed with the amount of skillful thought that guys put into fighting. She had no idea. And she could tell that Stevie left with some new confidence that he didn't have before. Watching this made her think of some feminist writings she read in college about the "social construction of gender." She wondered how much of male-aggression is taught and how much is driven by biology. Luke made the claim that boys are going to get violent to work things out and that he was just teaching Stevie the rules. After watching Luke teach Stevie to fight, she could see why people claimed that gender was a social construction. But she was intelligent enough not to reduce gender differences entirely to socialization. She wondered if there were ways to conduct controlled studies to determine what amount of male violence in the world was driven by their biological makeup and how much was learned. She stared past Luke imagining the details of such a study and didn't notice that Luke was staring straight at her. He was wondering what was going through her lake-drenched head, but mostly he was appreciating her lake-drenched body. River's thoughts were interrupted by Jules.

"You tryin' to win a wet T-shirt contest?" Jules yelled. "Your headlights are on!"

River looked down to see her wet t-shirt outlining her breasts perfectly. Her cheeks darkened. She suctioned her shirt away from her skin. "I have a sweatshirt, I think." Rummaging through her Jeep, she found a zip-up hoodie. Luke was still standing uselessly by with his thumbs in his pockets. Jules waved the back of her hand at him, "Move along, stud! Give the girl some privacy. Good lord!"

Luke smirked and wandered toward the group by the shore. In the distance, River could see Stevie punching the air practicing his moves.

As the sun went down, before the fireworks show, River sat by Penny and they talked about options for online classes and how the system worked. Luke spent some of his time playing the guitar, but the majority of the time he was throwing his nephew up in the air and around his shoulders and also play-fighting with Stevie and a couple other kids who wanted in on the action. River was amazed at how many kids could make a human jungle gym out of him at the same time. She thought it was sweet how he engaged with them.

For a Neanderthal.

BREATHING IN WATER

CHAPTER SEVENTEEN

River felt strangely relieved to usher Olivia off to complete the rest of her journey. The store was busier than normal that Monday; farmers and ranchers hadn't fully adjusted to the limited store hours. Cutting weekends out of the mix was particularly hard on the industry because Land & Cattle Co. was the only supply store within an hour's drive of Stillwater. Skippy was helping customers find what they needed and Luke was reviewing the inventory list behind the counter where River stood at the register. She was ringing up items for two men who were laughing as one man finished a joke he was telling. The joke ended with the word "faggot." Skippy looked up from the work he was doing nearby.

River spoke louder than their laughter, "Don't say that word in this store if you wanna shop here."

The laughter ended and one man looked at the tiny woman standing behind the register and asked, "Who the hell are you?"

"I'm the person who decides if you shop here," she said with fierce resolve.

The man sized her up and down again with narrow eyes and huffed. He looked at Luke and asked, "What the hell's going on 'round here?"

"You heard the woman. Leave that word at the door."

The man grunted an angry laugh and mumbled something to his friend.

When the men left the store, River looked at Luke. "Thanks for your help with that."

"Hey! It's your store. You make the rules." He paused, looked sideways at her and said, "Until the communist utopia arrives on a liberal platter. Then they make the rules."

His chuckle was annoying but she didn't give him the satisfaction of a reaction.

His voice took a more serious tone when he said, "You know, you're gonna see the same folks 'round here every day. Can't burn bridges like you can in the city."

Rivers eyebrows contorted.

"That guy owns the only car dealership in town. Let's hope your Jeep don't die."

This last point fueled her flickering fire. She raised her voice, "That's exactly what keeps hate goin', Luke, when good people do nothing. They just sweep it under the rug like it's no big deal. If everyone stopped tolerating hate then no one would have to worry about where to buy a Jeep, now would they?"

This made sense to Luke, actually. He could appreciate the logic. And her courage. The least he could do was agree. "I guess not."

Skippy turned his head away from Luke when a smile spread across his face. He'd never heard Luke concede a point to anyone before.

By late afternoon the store had slowed down significantly. Luke pulled his phone out of his pocket to read a text.

River felt kind of bad for snapping at him earlier so she joked, "I'm gonna write you up for taking care of personal business on company time."

He nodded mindlessly and started texting. She wondered who he was talking to. When he finished, he asked, "You ever been to The Farm?"

"The farm, as in, *The Farm*?"

He nodded.

"No. I thought that place burned down when we were kids."

"It did but folks still play music by the old shed."

Skippy was listening to their conversation and asked, "What farm?"

"The Farm, Skippy." Luke had little patience for Skippy's constant naivety. Skippy stared blankly at Luke. Luke cocked his head to the side and said, "Okay, how 'bout I tell you what The Farm is when you tell me what rock you been livin' under."

River smacked Luke's chest with the back of her hand.

"What? It's like he ain't ever had a conversation with someone in Stillwater before."

River gave him a look that made him feel obligated to behave.

He turned back to Skippy. "It's that farm outside of town where people been makin' music generation after generation. Where Red Dirt began. It's called 'The Farm'."

Skippy's curls bounced up and down as he nodded knowingly.

Luke assumed he was faking it. He slipped his phone into his pocket with a slight eyeroll and turned back to River. "Anyway, a buddy of mine is friends with Evan Felker from Turnpike Troubadours. They're passin' through town on the way to their gig in Tulsa 'n they'll be at The Farm tonight." Luke saw a silly grin spread across River's face, so he added, "Wanna come?"

River's stomach flipped. "Turnpike Troubadours? Yes! I saw them play in high school. I love them!"

"Well, it's really low key, so don't go tellin' no one. You neither Skippy, they don't want the whole damn town out there." He chuckled to himself remembering that one of their song's is called The Whole Damn Town. He added, "And don't worry, there'll be other girls there."

"Gals," she schooled.

"What?"

"Gals. Not girls."

Luke raised one eyebrow. "What's the diff'?"

"Same 'diff' there is between 'boys' and 'guys'," She raised one eyebrow and cocked her head to the side, making her short hair touch one shoulder.

He stayed completely still for a moment, amazed that there was no end to her feminism. "Don't make me regret invitin' you, River."

She said nothing.

He finally said, "Gals will be there, okay? Gals, River! Are you happy?" He shook his head and asked himself, *did I just say that?*

River's mind shifted. She stared past Luke. A few hours from then she'd meet the Turnpike Troubadours. She wondered if she'd make a fool of herself. She told Luke she'd drive them there to be sure that she wouldn't drink. She planned on staying sober and keeping her composure.

The night was cooler than normal. Jeans and a zip-up hoodie fit the mood. She pulled up to Luke's place as the sun was setting behind it. His house stood out in the neighborhood. It was like a log cabin had been dropped in the middle of suburbia. Luke jogged down the steps of the dark wood porch and set his cased-guitar in the back of her Jeep. It hadn't occurred to her when she was getting dressed that evening that she might match Luke's attire but, as it turned out, he was also wearing jeans and a hoodie. But he was sporting a baseball cap and she liked how his overgrown hair fanned out around the edges. He turned the cap around backwards to keep it from flying off as she picked up speed.

She mentioned the uniqueness of his house in the neighborhood.

"Ellie always wanted to live in a cabin. The old house needed new siding when we bought it. It's just a façade."

River wondered why he chuckled after saying that.

He finished the conversation in his mind. *A façade, like her affection for me all last year.*

When they got to The Farm Luke's friend Jerry was getting the bonfire started with a few cut up sections of wooden pallets. He wore his usual garb: a flannel shirt and long beard. She wondered what he looked like beneath all that hair. The fire was near a three-walled shed open to the elements. Its rugged exterior was contrasted by modern bulb-lighting that hung from the rafters above some folding chairs and benches.

The fire snapped when Jerry tossed more wood on the new flames, sending out waves of heat and smoke. Luke and Jerry talked about a song they were writing together, so River took the opportunity to walk around the vacant property, taking it in, almost like she was looking for something or someone. She came back when a car and truck pulled up the gravel drive. A few people got out and joined them at the fire and about ten minutes later the Troubadours tour bus pulled up. The band members got out carrying a host of instruments with them: guitars, a banjo, a ukulele and harmonicas. A couple of the guys looked like they would fit in anywhere in small-town America. Beards, jeans and flannel shirts, but a couple of them would have made hipsters jealous with their authentic farm-boy-going-to-church look: ankle-high slacks with suspenders and one had a brimmed hat. The lead singer was a committed Okie. He wore a classic western shirt with pointed pockets on the front. And River couldn't help noticing the large buckle at the top of his Wranglers. It screamed "tacky" at her. Not even Felker could make this gaudy man-jewelry look good, she decided.

The band members slapped hands with the men around the fire and nodded hello at the ladies. The fiddle player sported suspenders and held a guitar instead of a fiddle. He took a liking to River. She felt the bench move when he sat down next to her, shoulder to shoulder. She knew he was a pro on the fiddle but she didn't know he could work the neck of a guitar like he did. After impressing her sufficiently, he stopped and asked her if she played.

The question took her unexpected so she stuttered, "No. Yeah. I mean, no. I played the ukulele in a high school music class, that's all."

Before she could protest the guy jumped up, ran to the tour bus and came back with a shiny black uke. Luke could tell she was blushing even through the shifting light of the fire as the guy handed it to her.

"No, seriously," she protested, "that was like, five years ago. I can't even remember basic chords."

"Well, then, darlin', let me show ya." He reached around behind her to show her where to place her fingers on the strings for each chord. Luke wasn't sure why but he couldn't look away. He was relieved when the guy finally took his hands off her. River strummed the chords following the guy's lead on his guitar as best she could.

Someone offered River a beer but she passed. Luke took one, popped it open and enjoyed a big swig. He set it down and focused on playing his guitar. About thirty minutes in, one of the guys in the group had already drunk his share of alcohol. As he walked by the fire, he lost his balance and almost fell into it. The group shared relief when he regained his balance just in time. Felker celebrated by busting out

Johnny Cash on his guitar, singing, "I fell into a burning ring of fire." Everyone sang along,

> I went down, down, down
> and the flames went higher.
> And it burns, burns, burns,
> the ring of fire...

The last line Luke hit with vibrating bass, "the ring of fire." River's eyes widened; she'd never heard him sing before. Everyone gave him props for his low vocal range and some band members gave respects with a fist bump.

People went back to playing their own songs for a time. Felker walked back to the bus for something and River noticed, doing a double-take. She stood up and followed him to his bus. Luke watched them exchange a few words before Felker went inside the bus and came back out with a piece of paper, which River pocketed. This surprised Luke. He didn't take her for the type of woman to hook up with random guys. But maybe she was. She was a feminist, after all. And, anyway, it was none of his business.

He pretended not to notice when she came back to the fire and focused on strumming the uke. A few minutes later she felt a nudge on her arm. The guitarist held a thin joint between his fingers, offering it to her. Weed wouldn't make her act like a fool, she reasoned. She took a couple hits and passed it on. When it got to Luke, he shook his head and it passed him by.

He and Jerry had finally figured out the chords for the song they were working on. Luke began to sing the lyrics. His voice traveled across the campfire and got River's attention immediately. Jerry picked a fast and furious tune on his banjo while Luke accompanied with his guitar. It would have been a happy song if it weren't for the words:

Your little light, oh, so bright
Filled the sky in my head with angel light
But you killed the light, took it right out my head
You let the devil dance in our bed

'N he tries, but he can't dance 'round my head
'Cause I killed the devil, I killed him dead
Now he's lyin' in a liquid grave
'N I sing, Glory Hallelujah, my soul got saved

When your daddy racked his fuckin' gun
If he'd shot the guilty, you'd been the one
You shake the dice when lights go out
You're the girl mamas warn their sons about

Oh, the years were long, but that talk short
Just the sound of wood under foot when you walked
out
They say six-day creation made us water 'n dust
But, good lord, honey, it was spirit 'n trust!

Now no one can kill that light in my head
'Cuz life is good when the devil's dead
Yeah, life is good when the devil's dead

Oh, I said, Glory Hallelujah!
The devil's dead!

For River, watching Luke get lost in a song that exposed
his loss was like meeting him for the first time. Something
about him singing his own lyrics revealed his humanity in a
way that only music can. The campfire smoke moved her
direction and burned her eyes. She brushed it away. She
thought it might be impossible to keep Luke as a cliché in
her mind after tonight. Her mind focused on her strings and

the back of her head began to buzz as the cannabis kicked in. It deepened and widened her thoughts. She strummed and wondered what he meant by "liquid grave." And she wondered what the opposite of a liquid grave would be. Liquid birth? She thought about birth and she thought about thinking. She wondered what these might have in common. *Consciousness*, she decided. *Consciousness swims in the amniotic fluid of the mind. It gives birth to ideas that grow into reality.* She thought this sounded really brilliant. But maybe it was really dumb. It was hard for her to tell when she was high. But she thought it was sure to be one of the two. She wished she had a pen so she could jot it down and read it later.

Luke looked at her. He'd never seen her lost in her own world, paying no attention to the one around her. She strummed the uke carefully like it was the only thing in the world that needed to be done. He wanted to brush away the disheveled hair spread across her face. His stare was interrupted when the guitarist wrapped his hand around her thigh and made her laugh about something. Luke watched his hand linger there long after the laugh had ended. River felt Luke watching her so she looked over at him and their eyes locked. He didn't look away like he did when they were young; he kept his gaze on her. There was something about the campfire that made them both remember the night he'd told her she looked like Pocahontas. Their eyes broke contact when the guitarist asked her if this was her first time at The Farm.

"Yeah," she answered. "Well, actually, if it weren't for The Farm I wouldn't exist." She pointed where the burned down farmhouse used to stand, "My mom got pregnant with me right over there."

"I didn't know that, Riv!" Luke spoke up across the flames.

She nodded.

Everyone was impressed, including Felker who yelled, "We've got a farm-baby right here, folks!" His belt buckle glimmered in firelight under his guitar as he plucked a quick melody on his strings. He made up a silly song about harvesting farm babies that sprouted in the red dirt of Oklahoma. River was in disbelief that Evan Felker was singing an original song about her and her red-dirt roots. She was on cloud nine! She laughed from her gut and Luke laughed at her laughter.

As the night progressed, the crowd thinned out, the fire got smaller, the smoke got bigger and the guitarist found more and more reasons to touch River's thighs and waist. Luke wondered if River weren't high would she have let the guy keep touching her like that? The situation increasingly bothered him. It was past midnight so Luke suggested that they leave. He enjoyed seeing the surprise on the guy's face when he realized River had come with someone. Luke took River's keys away from her; she didn't seem to notice.

The Jeep top was down and dust flew behind them as he drove past squares of farmland. She was quiet as they drove the straight flat terrain, the night sky providing just enough light to see each other. He felt her watching him. He looked over. She was. Maybe it was the cannabis freeing her mind but she saw Luke differently that night. When he hung his head over his guitar and sang his experience into the night air he didn't look like a Neanderthal. She knew he wasn't perfect but maybe he wasn't the chest-beating gorilla she'd thought he was, even if he did vote for Trump. Her eyes were fixed on how the wind moved his hair around the rim of his hat. She thought he looked good driving her Jeep with his hoodie sleeves pulled halfway up his big forearms. He looked over at her and she didn't look away. He looked back and forth between her and the road trying to figure out what was going through her head, which was leaning on the headrest, her short hair whipping around her face. He thought she looked pretty damn cute with her bare feet on the dash, too. She didn't seem to notice that he was watching her stare at him. He grinned. Finally, she looked away and just chilled for the rest of the drive home.

I'll take her high over drunk any day of the week, he thought. *Or sober, for that matter.*

CHAPTER EIGHTEEN

Before River got to work the next day, she pulled a piece of paper out of her smoke-scented jeans from the night before. Evan Felker's personal cell number was written in his own handwriting. She smiled as she stuck it to her fridge with a magnet.

When she got to the store, she couldn't stop talking about how fun it was to meet the Troubadours and hear Felker sing a song about her. Luke had never seen her so excited. He also never saw her look at him the way she did the night before. Other than her manic mood, everything was back to normal.

When they closed the shop that evening Luke and River walked outside to find food trucks lining Main Street. The road was blocked off for "Food Trucks and Tunes," Stillwater's weekly downtown attraction. Luke asked River if she wanted to grab some food. The evening had a buzz to it so she agreed. She figured Loretta could wait.

Aroma-laden smoke wafted past as they walked down Main Street considering their options. River was glad to see Mediterranean food; she missed Boston's emphasis on healthy eating. She aimed in that direction while Luke focused his attention on the BBQ ribs.

They reconnected at an empty table somewhere in the middle. The sun peeked above the southern row of storefronts warming their arms and backs as they ate. Live music kicked in with vibrating strings from a stand-up bass, a fiddle, and a banjo; the three-man band was doing a Dixieland cover of Wagon Wheel. A few verses in, some folks danced the two-step in front of the makeshift stage.

"Go dancing with me tonight," Luke said before taking a bite of BBQ ribs.

Some time passed. He gave her a look that asked if she planned on answering him.

She waited a while longer before saying, "I answer questions, not commands."

He smiled and took another bite of ribs. He leaned his forearms on the table and looked her in the face. "Hey, River. You wanna go out dancin' with me tonight?"

She swallowed a mouthful of food. "I can't."

"Why not?"

"The Land & Cattle Co. has a strict no-dating policy for employees," she joked, for lack of a better reason, but also to make him clarify his intentions.

Luke grabbed his napkin and rubbed BBQ sauce off of his mouth. "Well, then, it's a good thing I ain't askin' you on a date. Just want to kick up some dust. You have something better to do, tonight?"

River thought for a while. Dancing sounded like fun but she was worried he'd get the wrong idea. "You promise you won't think it's a date if I say yes?"

"I don't date feminists."

She burst out laughing, even though she wasn't sure if he was joking or not. The man had a straight face. So, she agreed, "Okay."

River stopped by to see Loretta before going out. She told her mom about visiting The Farm and hanging out with Turnpike Troubadours. Loretta would have been impressed that Felker made up a song about River being a "farm-baby." If only for a moment, River forgot that her mom probably couldn't hear her. She was getting used to having a less-talkative mother who couldn't give unsolicited advice.

Later, when she was getting dressed to go out, she wondered why she'd agreed to let Luke pick her up. This wasn't a date, after all. And she didn't plan on drinking. It was a hot night but she decided against wearing Daisy Dukes. Too revealing for a non-date. She decided old jeans and a plain top fit the mood.

She opened the door to a resounding knock and found Luke wearing the entire cowboy getup: a cowboy hat, boots, a western blouse and one of those hideous belt buckles she told him she hated so much. It seemed he was trying to annoy her. Or maybe he actually wanted to be taken seriously. It didn't matter. Either way, she was relieved to know Luke wasn't trying to impress her. But she had to admit, he perfectly embodied a classic cowboy.

When they got to Outlaws, they practiced different versions of the two-step, the horseshoe shuffle, and a couple of line dances. River had some catching up to do. She barely remembered the Boot Scootin' Boogie. They laughed pretty hard when she turned the wrong way and landed squarely against the man behind her, something she figured Luke would put on his list of things to tease her about.

But the mood shifted as they stepped in time to the music and moved in unison across the dimly lit room. River had become attuned to Luke's subtle movements, and the fact that he led and she followed only mattered theoretically. Each of them skillfully managed their own role, which allowed them to achieve something akin to art, the kind of display that inspires awe in onlookers. When their equal-opposite movements were perfectly timed there was a kind of euphoria in it.

Luke became aware of the curve in River's waist and how it felt in the palm of his hand. He liked how her short hair exposed her neck. It looked perfectly consumable. Delicate, too, like everything else about her. When he spun her around, she gave off an intoxicating scent he could only describe as 'feminine.' With the slightest movement he pulled her in a little closer.

Maybe it was the vibe Luke was giving off but River became aware of the way Luke's bicep flexed under her hand before he spun her around. Being much shorter than he, River faced his chest directly. It was like a brick wall, solid and unmovable. She was curious what it felt like and was surprised when she imagined herself touching it. She decided Olivia would call Luke "toxic" simply by virtue of his muscle mass, even though he'd earned every contour by hard, manual labor. After a couple hours of close proximity, River finally admitted to herself: *this man is gorgeous.*

They took a break from dancing and settled at the bar for a drink. River ordered sweet-tea. No alcohol for her, no way!

What she didn't know was, the less alcohol she drank the more confident Luke became in making a move. He palmed his beer in one hand, his wrist rested on one of his thighs. One of his boots was behind her barstool. He almost straddled her at a comfortable distance. She felt an electric current moving between them. It was a little unnerving to feel that kind of sexual attraction to her once-childhood acquaintance, now annoying co-worker. But with the way he was sitting, she couldn't help looking down at his crotch.

He noticed.

He tipped back the remainder of his beer and said, "Thanks for comin' out tonight. I'm done here if you are."

"Yeah, I'm done." It was strange. The night was still young. Normally they would stay longer but somehow, she knew it would only get awkward if they didn't leave now.

The ride home was quiet. Only radio noise filled the warm air swirling through the open windows. River's heart was racing and she couldn't figure out why. He hadn't been flirting with her and he didn't try paying for her drink. He'd sent her no visible sign that he planned on making a pass.

When they pulled up to her house it felt natural when he walked her up the porch steps, but she made sure not to look at him before opening the front door and stepping inside. He took one step inside, too. He knew this was a risky move, like she might think he was being too aggressive and accuse him of harassment or something. But he was daring enough to find out. He had no plans of touching her, that was for sure! Well, not unless the coast was clear. He'd hoped she would see this move for what it was—a demonstration of courage and competence. Judging by the way she was looking at him earlier, Luke was 70% sure she wouldn't kick him out.

She turned around to face him but found she couldn't look him in the eyes. She kept her gaze on the keys in her hands. Clearly, she needed to kick him out. That's what needed to happen. So, she would.

River relied largely on reason to make important decisions. But in that moment, instinct took hold. She tried telling Luke to leave, but the words wouldn't come out of her mouth. Actually, the more she sensed his masculine energy standing there, the more she didn't want to kick him out. And the longer she stayed silent the more confident Luke became.

"River. Look at me," he finally said.

She looked up at his brown dilated eyes. Her legs went numb and her breathing quickened. The only thing she could feel was sexual tension moving between them like a gravitational pull. They looked at each other for a while before he brought his hand up to her face and moved his thumb across her lips. She involuntarily closed her eyes.

The coast was clear. He wanted to kiss her but she was so short. So he picked her up by the hips and pressed her against the wall. Her eyes flew open. She dropped her keys and held on to his shoulders. His lips came down over hers. She let herself feel his desire and his body against hers. She slid her hands through the back of his hair pulling him in and kissing him back. He smelled like shampoo, like sweat and like... Luke.

Their kiss moved with intention. His body kept her pinned to the wall and his hands cupped her neck and face. As their kiss intensified, he slid his fingers up through the sides of her short hair. Their kiss deepened and his hands traveled down to her waist, then up to the sides of her breasts. She felt like she had alcohol in her system but it was only adrenaline. He abandoned her mouth and moved to her neck. Her hands moved across his broad shoulders. Eventually, his cheek scraped hers when he said, "I'm gonna need your permission to touch your ass."

River laughed. The fact that he respected the boundary she had established made her want to give Luke an all-access pass. "You got it," she replied.

He moved his hands down her butt and cupped his hands around her thighs opening her legs around his waist while continuing to consume her neck. She jerked in a breath when he pressed in between her thighs with his hips, making her suddenly aware of his belt buckle. That's when River learned the usefulness of those damn things. Her legs rose with the sensation and she locked her feet around him. Luke chuckled, "You should take what I say seriously."

She unbuttoned his shirt a little and found a chest sculpted by years of manual labor. "Hard work looks good on you," she panted.

"Everything looks good on you," he whispered in her ear, but he imagined that nothing looked even better. Eventually, his hands found her breasts. Her subtle response made him feel like his desire couldn't be contained. The words came out before he realized what he'd said. "I just need one word from you, Riv."

It was hard for her to think clearly in that moment, but she knew she needed to. She didn't answer him right away. She worried if they slept together that he wouldn't take her seriously anymore, but she was equally concerned that he would. *Where could this possibly lead? Do I really want to sleep with Luke Thompson?* she asked herself. Her body answered. "Yes," she breathed.

"There's just one thing you should know."

Thinking clearly sounded more important suddenly. She pushed him away to look him in the eyes, "What?"

His eyes grinned, "If we do this, I'm in charge."

Her stomach jumped and her curiosity piqued.

"Do you trust me?" he asked, keeping eye contact.

She nodded.

He kicked the front door shut and carried her down the hall. He moved around a bed post and came down over her, careful not to crush her. They continued the intoxicating kiss they'd begun against the wall while the palms of his hands found hers and he pressed them down on either side of her head. Their kiss was full of unspoken desire and pent up frustration. He pulled her hands above her head and pinned them down with one of his forearms. Her strength couldn't have matched his if she'd tried and she knew feminists would write volumes protesting this move. But nature had already written volumes inside of her that no feminist tome could displace. She found herself thinking, *if masculinity is toxic, then poison me, Luke!* He enjoyed taking the driver's seat and he drove her to just the edge of ecstasy. But not over it.

At some point, animal instinct was the only thing Luke could see in River's eyes—pure sexual desire. Eventually, she said, "Just… finish what you started, Luke."

"Yes, ma'am!" he said. His belt buckle hit the floor with a thud. And that was the sound of River's shortlist getting shorter.

❖

They settled against the headboard his arm around her waist, her head against his chest, the sheet halfway up. Luke said, "You know, Riv… you're mine now."

She pushed away from his chest to look him in the eye. "What do you mean I'm yours? I'm not an object."

"I mean, I'm gonna take care of you now. Until you won't let me no more."

"Thanks anyway. But, I'm not a child either. I don't need taking care of." She laid her head on his chest again.

"What if it ain't about need? What if I want to?" She hated the fact that she swooned inside when he said that. Her eyes rolled back in her head. *I won't give up that easily*, she thought.

She changed the subject, "Aren't you supposed to feel guilty now? Christian man having sex outside of marriage?"

Luke thought about it. "Well, technically I'm not outside of marriage. Looks like you're the one that needs repentin'."

She laughed, "Why do you always have a smartass reply for everything I say?"

He stayed quiet just to prove her wrong.

She thought for a minute then said, "But, seriously. Aren't you worried what Pastor Jackson will say if he finds out?"

It's true, you would have found Luke sitting in church every Sunday as a child. But Luke didn't find God there. Luke found God sitting alone in a canoe only a few months ago when his traitor hands held a gun to his own head. Luke decided if he could find God looking down the barrel of a Glock 40 then he could find Him anywhere.

"If Pastor Jackson wants to talk to me about livin'-in-sin I'll just point to his tractor-tire belly and say, 'least the sin I'm living in has health benefits'."

River laughed from her gut, imagining Luke saying this to the pastor.

After a bit he ran his fingers down her bare chest and said, "Besides, God wouldn't of made sex if he didn't want us to have it."

She lifted the sheet a little higher. "Do you actually believe in God, Luke?"

He pulled his hand away and rubbed it over his scruffy jaw. *Topic change*, he thought. "Course I do. Talk to him all the time."

"It's hard for me to believe that God exists. And even if there is a God, why assume the source-of-all-things is a person, you know? A relational being."

He replied, "It's hard for me to believe everything comes from nothin'. And why would God make people relational if he ain't't?"

She hadn't thought about it that way before, from God's perspective, one might say. She would have to assume God is real to think about something from God's perspective. But if God is real then it would make sense to start from God's perspective and move toward people's, she decided. Her mind got all tangled up.

He could almost see the hamster-wheel in her brain turning, trying to rationalize this. "You won't find God in your head, Riv. God's an experience."

"An experience?" She raised her eyebrows.

He nodded.

She questioned what a gorilla might know about spirituality. "Okay, so, how does someone experience God, Luke?"

"Well… you gotta get to the bottom of your bucket first. When you get there, you look up—that's instinct. Then," he shrugged, "everything changes."

He could still feel the warmth of the sun on his face when he tipped his head back and brought the gun down to his lap. One word escaped his empty heart, "Help." In an instant, he became aware of someone sitting in that canoe with him. His eyes betrayed him; he saw nothing but an empty boat. But someone was there. If he never knew anything before that moment, he knew someone was sitting in that canoe with him. A warm sensation spread across his legs, like hands on his lap. A lifeline had been thrown to him and he held onto it with everything inside. Pain siphoned out of his soul and a strange peace replaced it. When the sensation lifted, a certain darkness left along with it, no longer infecting him like venom from a snake. No death-grip remained. He looked down at the handgun still in his grip, which then revealed itself as the enemy that it was. He emptied the chamber into the liquid grave, tossed his wedding ring in after it and paddled back to the shore. Luke continued, "People who don't believe in God haven't gotten to the bottom of their bucket, yet. Or, if they got there, they shook their fist at the sky."

River didn't think this was true. She felt like she'd gotten to the bottom of her bucket and didn't suddenly believe in God or shake her fist at anyone. But his statement reminded her of something she'd read in college by Carl Jung, something like, modern man can't find God because he doesn't look low enough. "People call that a crutch, you know? Religion as a crutch."

"You can shame a beggar for beggin', but that won't stop him from tryin' to get food."

Fair enough, she thought. "But how can you deny science for an archaic story like creation?"

"Never said I did."

She looked at him, "You're not a creationist?"

"I don't take the creation story literally, if that's what you mean. It ain't science. It's a deeper truth."

She hadn't imagined that Luke was an independent thinker, but she was happy to realize he was. "What deeper truth?"

"That God started all of this. You know? When everything came from nothin'. What do they call that? The Big Bang? It's kinda funny, the creation story kinda sounds like evolution if you think about it. First, he made light, then water and dirt, then plants, and animals and then people. But even if they didn't sound the same, it wouldn't bother me. I don't need to hate one 'n love the other."

She was surprised by this and a little impressed by Luke's reasoning. She liked the way he talked about truth. Like it existed and that it could be found. She'd previously assumed religion and science were mutually exclusive. The idea that they might not be had never crossed her mind.

But she decided to set all of this stuff aside and enjoy the moment she was in. The warmth of Luke's body against hers was comforting. And she needed comfort more than truth right then.

.

CHAPTER NINETEEN

River glanced at the phone number pinned to her fridge. Before dialing the number, she took a deep breath. Her stomach flipped when a man's voice answered.

"Hi. This is River. We met at The Farm last week."
"Hey, darlin'. How ya doin'?"
"Good. Is this a good time to chat?"
"Sure is."

River was happy to get some girl-time with Jules and even more excited when they pulled up to Nacho Mamas. She'd given up trying to find decent Mexican food in Boston. Stillwater's Tex-Mex was evidence that Oklahoma was closer to the border than Massachusetts.

She looked at the menu but found herself thinking about her Friday night escapade with Luke. She knew she would have to tell Jules before news got around and she heard it from someone else. River was scared that Jules would have a serious problem with her best friend and her brother hooking up. But this fact could not be undone, so the cards would have to fall where they would.

The waitress approached the table and they placed their orders. River took a drink of her sweet-tea before beginning, "So... how would you feel if Luke and I hooked up?"

"WHAT?" Jules yelled.

"Shhh," River looked around worried Jules hadn't invited eavesdroppers into the conversation.

"Oh my God! Did you sleep with Luke?" Jules yelled.

"For the love of God, woman! Keep your voice down! I'm just askin', how you'd feel if we did."

"Did you?" Jules persisted.

River paused, realizing there would be no soft-launch to this news. "Yes. Okay? We did."

Jules mouth hung open and she went completely still. Jules could be overly dramatic, but she'd really outdone herself this time. "I'm sorry." She finally said, "Give me a sec. Just tryin' to picture y'all together."

"Please don't."

"Yeah. No."

"Do you hate me?" River's eyes narrowed as she prepared for the worst.

Jules sounded really uncomfortable when she said, "No, of course not. But... I mean... you did sleep with a married man, you know?" Jules laughed awkwardly and took a very long drink of her tea.

River could tell Jules was trying to figure out what to say next. This was the first time River had ever witnessed Jules lacking words.

Jules picked up the dessert menu and flipped through it, as if she was actually seeing what she was looking at. "It's fine, Riv. Y'all are adults. It's not like I can stop ya. Just gonna take me some time to get used to it, that's all."

River nodded, glad Jules wasn't visibly angry.

"Frankly, I can't see the two of you mixin'. Tryin' to figure out how y'all made it to the bedroom without fightin' the whole way there." Both women laughed because it was the truth. Jules slammed the menu down and yelled, "Y'all were drunk!"

River shook her head. "Pretty damn sober, actually."

"WOW!"

"I know. I'm almost as surprised as you are," she shrugged.

Jules put a finger up. "Hang on." She pulled her phone out of her purse. It was Penny. "Hey, Pen, what's up?" Jules put her hand over her mouth, "Oh my God! What's wrong!" River's heart sank. It was Penny. River could hear her crying on the other end of the phone. Penny was one of the strongest, most responsible adults and could take care of herself, but they would always feel protective of her because of that traumatic night the three of them shared in their teenage years. That moment sealed a bond between the three of them that nothing could undo.

"Oh my God, Pen! Tell me what's wrong!" Jules fanned her face. "Are you hurt?"

She wasn't hurt. Jules' and River's shoulders dropped an inch. She didn't want to talk about it over the phone. Jules threw a ten-dollar bill on the table while River found the waitress to cancel their orders.

They got to Penny's house in record time. Jules had a key to Penny's house so they walked straight in and found Penny crying on her well-worn couch.

"Good lord, Penny, tell me what's wrong!" Jules demanded.

Penny sniffed, "Mr. Conner... Michael, came over to drop somethin' off. So, I invited him in for some tea. Stevie was sleepin'."

"Oh my God! He hurt you!"

"He did not hurt me, Jules! Calm down!" Penny slapped Jules' arm and gained some composure. "We talked right here on the couch for, like, an hour. Anyway, he kissed me and it was great. It was the best, actually." She started crying again and put her hands over her freckled face. Jules lifted her hands and looked at River with wide eyes. River shook her head and gave Jules a look that said, calm down and behave yourself. Penny looked up, "I ruined it!"

"How?" River asked.

"He started touching me and I wanted him to. I did. But, suddenly, instead of Michael it was Russel."

Jules and River looked at each other. They had never heard Penny say her rapist's name before. She probably only knew his name because of the trial where her brother was charged with assault.

"I couldn't get the monster out of my head. Instead of Michael it was him," she gasped, her shoulders rose and fell as she cried. "I told myself, stay calm, hopin' that feeling would go away, 'cause I knew what was happening. And I wanted it to happen. But… I was panicking inside, you know? When he climbed on top of me, I totally freaked out. I screamed and fought him off. I think I even kicked him in the stomach when he was gettin' up." She wiped the tears from her face with a ragged tissue. "I might as well have told him I was a man. That's how shocked he looked. He looked scared, actually! He left fast and didn't say nothin'. Well, I guess he said 'I'm sorry'."

"Oh, Pen," Jules said. "Does Michael know? You know? About how you got Stevie?"

Penny shook her head and tore off small pieces of the tissue in her hand.

"Do you care about him?"

Penny slammed the tissue down on the brown cushion. "Well, course I care about him, Jules! That's why I'm sittin' here cryin'!" She went back to tearing her tissue.

Jules looked at River like she had been tasked with parenting a hormonal teenager.

River put her arm around Penny's waist. "It looks like you're gonna have to tell him what happened if you wanna move forward with him. He seems like a good guy. I bet he'll understand."

"I wanted him to make it new for me, ya know? A good experience."

"He can't do that if he doesn't know."

"I know. But I didn't think he wanted to know about that." She started crying again, "But, now he thinks I'm a fucking head case. 'Cuz, I am!"

"Penny," Jules said, "I'd bet my life Michael would understand. You've been flirtin' him for two years, even though you've had it locked down like Fort Knox. That man has the patience of a saint!"

Penny looked at Jules through the corner of her red eyes, obviously unhappy with the observation. She said nothing. Her breathing calmed. The women sat in silence for a while. River looked around the room. Penny had obviously anticipated Michael's visit; the place was unusually organized. Eventually, Penny said, "I'll be lucky if he ever talks to me again. I don't imagine gettin' the chance to explain myself."

Jules didn't waste any time giving advice, "Just make it happen, Pen. You're the strongest woman I know. Just tell him what happened, even if you have to do it over the phone."

Penny nodded.

"The sooner the better."

She gave another nod. They offered to stay for support but she didn't want an audience, especially the judging type. When they left, Penny picked up the phone and called Michael.

Michael's phone vibrated on his table. He looked down at it. Penny's face lit the screen. The phone was a rattlesnake. He froze. It went to voicemail. He went back to pacing the dated floor of his apartment. The snake rattled again. He watched it shake until it went through to voicemail again. *What in the world does she want*, he wondered? He thought maybe she was calling to cuss him out and tell him she was pressing charges. He was 100% sure he'd scared her but he didn't know how he'd done it. He was going over the situation in his mind—over and over again. He thought she was enjoying the moment. And she was. Until she wasn't. He wondered if he'd be accused of sexually assaulting a student's mother. The accusation alone would get him fired. Would he ever find a teaching job in Stillwater again? The snake shook a third time and he seized it with a whisper, "Hello."

"I need to explain myself," Penny replied.

He said nothing.

She paused before saying, "Something happened to me when I was young. That's how I got Stevie."

Michael's stomach turned. He didn't expect to hear this. Of all the things he expected her to say, this was not one. When what she'd said sunk in, a queasy anger rose up in his gut. He knew he should say something. But, what? He was the calculated type. Everything he did was planned, even his words. He wasn't good with spontaneous, especially with important matters. He'd planned what he would wear that evening and even what he'd say. He planned to kiss her because he knew their attraction was mutual. And, he planned to take things as far as she would let them go. But he couldn't have planned for this.

She sniffed.

He finally said, "That shouldn't have happened to you." He put a sweaty palm on his forehead. He figured he'd said the wrong thing.

"It's okay if you never want to see me again. I just didn't want you to think you did somethin' wrong. 'Cause you didn't."

Relief didn't adequately describe how Michael felt when she said that. He wanted to record her saying that. She might as well have said, 'You won't be going to jail, after all. And you can keep your job.'

River and Jules made their way back to Nacho Mamas. Their stomachs punished them for the delay. They sat down and ordered as quickly as possible and ate all the chips and salsa within five minutes after taking their seats. They talked about Penny for a while and River used the phrase "women's issues" when discussing the effects of trauma.

"Trauma ain't just a woman's issue," Jules pointed out.

"Yeah, but women are victims of violence more often, statistically."

"Actually, men are victims of violence more often than women. And men make up half domestic violence cases. Plus, they don't have shelters like women do."

"That is not true! Men are not half of DV cases."

"They sure are! Forty-something percent. I know my stats, Riv. I'm a nurse, ya know?"

"You're seriously trying to tell me that women assault men as often as men assault women?"

"I did not say that! Men are assaulted by other men, mostly. But some are assaulted by women and no one talks about that. Everyone says domestic violence a 'woman's issue' but I see guys in the ER all the time for this. And, by the way, ain't nowhere to send 'em except back home. When's the last time you heard of a men's shelter?"

River was bothered that she couldn't remember the DV statistics she'd learned in her Women's Studies class years ago. But she knew the percentages were dramatically different from Jules'. She couldn't skillfully argue this point but she continued the debate anyway, "Well, there's no way men are even close to half of rape victims."

"True. Women are raped more often. But when men are raped, they don't go 'round talkin' about it, do they? So, who knows what the actual stats are? I'm just sayin', violence is a man's issue, too."

It was hard for River to tolerate Jules advocating for men when it seemed true that women were the overwhelming majority of victims. "Well, you can't fault feminists for working on women's issues, Jules."

"Feminists! Ha! You know what I hate about them?"

"Oh, here we go," River mumbled.

"They act like they represent women 'n they don't even represent half of us! They're waving their cardboard signs around, actin' like they speak for me. I don't remember votin' for 'em! Do you?"

"Of course, they represent women, Jules!"

"Okay, fine. They represent women. Except for ALL the women they don't, which is most!"

"Oh, my God!" River's hands covered her face.

"Feminists downright hate some women, especially ones like me. They're like, 'Y'all don't know what you want. Y'all don't know what's good for you, Y'all are workin' against your best interest.' They don't know my interest! Like, if you're pro-life they revoke your woman-card. Or if you stay home to raise your kids, they attack you. So much for sisterhood! They're probably just jealous 'cause some women found good men to depend on."

"Depending on men is dangerous, Jules. Even a good man can change. Plus, who got you the right to vote pro-life? Feminists!" River said, smugly.

"Feminist wasn't even a word when women were workin' on getting the vote."

"Well, you know what I mean."

"You know how Elizabeth Cady Stanton was able to work on the vote? By depending on her husband, that's how. And, she raised seven kids, by the way. No one ever talks about that."

"Susan B. Anthony didn't have kids or a husband. And, by the way, the only reason Stanton had seven kids is 'cause she didn't have birth control!"

"Well, feminists didn't invent birth control, now did they? Men did! If feminists wanna make a difference in the world they can put down the cardboard sign and pick up a microscope!"

Spoken like a scientist, River thought.

"You give a feminist a microscope 'n she's like, 'Oh, my God, I see a micro-aggressions'."

River laughed, even though she didn't want to.

Jules laughed, too. "But, seriously, though! They've run out of issues and they're still screamin' in the streets. Name one thing that men can do and women can't in this country."

The waitress arrived with their steaming hot plates of Mexican food; their senses were on high alert. Suddenly, all they could think about was cheesy-goodness.

River kept her eyes on her plate but tried to think about Jules' question. What can men do that women can't do? *Pee standing up?* she laughed to herself. Technically, the answer was "nothing," but she didn't like conceding a point. And she was enjoying the intellectual banter. Plus, she knew there was more to the topic but her stomach was overriding her brainy-part. She managed to add, "It's not just about opportunity."

"HA! You can't!" Jules announced victoriously.

"Just eat your damn burrito, Julie!"

Jules reached across the table and slapped the fork out of River's hand. "Don't call me that, you little brat."

They laughed off the tension and appeased their stomachs, which had become a vocal part of the conversation.

River swung out of her Jeep holding onto the roll bar above and walked around the side of the farmhouse where a creek bed ran. She settled onto rock in the shrubs and watched her younger self playing in the water, trying to catch fireflies at dusk. It would have been a typical summer night as a child. As the summer air darkened, they bobbed and played like old friends in a game of hide and seek. In her trancelike state, River half expected to hear Loretta calling her inside for a bath.

River missed her mama, the one she'd known before the accident, which by then had been many weeks before. She'd begun wondering if her mama would be one of those coma-cases where someone sleeps for decades before waking up. River put the thought out of her mind as quickly as it arrived. Then, as if willing it to happen, she told herself, *mama will wake up soon. She just has to.*

CHAPTER TWENTY

Anytime the outdoors reached triple digits the old store got uncomfortably hot before noon. Business was as still as the hot air, so she sent Skippy home early.

Luke was stocking heavy bags of animal feed directly in front of the counter where River was slumped. He'd sweat through his shirt, so he took it off to finish the work. River found herself watching him stock the shelves. She figured this might be the closest she'd ever come to a religious experience, meditating on God's creation in the form of Luke Thompson. She imagined Pastor Jackson adding an eighth day to the creation story saying, "And, on the eighth day, God created Luke Thompson and he said, 'It is good'." Her imagination left church pretty quickly as she watched his muscles flex under his sweaty skin.

Luke interrupted, "You, like havin' a Greek god 'round to do your heavy liftin', don't ya?"

Her cheeks darkened and her eyes darted away. "Don't flatter yourself, Luke" She organized the papers in her hands.

"Well, someone's gotta do it!"

"Do they?"

He put his hands on his hips. "Wow! You really know how to stroke a man's ego."

"Why the hell would I want to do that, Luke?"

He looked from side to side then walked around behind her. He cupped one hand around her waist and leaned his other on the counter in front of her. "Because his confidence follows him to the bedroom, darlin'." He smacked her thigh which made her knees go a little week.

She elbowed his stomach as the bell on the door rang. "Hello, Mr. Robertson," she said awkwardly. Luke went back to stocking the shelves, looking at her from the corner of his eye. Even though she was making small talk with Mr. Robertson, her mind was considering what Luke had just said. *Does stroking a man's ego actually affect his performance in the bedroom?* She decided to test this theory on him.

Just outside of Stillwater, Carl parked in front of a run-down bar on his way home from Texas where he had unsuccessfully searched for Linn. The Corral had a flashing sign on top but the C no longer lit up and the L flickered off and on in no particular pattern. This dive always had a handful of truckers and prostitutes lingering inside. Carl hung around there sometimes when he was avoiding a Stillwater local to whom he owed money. It was also a fairly anonymous place to find a hooker.

The bar was dim, just a few lights hung around the room and a couple above the bar. The beefy bartender wore his usual bandanna with sleeves pulled halfway up his tattooed arms. His face had a thick scar down the left side. He didn't talk much. But when he did you listened. "The Man," they called him. If The Man said it was time for you to leave the bar, you left. He took shit from no one; rumor had it he used to be a Hell's Angel. Carl didn't take him seriously until one night when he actually witnessed The Man shoot a guy who wouldn't leave the bar when told him to. The Man only shot his arm, but still. That was enough to convince Carl of The

Man's dominance. Plus, The Man had dirt on everyone who frequented his bar, so no one ever snitched.

He poured a few shots of Jack when he saw Carl walk in. Carl took his place at the bar and tipped all three back, one after the other, and then ordered a beer. The Man was only a little surprised at Carl's speed. He usually paced himself more slowly. But Carl was agitated. He didn't know where to go from there in his search for Linn. He was almost out of money and the farm had stopped generating revenue. In fact, it had come to a complete stop. He hadn't even fed the animals in a long while. Anywhere else he would search for Linn would be a shot in the dark. He feared he'd run out of resources before he'd run into Linn.

A woman who went by the name Candy was trying to make eye-contact with him but he knew he couldn't afford her that night, so he ignored her. The rest of his dwindling cash would go entirely to finding Linn. And drinking, of course. He thought about Linn. He wondered where she was and who was with her. He imagined her being with another man. Heat emanated from his entire body. He gulped the beer and slammed it down on the counter. Candy walked over to Carl and promised she could cheer him up. He was just about to say "go to hell" when it occurred to him, she might be able to help him find Linn. He realized there was still one place in town he hadn't looked for Linn—the Women's Shelter. That's because he didn't know where it was. Its location was unknown to the public, unless you were a woman who needed it. He'd already called the place pretending to be her brother needing to inform her about a family member's death, but they "would neither confirm or deny" that she was staying there. They certainly weren't going to give him the address. But, Carl reasoned, they would give it to Candy, wouldn't they?

He looked her up and down. Her cheap shirt looked more like a bra and she was twitchier than normal. He told her he had a job for her and not the usual kind. When he explained it, she told him she hadn't been to the shelter in Stillwater, but she'd been to plenty of other shelters and she knew how they worked. They didn't just tell people their address, not even women. Candy explained that she would have to meet a shelter worker at a random location, tell her a sob story and then ride with the worker to a secure location where she would stay overnight. Candy didn't have a car so she couldn't just follow the worker there and then leave. He told her he'd let her use his truck but he would keep her ID to make sure she'd return with the vehicle. He'd pay her to talk to the worker and follow her but not stay there overnight. He'd give her half up front the other half if she came back with the address. But he warned her, it'd better be the correct address because he knew where to find her and he knew who managed her, too. She agreed to do it, only so long as Carl didn't tell her pimp about this. The last place he wanted Candy to go was a shelter. Carl agreed.

She almost felt bad for the broad Carl was hunting. But if she didn't pay her pimp $1,500 by the end of the week, she would need that shelter worse than Linn did. She figured it wouldn't be a problem to make up a believable sob-story for the shelter worker. Actually, she'd just tell her the truth about her life. But she wouldn't use the shelter because she really wanted her next fix and her pimp kept her supplied as long as she met her quota each week.

Luke and River needed to work on the store's finances, so they brought the work to Luke's air-conditioned home that Friday evening. At some point, she remembered the male-ego experiment she wanted to conduct. About an hour into their work, she complimented him a few times on the work he'd done around the store. She also mentioned how good he was at figuring out the books.

This took him off guard. He paused and flipped his pen through his fingers a few times. "Did I just get a compliment from Miss River Novak?"

"Damn Straight!" she smiled, trying to sound like him.

A smile crept across his face and he went completely still. He said in his best John Wayne, "Come 'ere. I got som'thin' to show ya." He stood up, grabbed River and flung her over his shoulder, her butt to the sky. She screamed and laughed as he carried her to his bed. He tossed her on the mattress, straddled her and held her wrists down. She laughed and tried to sit up a few times without success. She dug her heels into the bed and tried bucking him off but he didn't move an inch. His smiling face hovered over her. She struggled some more and then realized it was pointless. When she gave up, Luke said, "Please say yes." His eyes were pleading. His hair was hanging down around his face. The contrast between his physical position and his emotional disposition struck her funny bone and she started laughing. Then it struck her—the experiment. This made her laugh even harder. She didn't expect the results that fast. This was no ordinary laugh. It was the kind people get at church or at a funeral, when they shouldn't be laughing at all, but the more they try to stop the more they have to do it. Half of the time Luke was laughing with her and the other half he was begging, "Please," which only made her laugh harder until tears streamed down her face. She worried she would pee her pants.

Eventually, her stomach muscles hurt enough to bring her laughter to an end. She finally responded, "You need to get off me." He rolled to one side and put his hands behind his head. She scooted up next to him and laid her head on his arm. She yawned and said, "I don't know why that was so funny."

He was still smiling, even though he figured he wasn't going to get laid. There was something about the way he could make her laugh that filled his soul all the way to the top. It was almost as good as sex. Almost! He needed a new strategy for getting that. He put his arm around her waist and kissed her head. River breathed him in. He smelled like home—like everything she ever cared about was contained in the smell of his skin. She was exhausted. She yawned again and fell asleep within a couple minutes of laying on him.

About thirty minutes later she woke up surprised that she'd fallen asleep on him and even more surprised that Luke was awake, just letting her sleep there. She thought this was incredibly sweet so she climbed on top of him and gave him a kiss. He ran his hands up her thighs and got frisky with her. Before she knew it, she was ready to read the results of her study. She found the experiment to be conclusive: stroking a man's ego was definitely worth it! She figured it would pass any peer-review.

Luke read the results of his own experiment: Patience and Persistence.

CHAPTER TWENTY-ONE

River woke up early, as usual. She carefully removed the blanket and got out of Luke's bed. Once she'd finished brewing coffee, she opened the laptop she'd brought to his place and began typing:

> Country music is rural music. Distinct genres emerge and cross-pollinate in different regions of the U.S. but together they produce the sound of small-town America.

> Oklahoma's unique sound is called Red Dirt. It began in the small town of Stillwater. Okie country has so much grit it makes commercial country sound like pop. It was named for the iron-rich soil in which it sprang up, at a place aptly called "The Farm." This stretch of earth has attracted amateur and hopeful musicians for decades.

> Red Dirt's sound is best embodied by Turnpike Troubadours. Their song Gin, Smoke & Lies has a sort of poetic hypnosis that could make even the most committed saint tap their foot to murderous jealousy.

Lead singer/songwriter Evan Felker says he wrote this song on the front porch of his parent's farmhouse in southeast Oklahoma. He said, "I was watching this rooster wrangle twenty hens and I thought, man, I can't even wrangle one woman!"

Their music is roots-music. And its grit is enriched with a whole lot more than iron— it's got time. Felker says their songs are an interpretation of what people have been doing for a couple hundred years. "We take a theatrical approach to songwriting. Music as a literary device is

River stopped typing and pulled her earbuds out. She looked over her shoulder and found Luke standing there.

He put his hand on her shoulder. "What's this?"

She paused the audio she was transcribing. "A freelance piece I'm writing for *The Oklahoman*."

He kissed her head and sat down next to her wearing only shorts. "Your brilliant mind doesn't have enough work to do, does it?"

She shrugged. "This is fun for me. It's not work, really."

"I read some of it. You're good, Riv." He looked down at the oversized mug in his hand and swirled the steaming liquid. "You put words to things I feel but wouldn't know how to say." He looked at her. "You can't learn that. That's a gift."

This was the highest compliment someone could give River. She measured her success by whether or not people could find their story in the pages of her work. She looked down and smiled. "Thanks, Luke."

His word "gift" lingered in her mind, trying to catch her attention. She sat with it for a while until it made its purpose known. She recalled Loretta was going to give her a gift before the nearly fatal accident. River remembered her saying she was nervous about it. She wondered what it could possibly be. And where it was.

She sat at Penny's table reviewing paperwork. Penny was beginning to understand the admission and course selection process.

As River finished up Jules said, "So? What's the update with Michael?"

"I told him what happened 'n he still wants to see me." Penny smiled, "Actually, he comes over regularly now after Stevie goes to bed."

"AND?" Jules demanded more information.

"Well, I'm not givin' out details! But we're figurin' it out. Slowly. 'Cept I'm worried cuz Blake saw Michael's car parked at my house one night and now he's gettin' involved."

"How's he getting involved?" River asked.

"He told dad. Now dad's having us over for a BBQ next weekend. And I know what's gonna happen! Blake did it to the last guy I brought to a BBQ and he wasn't even datin' me!"

River was confused. She couldn't imagine what Blake would do at a BBQ other than grill meat.

Penny continued, "He's gonna toss Michael a pair of boxing gloves and tell him to meet him in the garage."

River almost burst out laughing but she contained the urge because she knew Penny was seriously worried. River suggested, "Just tell Michael not to take the gloves."

"Oh, Riv! Shows what you know 'bout men! 'Course he's gonna take the gloves! Men don't turn down a challenge like that. They'd rather die tryin'."

Jules injected, "So what, Penny? So, they have a little spar. How much damage can Blake do with gloves on?"

"Even if Michael could see without his glasses, Blake could knock him out with one swing! Michael doesn't know the first thing about boxin'. He ain't the sporty type. He's the thinkin' type. I'm worried."

River held back laughter when she said, "Maybe you can warn him so he can practice his moves." She couldn't believe they were having this conversation. There was no way women would plan a BBQ and anticipate it getting violent before it had even started.

Jules said, "Penny, if Michael gets hurt you can just lick his wounds!"

Penny practically yelled, "If he's gonna indulge in the foolishness of manhood, he can lick his own wounds!" River nodded and pointed at Penny as if to say, 'Exactly!'.

Jules shook her head. "I like men bein' men and women bein' women."

"Oh Jules," River was exhausted by her friend's conservatism. "What would patriarchy do without you?"

"Exactly! That's what I'm sayin'," Jules replied.

River tipped her head. She was pretty sure they were not saying the same thing. But, since Jules was a proud supporter of the patriarchy and River was having a hard time taking the conversation seriously, she patted Jules shoulder and said, "Well, since I don't know much about manhood, I'm gonna leave this one to you." Jules gave her a look that said, 'thanks a lot' and River smugly left the house.

The contrast between male and female engagement struck River's funny bone on the drive home. She pictured her mom inviting one of her friends over for a BBQ, and when her friend arrived Loretta tossing her a pair of boxing gloves and saying 'meet me in the garage.' She drove down the street laughing so hard she had to wipe a couple tears away.

The only thing lighting up the horizon was The Corral. It got brighter as Candy approached it. After she parked Carl's truck out front, she opened her purse. The only things her pimp let her carry were a phone, some condoms and a knife, just in case she needed to escape a sadistic john. She double checked to see that the address of the women's shelter was still in her purse. It was.

What she didn't know was that included in her purse was a GPS tracker, tucked just inside the lining, courtesy of her pimp. Unfortunately for Candy, he knew the location of the women's shelter, and he could see that she had been there that night. She wasn't the first bitch he'd groomed and lost. He'd watched the GSP signal land at the shelter that night. He knew he could lose her to that place. That is, if she could resist getting her next fix. He'd only ever lost one of his girls to the shelter. They usually stayed a couple nights and then came right back to him, so he was genuinely surprised to see her GPS moving back toward The Corral that very same night. Bottom line. She knew where the shelter was now, and he needed to teach her a lesson. He was in charge!

As she approached the door of The Corral, her pimp stepped out from behind a vending machine, grabbed her hair and swung her around by it. She screamed as he threw her up against the brick wall. In the unexpected assault, she'd dropped Carl's keys in the dirt. The pimp spoke close to Candy's face, telling her he knew where she'd been that night. He told her what he was going to do to her; she wouldn't survive it. He didn't need her anymore; she was washed up. He'd groomed a younger bitch who was only fifteen. She could bring in twice the money Candy ever could. Candy tried explaining what she's been doing but he punched her in the mouth mid-sentence. The impact was so blunt a tooth loosened when it cut through her upper lip. The bar doors swung open. A few guys, including Carl and The Man, stepped out. The pimp grabbed Candy's arm. She screamed, "Help," as he shoved her into his car and sped into the night.

Carl cursed God a few times. His last chance to find Linn had just gotten away. Carl picked up his keys and took Candy's ID out of his wallet as the other men went back inside. Jessica Spenser, was her name. Carl flicked the ID onto the ground.

The liquor store would close soon. He'd get there first.

CHAPTER TWENTY-TWO

Luke and River woke up to his phone buzzing on the nightstand. He grunted as he picked it up. After looking at the screen for a moment he said, "My folks are grillin'-out this weekend. Wanna go? Kev 'n Jules will be there."

"Yeah, that sounds fun! I haven't seen your folks since I got into town." She flipped the covers off and sat up. Luke decided she was way too perky first thing in the morning, so he pulled her back down, threw the blanket back over her and locked her down with one arm.

"Hey!" she yelled.

"Where ya goin' so fast?"

"It's time to get up!" She pushed unsuccessfully on his arm. "Let me go."

"What's the magic word?" He determined the magic word would not be 'please,' but he didn't know what it was yet. He was hoping she'd change her mind about getting out of bed.

"Coffee. Coffee is the magic word," she said confidently.

She was right. That was the magic word. He groaned and let her go.

That evening they drove to the Thompson's house, which was Luke and Jules' childhood home. Having spent so many summers with the Thompsons, this old home also marked

River's childhood. The smell of that 70's ranch-style home brought River back to a state of youthful vigor, and the recollection of naivety on a level that could only be surpassed by her new-found understanding of life's tragic nature. Other than professional landscaping, the kitchen was the only thing that told the tale of time having passed. It had been updated with the addition of a granite-top island and stainless-steel appliances.

River complimented Mrs. Thompson on the beautiful updates as she followed her into the kitchen where Jules was prepping side dishes. The smell of a well-used grill wafted through the sliding door as Luke joined his dad and Kevin on the deck where they were warming the grill for steaks. Mrs. Thompson was making a macaroni salad and River had brought fruit to make a salad. River washed the fruit and Jules helped her cut it up. They reminisced about the years they had spent together at the lake house. Mrs. Thompson was horrified to learn that the boys had skinny-dipped and even more horrified that the girls spied on them. But she let herself laugh about it now that they were grown.

Luke came back inside the house to get a plate of raw meat out of the fridge. Before he took it outside, he put his hand on River's waist and kissed her cheek. River looked up at Mrs. Thompson from across the island. River had been like a second daughter to Mrs. Thompson, however now she was sleeping with Luke, who was technically still married to Ellie. River knew Kathy was very religious, so the dynamic was very uncertain. As soon as their eyes met, Mrs. Thompson looked down with disapproval. River could feel it.

The discussion died down a bit. Drew cried out from the other room. "Lil' bugger's awake already." Jules complained, "He probably messed his diaper."

Mrs. Thompson didn't waste any time when Jules left the room. She looked at River, "It seems like you and Luke are intimate. Is that right?"

River's shock came through in her face. She couldn't believe Mrs. Thompson would ask her this. Loretta would never stick her nose into other people's business so directly, not even her own daughter. River simply nodded, for lack of another response.

"You know, honey. Intimacy is best done in the context of marriage."

River breathed an angry sigh. "That didn't work out so well for Luke, did it?" She wouldn't normally talk to Mrs. Thompson this way, but she was being judged. And she didn't appreciate it.

Mrs. Thompson replied, "Well, it's just that, the dust hasn't settled for Luke yet and there's just proper ways to go about things."

River wanted to say 'Look, we're just having fun,' but she knew Mrs. Thompson would only have more judgement so she stayed silent. And angry. The strawberries she was cutting weren't so much sliced as they were crushed.

Mrs. Thompson stirred the macaroni salad and continued, "You know, honey, Luke already committed himself to someone…"

"Ellie isn't coming back, Kathy, okay? And even if she did, is that really what you want for him?"

Kathy's eyes shot up from the macaroni salad and locked with River's. River had never called her Kathy before. Even after all these years, she maintained the respect of her title. River leveraged this move strategically and Kathy understood her meaning. She was saying 'I'm an adult! Back off!" Kathy's surprise was surpassed by the weight of River's question, did she want Ellie to come back for her son?

"No," Kathy answered. "I don't want that."

Jules came back into the kitchen with a sleepy toddler on her hip. Both women went back to their food preparation. Jules looked back at forth between them. She could feel the tension in the room.

It struck River that Kathy had chosen to give *her* this little talk about commitment, and not her own son. This fact angered River even more. She excused herself and joined the men on the deck. Luke put his arm around River's waist when she arrived. She had never been so satisfied with a public display of affection. She put her arm around Luke's waist, too. He bantered with his dad and Kevin about which is harder to do, grill venison or buffalo. River envied the mindless chatter that men engaged in. She remained outside until it was time to eat.

Not consciously, River had gone to the Thompson's house hoping it would feel like it used to feel, like she had an extended family beyond Loretta. With her mama wasting away in a hospital just down the road, Kathy's rejection of River delivered a blow to her psyche that was deeper than it would have been under normal circumstances.

At dinner Luke could tell that something was very wrong with River. She'd gone strangely quiet and distant. Luke found a reason to leave as soon as he could after dinner. He asked what was going on. She decided not to tell him about the lecture she'd gotten from his mom. At least one of them could live blissfully ignorant of Kathy's disapproval. She explained her mood by saying, "I just need to see my mama."

Luke joined her at the hospital. It was the first time he'd seen Loretta since the accident. He was taken aback the moment he laid eyes on her. The person lying in that bed looked nothing like Loretta Novak. Her face was sunken in and developing scars. He struggled to find familiarity about her. Her missing limb was a notable void. He imagined the effort it would take for her to learn how to do basic things again with only one arm. That is, if she ever woke up. He'd known Loretta was in bad condition. But seeing her this way made River's pain resonate deeply within him. He looked at River who was slumped in a chair with eyes fixed on her mama.

As she stared, she questioned something she had only ever assumed. Could her mama really go missing for so long and return with her memories and personality intact? She hoped this would happen. She willed that it would. She even considered talking to someone who seemed less likely to hear her than Loretta--a supposed God.

River's mind did the loop it always did, but it landed in a less hopeful place this time. Where had Loretta gone? Her body was right there. River could see it. She could touch it. And, yet, Loretta was nowhere to be found. Her mama's body might fail before she had a chance to return to it from the undisclosed location she now inhabited. If her body failed, Loretta would be done. Erased like a hard drive. Annihilated. The inevitable fate of every human being.

This terrifying truth seized her every fiber. Gravity seemed to fail her. She was floating. River stood up suddenly. "Let's go!"

They moved silently through the cold, empty hallways of the Stillwater Medical Center. When they got to the parking lot Luke paused before getting in his truck. He didn't know how to help her, but he could see that she needed a distraction from her thoughts. "Hey, I have an idea," he said.

"What?"

"You'll see."

CHAPTER TWENTY-THREE

She was glad Luke had a plan. Her mind felt glitchy. She had a hard time placing one rational thought upon another. Her vacant stare watched Luke through the truck window pulling a tandem kayak out of his garage. Yes. Watching the Oklahoma sky bid her farewell seemed like the perfect way to end a soul-crushing day.

McMurtey's Lake was the nearest body of water. They carried his kayak through the dimly-lit warmth to the water's edge. They abandoned their shoes before setting out on the glassy lake that reflected the emerging artwork above. Stratus clouds moved outward, slowly expanding like ripples in a pond from a stone's throw. They changed color over time from yellow to orange to darkening shades of pink. About mid-lake, Luke and River stopped paddling and stayed completely still, almost reverently watching the sky speak from above the expansive horizon. It suggested there was more to this tragic life. That there might be a great artist who, even though seemingly unable to control the growing chaos, at least had some sort of a purpose in it.

Their silent drift ended when the sky stopped speaking. They paddled back to the shore where the full moon aided their efforts of securing the kayak in the back of the truck. It occurred to Luke that neither of them had spoken since they'd left his house. He'd never seen River so withdrawn and lifeless. She was about to climb inside the cab when Luke stopped her. He put the key in the ignition and turned up the radio. He pulled her close, so she rested her head on his chest. He led them in syncopated steps to the slow song that was playing.

Everything made sense to her when they danced. When he stepped forward, she stepped back. When he stepped back, she stepped forward. There was comfort in knowing what came next. There was a method. He was an anchor. Their mirrored movement made her feel like she was part of something bigger than herself. Luke's chest vibrated on her cheek as he began singing to the song. She looked up. He was looking down at her.

> I sat in darkness
> You broke through and saved me
> You're an angel. Tell me you're never
> leaving
> 'Cause you're the first thing I know I can
> believe in
>
> You're holy, holy, holy, holy
> I'm high on loving you,
> high on loving you
>
> You made the brightest days from the
> darkest nights
> You're the riverbank where I was baptized.

She looked away. His eyes suggested he meant what he was singing to her. She looked back up again.

> You're the healing hands
> Where it used to hurt
> You're my saving grace
> You're my kind of church

You are holy

On the drive home, River's mind had shifted from Kathy's rejection to Luke's affection. She could imagine herself falling in love with him. This freaked her out. They weren't supposed to be together. Everyone knew it. His mom knew it. He knew it. And, so did she. Almost as fast as she wondered if he really meant what he sang to her, she decided that, being the artist-type, he was just really good at romance. Luke invited her to stay at his place on the drive home but she declined.

She needed solitude. Or at least, she thought she did.

The next morning Olivia rang. River was curious to find out how her adventure across the U.S. went. Olivia told her about ditching the rental car in California and flying back to New York. She couldn't take another four-day drive through corn fields, she said.

River responded, more jokingly than seriously, "Well, I'm glad you survived the patriarchy out there on your own."

"Yeah, I survived the patriarchy. Barely. There are some fucked up places down there in the south. I don't know how you can stand living there. I mean, I know you have to right now, with your mom and all. Just sayin'! I saw all kinds of racism and sexism on this trip, but nothing compared to what I saw in Stillwater."

Olivia's stab at her hometown made River feel defensive. Stillwater folks were the only thing keeping her alive. Keeping her mama alive. But River knew who Olivia was really talking about. Luke. And she thought it was an unfair assessment. Olivia basically provoked the predictable response from a southerner by not standing for the national anthem. And then she found a way to make the conversation about race.

River's heart sped up. "Luke's not a bad guy, Liv. Sure, he's got some things to learn. But he's not a racist."

"Are you kidding me? That man was practically dripping with white supremacy."

"Liv, you were hating on white people. That's why he asked, 'What's wrong with being white'?"

"I can't even believe you're defending him, River. His question just proves how much privilege has. And his refusal to acknowledge his privilege is straight up white supremacy. The man might as well have been wearing a white hood!"

"You have GOT to be kidding me! He doesn't hate people for their race. He just doesn't like being hated for his. Luke is actually a really good guy!"

Olivia went silent for a moment. "Oh my God! You're sleeping with that man, aren't you?"

River didn't respond.

"You are! You're sleeping with him!"

River could have lied to Olivia. She thought about it. Being honest would mean that Olivia's judgement of Luke would apply to her as well. She'd be guilty by association. But River valued truth more than good friends. And she didn't think those should be mutually exclusive. "Olivia, you were ready to fuck the only real racist in Stillwater that day, an ACTUAL racist! And you're judging me for sleeping with Luke?"

River could practically hear Olivia's head shaking back and forth. "I don't know what's happened to you, River. I really don't. You used to care about justice, I mean, really care. And now… I just don't know."

"How the hell does sleeping with Luke mean I don't care about justice?"

"BECAUSE HE'S A RACIST! You're literally sleeping with the enemy!"

"I'm sleeping with LUKE! Did you hear what you just said? You just called another human being 'the enemy.' It's people like you who are going to start an actual war in this country if you don't stop talking like that."

Olivia's voice lowered and took a threatening tone. "What do you mean, people like me?"

River couldn't take it anymore. "I MEAN THE RACIST-TYPE! The type who hate people for their skin! Next time you're looking for a racist, take a look in the mirror!"

CLICK. Olivia hung up.

River exhaled. She almost called Olivia back, but realized they both needed some time to cool off. She stood in her living room for a while, hoping in vain that her phone would ring.

River thought about the big picture of Olivia's friendship in the moment that she feared she would lose it. What would she lose exactly? She'd lose a friend who checked in on her sometimes. She'd lose a storehouse of happy memories from college. She would lose a friend who was mostly self-consumed and increasingly monitoring River's behavior and speech. Olivia's ideology had become burdensome to River. Its purest form, it was impossible to achieve. And at each new level of achievement, there was a purity-test chastising her for falling short. But the testing was over. River had failed. There was no going back now. Somehow, River knew that even if she hadn't slept with Luke, her refusal to adjust her pronoun usage would have corrupted her virtue beyond repair, in Olivia's mind.

River was surprised at the relief she felt at the thought that Olivia might be done with her. But her grief outweighed relief. She would miss the contagious laughter of her eccentric friend. She remembered when Olivia was the kind of liberal who was open to debate for the sake of learning, before she'd committed herself to a prepackaged set of ideas. And then it struck her. Olivia wasn't a liberal anymore. In fact, Olivia didn't claim that title for herself. She wanted to be called "progressive." Then, it occurred to River that progressives are to 'the left' as white-supremacists are to 'the right.' They are the far-left. She thought it was strange how much these two extremes had in common. For one, River realized, they're both obsessed with white people. They both identify their enemy by looking at their skin color. And, they consider all who dissent from their extremism enemies just the same. That's when River realized that Olivia would not be calling back. Ever.

If the soul had weight to it, River's got heavier that day. In the current state of her tragic existence, she couldn't afford to lose meaningful friendships. So, despair took Olivia's place as companion in a room where the only thing piercing the cold, dead silence was the ticking of time on the wall.

She set her phone on the coffee table and moved through the living room mindlessly. Her bed was a womb that carried her into a deep and immediate sleep.

River woke up many hours later, disoriented. It was almost seven o'clock, but was it morning or night? It took her some effort to find the PM on her phone.

CHAPTER TWENTY-FOUR

Maybe it was all the sleeping she did the day before, but she woke up earlier than normal that Sunday morning. She brought her coffee outside to watch the sun rise. She climbed onto the hood of her Jeep and appreciated how the sky spread itself across the grassy expanse behind her childhood home. Hues of orange and blue clashed and complemented each other for the proper mix of intrigue and conflict. It made her think of Luke. She considered what she liked about him. And also, her reservations. She wondered what her mom would say about her dating Luke. She knew her mom would accept the relationship, despite his marital status. But was Luke right for her? No one was available to help her make big decisions or even point out blind-spots.

Her thoughts were interrupted by the buzzing phone in her pocket. It was the hospital. An on-call doctor told River that her mother's health was wavering. Loretta had developed bedsores from weeks of lying in bed. The hospital staff had managed to keep them under control, but the doctor told River that Loretta had developed a staph infection in one of the bedsores on her left leg and it was spreading rapidly. They wanted River to know that this type of thing can easily get out of control and require the amputation of a limb. She already had her keys in her pocket so she swung from the hood into the driver's seat of the jeep and drove straight to the hospital.

When she got there, she turned her phone off and stayed in Loretta's room the majority of the day reading a disinteresting book she'd found in the hospital gift shop. She watched when nurses attended to Loretta's routine needs. But when the physical therapist came by to move Loretta's limbs around River stepped out. It bothered her to see her mother moving around in her unconscious state. At some point during the day when River was alone with Loretta, she said, "You need to wake up, mama. You need to pull through this. I can't do life without you. I just can't!" Thinking maybe her voice could prompt her mother to wake up, River spent the good part of an hour reading out loud to her mom. By the time evening rolled around, River had decided to take the next couple of days off work. Maybe if she spent more time reading aloud and talking to her mom it would make a difference. She called Luke and made arrangements.

The next day Luke came in to the shop early to make sure the store was ready for the day. The store was busy all morning so he was glad that Skippy was there and was good at what he did. It slowed down in the afternoon so Luke was able to restock the shelves. As he lifted a bag of soil onto a shelf, he felt a solid slap on his back. Quinn was standing there with one thumb in a pocket.

"Luke, my man!" Quinn said. They slapped each other's shoulders firmly. "I saw your truck out front. Thought you were workin' at Cramer Ranch this summer."

"Not this year. Manage this place now." Luke went back to stocking the shelf.

"Hey, I know some college girls stickin' around this summer. Curt and I are gettin' them drunk tonight? Wanna come?"

"Nah. Can't make it." He threw another bag of soil on the shelf, disgusted that Quinn planned on getting women drunk to sleep with them.

"That's right! You screwin' that River girl, aren't ya? Must be a pretty good lay for you to put up with that mouth a hers."

Luke's temperature spiked, but he tried not to show it. "Least I don't have to get women drunk to get laid."

Quinn paused. He felt that. The truth was, he couldn't figure out how Luke got River into bed. She was out of Quinn's reach. He finally said, "Looks like she's turned ya into a feminist."

"Hardly. What's it to ya, anyway?" Luke tossed another bag on the shelf.

If Quinn couldn't dominate River, he would be satisfied knowing someone else would. "Just wouldn't put up with that mouth a hers, that's all."

Luke's temperature spiked again. He threw another bag on the shelf, harder than he needed to, "Least I'll see it comin' if she's gonna walk."

"There's better ways to keep a chick from walkin' than being her bitch. You're gettin' soft."

Luke straightened up, locked eyes with Quinn and said, "Why don't you step outside 'n I'll teach you to keep your mouth shut!"

Quinn kept his eyes locked on Luke's, trying to figure out if he was seriously challenging him or if he was just saving face. Quinn decided not to take him seriously; he didn't want to fight a friend over something trivial. He said firmly, "I'm just sayin', it's best to show a woman who's in charge right up front."

Luke stepped forward and yelled, "And, I'm just sayin' it's best for you to keep your damn mouth shut!" The men kept eye contact a while longer without blinking. Quinn didn't like being talked to that way, and he thought Luke deserved to be taught a lesson for it. But, frankly, he wasn't sure what they were fighting about. If it was River, she didn't seem worth it. Quinn finally shook his head in disgust and walked away.

Luke watched the back of his head as he left the store, hoping Quinn would take him up on this challenge so he could land a few punches on the bastard's face. As Quinn left Luke realized the only reason they were friends was because they were both wrestling champions in high school. They had nothing else in common and he was happy to realize it. It was time to put childhood things to rest.

Skippy was watching this clash of the titans from across the store, quite worried it was going to get bloody. Luke shot eyes at him. Skippy grabbed a push-broom and swept the floor better than he had ever swept it before.

River emerged from a three-day hospital visit in a wavering emotional state. That much time thinking about your mother's mortality will tilt the strongest soul off its axis. She'd also spent too many hours thinking about what Kathy said. And she knew Kathy was right. The dust hadn't settled in Luke's life yet, and she wondered what the hell she was doing, messing around with him.

The emotional distance she put between herself and Luke was tangible. But by the end of the week she was engaging him more often in conversation. They both got texts from Sarah saying there was a group of people going out that night and invited them to come. A stiff drink was exactly what she thought she needed. He could see she wasn't emotionally stable, so he wondered how the evening would go. He figured he'd be driving drunk-River home soon after getting there. So, he mentally prepared to do just that.

When they got to the bar the group did shots on a ski and River ordered another cocktail immediately afterward. Luke had learned that questioning her choices got him nowhere, so he didn't. But he found it hard to enjoy the scene. He could see the night coming to a swift end. He didn't want to watch every moment of the train wreck that was surely coming, so he distracted himself by challenging Sarah's boyfriend to a game of pool. Turned out Sarah's boyfriend was a pool shark so Luke's competitive streak meant the pool game got his undivided attention.

The world tipped right for River. It was hard to arrive at a destination that was straight ahead. She followed her ears to a corner of the room where there was a loud group of men. She started dancing to the music right in front of them. The men gladly focused their attention on her. She slid her hands down the front of her shirt while she moved to the beat. One of the men yelled, "Take it off." Drunk-River didn't even hesitate. She pulled her shirt off and swung it around above her head and then threw it at them. They cheered. A couple of them stepped closer just as Luke looked over to see what the cheering was about. He walked over and yanked her shirt out of a guy's hand with a threatening glare and then pulled River to the side of the room. "That's enough, River!"

"What's enough?" She slurred and stumbled sideways a bit. "I can tell myself what's enough."

"Clearly! Put your damn shirt on. It's time to go."

"Don't tell me what to do. I'm fine!"

The volume of their conversation got louder and drew the attention of their friends and some other onlookers.

"You're not fine, River! Some men take advantage of women when they're drunk, you know that! I'm just protecting you."

"Don't protect me!" she tried pulling her arm out of his grasp.

His hand tightened as she swayed, "You need help when you're drunk, Riv."

"Dammit, Luke, I don't need your help. Don't tell me what I need! I'm not your fuckin' child!" She yanked her arm out of his hand and stumbled sideways.

Luke threw his hands up. He understood conflict with men. When a man's being unreasonable there's a quick fix for that. But he didn't know how to do conflict with women. He'd only hit a girl once and that was his sister. As teenagers, Jules called Ellie a slut, so Luke punched her in the stomach. When Mr. Johnson saw Luke make contact with Jules, fury put him on like a glove. Before Luke knew what had happened, he could taste the pain radiating in his head. He found himself flush against the wall where his dad had slammed him with unusual force, still holding him a foot off the ground, his eyes wild like a lion who'd just snagged its prey. Mr. Thompson's baritone voice yelled, "Never hit a girl! You protect 'em! Ya hear me?" He dropped Luke to the ground and walked away before he did any real damage to his boy.

Luke never forgot that lesson. His job was protecting women. But his dad never told him what to do if women didn't want his protecting. One thing was for sure, though, he wasn't going to wait around to find out. He couldn't watch River put herself in danger and do nothing about it. He tossed River's shirt at her, turned around and aimed for the door, pausing only briefly to say something to Jules.

Jules walked over to River and led her away from the men. "Mama-bird's here, darlin'" Jules made a bird-like sound, "Caw-caw. Caw-caw."

Somehow, River didn't mind Jules' protection. She knew Luke was right about needing supervision when drunk. But there was no way in hell she was gonna let a man tell her what to do, like she was his child or something.

Her head punished her for her excess the next morning. She walked a little sideways until noon. The entire weekend she spent alone or visiting her mother. One was much like the other. The only human interaction she had was when Jules caught her in the hospital hallway one evening.

"Riv, I just have to ask. What's the big deal with letting Luke protect you?"

"It makes me feel like a child."

"It makes me feel like a queen when Kev protects me."

River's patience for Jules' conservatism ran thin that evening. "I'm just independent, okay? Don't like men telling me what to do."

"He's not that type of guy, you know? Controlling. He just wants what's best for you."

River snapped, "He might WANT what's best for me, but I KNOW what's best for me."

"You tried to give a bachelor party a strip tease. Is that best for you?" Jules laughed.

"Oh my God!" River put her hands over her face as she remembered the moment.

Jules continued, "I mean, if you're gonna do that kinda shit you might as well get paid for it!"

Both women laughed. River tried to imagine herself stripping. She couldn't do it, even for money.

Jules added playfully, "You're, like, the smartest dumb-person I've ever met."

They laughed some more.

Jules sobered, "But seriously, Riv. What's the big deal? He's just watchin' out for you."

River got defensive, "It feels like he's trying to parent me, okay?"

"Well, someone's gotta do it!"

That cut a little. River could feel the ever-present absence of her mother. She was ever near, and yet so far away.

"You can't just get drunk off your ass and expect to get home safely, all by yourself."

River looked away at the spoken truth.

"Frankly, River, if it weren't for Kev and I, God knows where you would've ended up Friday night." She paused. "Probably in the back of some Farmer John's truck."

Both women laughed again, nervously.

"You're welcome, by the way. Just let Luke do his job."

"His job?" River's gaze met Jules'.

"Yeah. His job. Women make life. Men protect it."

"Oh my God, that is so archaic!"

"It is! It's been happening from the beginning of time! Men's instinct is to protect women. It's as natural as women givin' birth. How do you think we've survived all this time?"

River really didn't have the energy to argue with Jules but she couldn't help it. "If men's instinct is to protect then how do you explain men who harm women? 'Cause plenty of them do!"

"Their brains flip. They hurt what they're supposed to protect. Women do it, too. Women hurt their kids when they go crazy. Male brains have more variability than women. That's why men go crazy more often."

It seemed to River that Jules was speaking as a scientist as well as a conservative, which somehow made her message more tolerable. But still, she argued back. "Just because something has always been done doesn't mean it should continue. That's why we're evolving."

"True. But you gotta leave something important for men to do. Women make babies. That's a powerful thing! Women don't appreciate it, probably cuz it's hard work. But anything worth doin' is. Women run around acting like whatever men are doin' is better. Talk about 'penis envy'!"

"Jules, it's about economics, okay? The reason women value what men are doing is because it is *literally* valuable— it's monetized. People need money to survive, you know?"

"Okay, but look. I work. I'm standing here in my scrubs. But Kev don't make babies. I do! 'N I expect him to protect us if there's danger. And he wants to. He's literally built for it. Men are stronger than women; there's a natural order to things."

River wanted to roll her eyes but for some reason she didn't. Jules' trite explanations of life sounded overly simplistic, but something deep inside of her longed for this kind of simplicity. She almost hated her own resistance to it.

"All I'm saying is, guys need somethin' important to do. Don't deny 'em that. Plus, when you take their job away, you're puttin' yourself in danger."

River still hated being referred to as Luke's job, like she was some sort of project that needed fixing or something. But then she considered whether she was really as put together as she imagined herself being. River looked away, hoping their little talk was done.

CHAPTER TWENTY-FIVE

Carl moved through the store in a disheveled manner. He'd been in a constant state of drunkenness for a week. The anger that bubbled just below the surface threatened to spill over with the slightest nudge. He figured he'd feed his animals for lack of something better to do. It was the only store he could still shop at without money. He dropped a fifty-pound bag of feed at the register and leaned into River's personal space. His whisky-tinged breath hit her when he said, "Li'l Miss Yankee. Think you can run the store like your mouthy mama did? I hear she's dyin'." One corner of his mouth went up slightly, as if he were amused by the idea. Luke was at the end of the counter. He'd heard what Carl said, but he pretended to be immersed in the inventory list. He figured, if River didn't want his help, he wouldn't give it. She'd need to figure this out on her own.

River's face hardened. She used all of her strength to push the weighted bag of feed off the counter, then pointed to the door and shouted, "Get out of this store and never come back! We won't serve you here no more!" Her Okie accent came back in her rage. "Go find another store to keep your failin' farm goin', Carl!" Telling him he couldn't shop at the store anymore was a big deal because the nearest supply store was an hour away and they probably didn't run on credit. But she was angry and she didn't care what Carl would have to do. How could he talk about her mama that way?

Carl looked over at Luke who was making it clear that he didn't care about the situation. Carl looked back at River, tilted his head and said. "You cain't stop me from buyin' feed here, Sweet Cheeks!"

"GET OUT before I call the police!" she yelled. "I hear they're on a first name basis with you," she added.

Carl huffed a chuckle. His eyes got small. It had been two months since Linn went missing. He'd lost patience, hope and resources. His fridge was empty and he had to sell a couple of his guns to afford the alcohol that was keeping him alive. He reasoned if he couldn't take Linn with him to the grave that River would be a satisfying substitute. "You'll see me again. Won't deny me service for long." He walked past Luke toward the door and mumbled something under his breath. Luke shot eyes at Carl just as Carl glanced over his shoulder at River.

When Carl walked out Luke went back to pretending to be busy. River looked over and put her chin up. He pretended not to notice. It bothered her that Luke didn't engage in the situation. It seemed like something he should have gotten involved in, even just as an employee. But she figured she knew why he didn't.

I can take care of myself, she thought. *Some assembly required. Man not included!*

River was more exhausted than usual when she got home from visiting her mom that night. The emotional and physical strain of the weekend still lingered, and her interaction with Carl earlier that day didn't help. But, hearing the hustle and bustle of hospital staff gave her the feeling of having community.

She yawned as she closed the farmhouse door behind her. She threw her keys and phone in the tray by the front door and opened the fridge where a cold beer sat waiting for her. She set it on the island and began sorting the mail. There was a strange feeling in the room, like the silence had a presence. It seemed as though she'd entered into a movie scene, like she'd begun watching herself from a distance. But maybe it wasn't her that was doing the watching. A deep awareness of her surroundings engaged to a degree she'd never experienced. All of her senses were on high-alert, though she saw nothing, heard nothing nor smelled anything unusual. The sensation of not being alone in that room grew stronger, though without cause. She went back to sorting the mail and told herself to stop being paranoid. She reasoned that high-stress and a lack of sleep could make the most committed rationalist behave irrationally.

It was her sense of smell that first confirmed danger. The smell of alcohol filled the air, though her beer remained sealed. Carl's voice sounded behind her.

"Lil' Miss Sweet Cheeks is all alone in her mama's big house."

River jumped, dropped the mail and swung around grabbing the island behind her. Carl staggered towards her, dangerously close. A lethal amount of alcohol seeped from his pores and orbited the air around him.

She stepped back around the island yelling, "GET OUT OF MY HOUSE!" He stepped closer and she realized he'd stepped between her, the door, and her phone. He got within reaching distance, crossed his hand over his shoulder and backhanded the side of her face with full force. River's head swung to the side and pain radiated from her cheekbone. She screamed as he grabbed a handful of her hair in his oversized hand. His free hand he grabbed the beer on the island and smashed it in half on the wooden edge. She

189

jumped and screamed again as glass and beer flew across the kitchen floor. He held the jagged bottle up to her face and walked toward her. She grabbed his wrists and stumbled backwards into the dining table. He let go of her hair and grabbed her throat. She grabbed his wrist and tried pulling his hand away from her throat but her strength couldn't match his. She wanted to kick him but he'd stepped between her legs, rendering them useless. He pressed the jagged glass against her throat.

"Please!" she gasped. "Y-you can shop at the s-store. I'm sorry!"

"The Yankee's apologizing. Well, you're gonna serve me tonight, you little bitch," He put pressure on the glass against her neck.

She knew there was very little chance of escaping his grip, so she tried negotiating again. "PLEASE," she begged, "I, I'll cancel your debt at the store. No one will ever know about this."

He chuckled. It amused him that she thought he cared what people knew about him. And she thought he had something to live for. "How 'bout I get started by carvin' my initials in that pretty lil' chest o' yours?" Carl tightened the grip on her throat and moved the shard down her chest right above her breasts. She tried screaming in vain; his grip on her throat had tightened. Even if she could've screamed, she knew no one would hear her on 21 acres outside of town. Every second was a minute. Penny's face flashed through her mind; it got replaced by her own. The front page of the morning newspapers and all of Stillwater would have her name in bold print. She used every bit of her strength to pull his hand away from her neck and tried contorting her body out from between him and the table, but she simply couldn't match his strength. The harder she pulled away the tighter he squeezed her throat, making her gag even more. He pressed the glass hard against her chest and a warm sensation spread all around it. Oxygen hadn't found her lungs for a quite a while and this was darkening her vision. The room dimmed black around the edges.

Even though Luke didn't think River deserved his protection, he'd followed her home that night because of what Carl mumbled as he left the store that afternoon. Something about "tonight." Luke's protective instinct overrode his anger. When he pulled up to the farmhouse the only vehicle Luke saw was River's Jeep and Loretta's truck so he killed the headlights on the way down the dirt drive and parked outside. But when he heard glass break and River scream, adrenaline shot through his veins like kinetic shrapnel from a shotgun. He kicked his truck's door open with so much force that he later he would find the hinges bent. When he came inside, he saw Carl pressed up against River who was pinned to the dining table and struggling. Luke's single-minded focus became taking Carl out. He ran across the room in a few bounds and grabbed Carl's overalls, throwing him sideways, his head hit the wall so hard that Carl fell limp. Luke woke him up with a swift kick to his ribs.

Luke only subconsciously heard River gasping for air. The sound fueled his rage. Carl came-to, coughing and grabbing his ribs, protecting them from the second, third and fourth blows Luke delivered. Luke shoved Carl's shoulder with his heel, turning him onto his back, then straddled Carl's chest, pinning his arms down. Luke drew back his arm like a lethal weapon and Carl was only conscious long enough to see that it was Luke who was attacking him. Luke sent every ounce of his upper-body strength down at Carl's face which swung limp to one side on impact. The skin on his cheek split open. Blood ran down Carl's face as Luke delivered one blow after another.

The sound of Luke's knuckles hitting Carl made River's choking cough turn to a panicky cry. Luke came to himself momentarily, realizing River shouldn't have to see what he was going to do to Carl. He stood up, grabbed one of Carl's overall straps and drug his limp body across the room and onto the front porch. Luke kicked Carl's unconscious body, which rolled down the stairs and into the dark. This is where Carl would get what he deserved. But the sound of River coughing and panicking got Luke's attention. Was she hurt? He didn't know. Carl was still unconscious. He went back inside to see if River needed help.

She was sitting on the floor hyperventilating, her head between her knees. "YOU OKAY, RIVER?" he shouted, louder than he meant to. Even if she could have spoken through the short, quick breaths she wouldn't have known how to answer him. She was panicking and needed help calming down. It was obvious to Luke what Carl's intentions were. Luke scanned her body. Her clothes were still on. He didn't see any blood. He picked her up and put her on the couch, keeping his gaze at the front door. He wasn't sure how long Carl would remain unconscious. Forever, he'd hoped!

"Shhh. Breathe," he said, as calmly as his rage permitted. He looked back and forth between River and the front door. Luke stood near River for less than a minute but it seemed like an hour. He was in active combat mode. Carl was still outside and he hadn't gotten what he deserved yet. Luke rushed onto the porch but stopped at the edge.

Carl was gone.

Luke swung his head back and forth, straining his eyes to see into the darkness.

He saw nothing. He heard nothing.

Luke stepped down each porch step carefully. Ears alert. Luke's head jerked sideways to the sound of a truck starting around the side of the farmhouse. Carl's flatbed peeled out, shooting rocks behind it as it swerved uncontrollably down the dirt-drive, back and forth.

Luke's instinct was to chase him in his truck; he had a gun in the cab. But he couldn't leave River. He didn't really know what condition she was in. "YOU FUCKIN' BASTARD!" he yelled. He swung his foot at nothing in particular, kicking up dust in the night air. Carl hadn't gotten what he deserved, yet. But Luke determined that he would. Eventually.

He went back inside to find River sitting on the couch with her face in her hands, crying. He pulled her head against his chest and within minutes her breathing calmed. As he held her, he said nothing but he felt everything. Sadness, hearing her cry like that. Fear, imagining what would have happened to her if he hadn't shown up. And anger, because River made it so damn hard for him to protect her. And rage, because Carl was a dead man!

Her chest felt wet. She touched it and found crimson red on her fingers. She pulled her shirt up over the wound. If Luke saw blood, she was sure he'd go after Carl and God-knows what would've come of the night. She sat up and looked at him with red eyes, still holding her shirt up. She didn't recognize the look on Luke's face. His eyes were vacant. His neck was bright red.

"How'd you know he would be here?" she sniffed.

"I heard what he said as he left the store." Luke ran his bloody knuckles through his hair.

"I didn't," she admitted.

He looked at the way she was holding up her shirt. She looked violated. "Did he hurt you?" His blood boiled at the thought of it.

She looked down and saw no blood on her shirt. The situation had gone far enough. River reasoned that Carl must have left with a broken nose and a few broken ribs. His face would need stitching and he probably had a concussion. She figured any more action Luke took would just land him in jail. She shook her head.

Luke sat for a long time with his head in his hands and finally said with sober concern, "River, I need you to let me protect you. I couldn't stand losing you that way. Especially knowin' I coulda stopped it."

She looked at his hands which were shaking a little.

"Plus, what if he had a gun? It's hard enough to deal with this shit when..." he paused before saying, "when you let me."

For the first time in her life, River imagined what it would be like to be a man with superior physical strength. Would she have the courage to protect others, spontaneously risking her own life to save theirs? It seemed impossible to squeeze out a feminist protest in that moment. "Okay," she agreed.

Luke stared vacantly ahead and said, "If he'd hurt you, I'd have killed 'im. Bastard knows you ain't got a daddy or brothers to come after him. Thought you were easy prey." He shook his head with rage in his eyes. "Can't believe that bastard got away."

She took some control of the situation by saying, "Don't tell anyone about this, 'kay? You know how it is 'round here."

He shook his head. He wouldn't agree to that. "The people who find out are the people who need to know."

Luke would make sure he wasn't the only guy in town monitoring Carl's proximity to River.

She nodded, understanding his meaning.

She needed to check her wound, unsure of how bad it was. On her way to the bathroom, she realized that Luke hadn't actually seen Carl hurt her. And thank God! Luke's capacity for aggression was almost as frightening to River as Carl's, although she didn't fear it. She wondered if Luke really would've killed Carl like he said. She took her shirt off and assessed the cut. It was about an inch long but not deep enough to need stitching. It turned out there was some blood on her shirt where it had pooled beneath her breasts. She stuffed the soiled shirt at the bottom of the bathroom garbage, along with her bloodied bra. Her hands shook as she cleaned the blood off her skin and bandaged the cut. She went to her room to get dressed, wondering if Luke would notice her wardrobe change. She guessed that he wouldn't. She was right.

Luke noticed other things: the broken glass, the liquid on the floor. When she came out his eyes scanned her again for signs of abuse.

"You sure you ain't hurt?" he asked again.

"I'm fine. I just..." she paused. "Would you stay here tonight?"

She'd barely finished asking before he replied, "Plan on it!" Luke would never have wished this scenario on River, but there was something satisfying about hearing her ask for his protection, fully aware just how much that she needed it.

Luke reached in front of her for a dish towel on the island to clean up the beer on the floor. When his hand passed by, she flinched, as if he were going to hit her. His heart sank. Carl had hit her! That much was clear. And she wasn't going to talk about it. He pressed the towel down over some beer on the floor but kept his eyes on her. Her hands shook uncontrollably as she picked up a large shard of glass from the floor. As she bent, her shirt came down away from her chest and he saw bloodied bandages stuck to her skin. His neck turned fire-red and his breathing quickened. He looked down at the towel in his hand, but he didn't see it. What he saw was Carl's bloody face struggling to breathe. His hands clenched around Carl's neck would be the last thing that bastard ever felt. His limp body would make a splash falling into the lake under a starry sky. But, the next morning, birds would still sing and the store would still open at eight. And nobody would miss Carl.

The rest of the night was silent. They both felt contaminated by the situation. Bloodied. Each of them showered. They climbed into bed exhausted, but neither of them could sleep immediately. A vivid scene ran through Luke's mind on repeat. How the night would have ended if Carl hadn't gotten away. How it should have ended. How it would end. Eventually.

When River laid her head down on her pillow her cheek throbbed, warning her of a developing bruise. She worried she'd be unable to hide it. She wasn't sure exactly why she didn't want Luke knowing how Carl had hurt her. Maybe she feared Luke's aggression would get him into trouble. Or maybe admitting this to him would mean admitting it to herself. Or maybe she felt guilty about everything, about putting Luke and herself at risk. But, was it her fault? She reasoned that it wasn't. But it felt like it was, somehow.

Just as her eyes closed, Carl lunged at her with jagged glass. Her eyes shot open with a jolt. Her heart raced. Carl wasn't really there, but she could feel his hand around her throat. Her entire body began shaking. It was happening all over again—over and over again—each time she closed her eyes. This was assault, she realized. And she was glad she'd reserved a word potent enough to name the terror that then seized her.

Luke felt the bed shaking. He wrapped one of his arms and legs around her. His body was an immovable fortress. She felt as though she could hide there. Her mind was still exposed. But her body was safe.

For now.

CHAPTER TWENTY-SIX

Pain shot through one side of her neck as she got out of bed that morning. She couldn't turn her head very far right and that same side of her face was sensitive to touch. The mirror revealed a swelling purple bruise on her cheek going all the way back to her hairline. She didn't always wear makeup but she would that day. Makeup mostly covered it and she used her hair as a second layer. When she opened her mouth to brush her teeth, her jaw ached, too. As she brushed, she examined her neck for marks but didn't see any. She thought she might be able to conceal the assault.

Luke was finishing up making breakfast when she came out. He shut a cupboard door near her head and she jumped. Luke made small talk with her, trying to get a good look at her face. He could see the bruise she was trying to cover on her cheek. His rage kicked in again, imagining the moment Carl's hand made contact with her face.

He tried to sound calm. "How ya feelin' this morning?"

"Fine. Thanks for... everything."

"'Course." He went to kiss her forehead by cupping his hand around her neck, but the second he touched her she lifted both of her shoulders and slapped his hand away. He stopped his kiss midway.

"Sorry," they both said.

Luke watched her carry her plate to the table, keeping one hand on her neck.

When she moved her hand, he could see a couple of dark spots on the side of her neck, finger marks. Luke recalled the choking sound he heard when he was kicking Carl. *Bastard was choking her!* Luke couldn't believe River was trying to conceal this level of assault. He tried not to direct the rage bubbling just beneath the surface at her. He sat down across from her and stabbed a mouthful of eggs. He looked at her with a fire-red neck. "Is there somethin' you wanna tell me?"

"What?" She looked up, surprised.

"I mean," he shook his head and tried not to sound as angry as he was. "Wanna talk about it?"

"No." Her fork moved her eggs around her plate.

He gulped some coffee before saying, "Why won't you tell me Carl choked, hit and cut you?"

She exhaled completely and leaned back in her chair. She paused, "Because, Luke. I don't need you doin' something stupid, okay?"

He kept his eyes on his plate. "Like what?" He knew exactly what but he figured he'd play dumb.

She shook her head. She wasn't going to say it. Her fingers combed her hair down over her cheek. "I just want the situation to be done with." She went back to picking at her plate.

"Consider it done." The words came out sounding ominous, even though he didn't mean them to.

She did a double-take looking up at him, but he kept his eyes on his plate.

He looked up. "You gonna press charges?"

"Why? So I can talk about this with a bunch of people I don't know? Then I'll have to see his face in court, like, a year from now. Then after all that, maybe he'll spend a few nights in jail. There's no money to get from him. What's the point?"

Luke was silent but his thoughts were loud, *that's why back-country justice is in order, honey!*

After breakfast River decided to spend the majority of the day in the hospital with her mom. At one point a nurse came in to re-bandage her mom's bedsores. The nurse kept clearing her throat, then coughed suddenly. The sound made River jump almost completely out of her chair. The nurse apologized profusely. River felt like such an idiot for being so dramatic. There was no way to explain her strange behavior. She couldn't reason how an ordinary noise could scare her like that and why she would react before she knew what it was.

When the nurse left, River told her mom the store was doing fine and not to worry. She didn't mention Carl, mostly because she didn't want to talk about it, but she also thought that if her mom could hear, she would just worry.

Instead she said, "Mama, what the hell is wrong with men? Why are they so violent? I really don't understand it. Is it testosterone? Is it the fucking Y-chromosome, or something?"

The hospital cafeteria wasn't the best place to get lunch in town but it was convenient. And safe. The macaroni salad River was holding almost flew out of her hands when the people behind her in line burst into laughter. Terror shot through her veins, in rushes of waves, as if Carl had just broken the bottle on the island. Her heart raced. The people next to her were having a great time. But her body's reflex was simply faster than her mind's ability to consider the noises she was hearing. Waves of terror still seized her while they laughed from their guts. They seemed to exist in a completely different universe than River. She had never felt so far away from people she could reach out and touch.

She remembered learning about "trauma triggers" in a psychology class, things that cause flashbacks or symptoms in trauma patients. These would be different for each patient. A strange example the book gave was a trauma patient being triggered by green shirts because he was attacked by someone wearing a green shirt. She recalled her disbelief in this particular trigger. It sounded made up. But, right then, nothing sounded far-fetched. Her trigger seemed to be loud noises. She despaired. There were a lot more loud-noises in the world than there were green shirts. "I'm a fucking head-case!" she whispered to herself. She hated herself for this. And she hated the fact that she hated herself for this. It wasn't her fault and there was nothing she could do about it. And no "trigger warning" could help her because people didn't know when they were going to laugh loudly or cough. And even if they did, what were they supposed to do? Say, "River, I feel a laugh coming on" or "I'm about to close the door." Would this reflex ever go away? Frustration brought tears to her eyes.

Her soul weighed her body down; even her eyelids had weight to them. When she got back to Loretta's room, she set her food aside and curled up in the corner chair. She slept for a good chunk of time before she woke with a text from Jules inviting her to Penny's place on Tuesday night.

Her food called out to her from the chair nearby, but she had no appetite. Her lunch found its home in the garbage when she finally left the room that evening.

The jumpiness decreased slightly with each passing day, but it didn't leave entirely. Luke had slept in her bed every night that week, which brought her a lot of comfort. She felt safe with him. But he had a camping trip planned for that weekend with his fishing buddy Cliff. They were headed down to Broken Bow Lake for the weekend. When she found out he was canceling the trip because of her, she insisted that he go, telling him that she wouldn't let him stay at her place that weekend if he stayed in town. She'd be damned if Carl was going to disrupt Luke's life as well.

He was still concerned for her safety and he reminded her she agreed to let him protect her. She suggested getting someone else to stay with her for the weekend, maybe Jules. Luke reminded her it wasn't about comfort; it was about safety. He wanted a guy there. He considered which one of his buddies would be willing to kick Carl's ass if the bastard showed up at River's house again.

It was hard for him to think about one of his friends staying overnight with River. Ellie messed him up that way. But he knew his concern was irrational, especially given the circumstances. He decided to arrange this sleepover himself. It would be a step in the right direction. They mutually decided that Jerry would be a good fit to stay with her for the weekend. He was trustworthy and tough as nails.

Luke called Jerry and explained the situation. Jerry agreed to the arrangement knowing the risks. He had no problem kicking Carl's ass. He'd be happy to do it, actually.

That Friday evening when Luke left town, Jerry came over promptly. River wasn't surprised to see him in his standard garb, a flannel shirt and a beard. He reminded her of a Sasquatch.

He pulled a banjo out of his truck when he arrived and sat on her couch, saying only one word, "Howdy." He wasn't much of a talker, which River appreciated because she wasn't either. As River continued her effort of cleaning dishes, a skillful banjo melody filled the room. It would have made the average person feel like dancing. But she wasn't the average person. Not anymore. Having Jerry around made River feel unsettled, which was strange because he'd never made her feel that way before. But River felt that he could be a potential predator. She now believed in what they call "the sixth-sense." It had warned her about Carl.

She was always aware of Jerry's position in the room. He was still sitting on the couch, playing the banjo, paying no attention to her at all. Her heart raced as her clammy hands scrubbed the dishes. She kept looking over at him to make sure he still hadn't moved. She had mapped out a plan in case he did. If he stood up and walked toward the kitchen, she would grab a knife and run in the opposite direction before he could reach her. She was ready.

On second thought, she wondered if this was her sixth-sense or if she was experiencing irrational panic. She couldn't tell. She felt exposed, body and mind.

When the dishes were done, River quietly moved to the edge of the room near the hall. As she moved into Jerry's peripheral vision, he turned to look at her. She quickly said goodnight and went straight to her bedroom without even brushing her teeth. Her rational mind finally spoke up. *What are you doing?* It occurred to her that she was being totally irrational. The man was there to protect her. Her rational mind was confident that Jerry wouldn't hurt her. Luke wouldn't have trusted him to stay with her if there was any question about that. But her mind wasn't in charge right then. Her body was.

Everything inside her screamed, "Lock the door! Now!" The cold metal clicked between her fingers. "Cognitive Dissonance," she said out loud, remembering the psychological term for having an inconsistency between thought and behavior. She wondered how awkward Jerry would feel if he knew that she'd locked her door to keep him out, as if he were a predator. She was glad he would never find out, because that was just the thing: she knew he wouldn't try opening her door. But she'd locked it anyway, making it one of the most irrational things she had ever done. Irrationality was new territory for River. That was for weak people. "I'm a fucking head case!" she almost yelled. Penny came to mind. She realized she'd have so many additional issues if Carl had successfully raped her.

Not long after River went to bed, Jerry pulled his handgun out of the camouflage bag by his feet and laid it on the coffee table near the couch where he would sleep. Jerry figured if Carl showed up at River's house again after what he did, he obviously deserved to die. And Jerry couldn't think of a person in town who deserved death more. Not even Carl's messed up kids would miss him. He'd be doing the town a favor, actually. Jerry reasoned he could claim self-defense, since Carl would be trespassing. Plus, the Chief of Police was his dad's best friend.

Jerry slept ignorant to River's fear of him. He thought he was helping her. But the truth was, nothing could help River right then.

CHAPTER TWENTY-SEVEN

That first night at the lake Luke had a hard time sleeping and it wasn't just because of the hard ground under his small tent. He kept wondering if River was shaking in bed, but more importantly whether Jerry was paying close enough attention to his surroundings. He imagined what Jerry would do if Carl showed up at the house. He imagined what *he* would do. He saw himself rolling Carl's dead body off his boat into the lake. There were new lyrics moving around in his head. They weren't fully formed but he would finish them and turn them into a song when he was ready to face his dark side.

> You knocked; my shadow answered
> Say "hello" to that ol' lake floor
> We laughed your eulogy
> "He's got concrete boots 'n gravity"

Luke knew Jerry would notify him if there was a problem, but he still wanted to text him to see how the night went. At the risk of seeming needy, he texted Jerry. Sure enough, Jerry confirmed the night went by without incident.

That morning Luke and Cliff pushed their canoe into the lake and set out to a hot-spot. They hooked their bait, tossed in their lines and waited for the bobbers to move. Cliff spit tobacco juice into the lake created by the lump in his lip and Luke spit sunflower seed shells, as they waited.

After some silence, Luke told Cliff what Carl did to River and how he hadn't gotten what he deserved yet. Cliff said he dated Carl's oldest daughter in high school, and he'd always wanted to kick Carl's ass ever since he found out what he'd done to his own daughter. The men talked, theoretically, about what back-country justice might look like for Carl.

Guilt plucked Luke's conscious like a guitar string. He was sitting there as Carl's judge in the very canoe, the very location where God had revealed himself in his time of need. It was as if God were asking him, *Luke, would you judge when I haven't? Are you more just than I am?* Luke swallowed and almost choked on a sunflower shell. He was relieved when Cliff changed the subject.

Cliff told a story about how he was fishing with a buddy last year and they got into a yelling match with this old man who was drunk, so they kicked his ass. Then Cliff told another story about a hunting trip he took a couple years ago with a city-buddy who was new to hunting. Cliff said, "Idiot don't even know how carry. He ended up shootin' the dirt right next to me."

Luke laughed, imagining this.

Cliff only chuckled. "Idiot kept pointin' his rifle at me. I told him, if I saw 'im aimin' at me again, I'd fuckin' knock him out."

They both laughed.

Cliff continued, "He was like, 'What, it's not even chambered' 'n I said, 'Stop bein' a fuckin' girl and learn some gun etiquette'."

Luke laughed again. This struck his funny-bone. River surfaced in his mind. He could hear her saying, "Gal, not girl." And then he laughed again at the thought of replacing the word girl in Cliff's sentence, "Stop being a fuckin' gal."

He decided the next thing River would do is chastise Cliff for using women as a put-down. And then it struck him, the woman had gotten into his head. He knew that she'd gotten under his skin, swam in his sheets and even found her way into his heart. But it was news to him that she'd moved in upstairs.

At the campfire that night Cliff took over cooking the small bass they'd caught, so Luke pulled out his guitar and tried finding a tune for new lyrics moving around his head.

> You shake your head when I nod mine
> When you push, I pull; we fall intertwined
>
> I brought you in to share my bed
> But you're takin' up space inside my head

Even as he zipped up his sleeping bag that night, more lyrics came to him like haunting spirits in the night. He snatched them up, as if to possess them before they could possess him.

He eventually fell into a deep sleep but not even waking up to the crisp lake air and the sound of chattering birds could shake the woman from his mind. It amazed him that he could spend three days and two nights thinking about one woman who wasn't even there.

That Saturday morning River's phone reminded her that she had a lunch date with Thelma Woodson. She was happy she had somewhere to be so she didn't have to hang out with Jerry all day. She stopped by the market to buy flowers for her host.

Thelma's home was located in the north center of town in a neighborhood developed in the 70s. River had been to her house one time as a youth when Thelma and her late husband hosted a church youth group party that River happened to attend. So, it felt somewhat familiar when she arrived that afternoon.

Thelma gave River a warm southern greeting and brought her in to enjoy some egg salad sandwiches and fruit salad for lunch. Being around Thelma put a person at ease. She had the demeanor of someone you could tell anything to and not feel judged. She was unlike Kathy that way.

River told her about her life in Boston and the journalism degree she was pursuing before the accident. After they ate lunch Thelma mentioned she needed to make bread while they talked. Ms. Thelma told River about some significant events since she'd left town, including her late husband's passing. She said the service was beautiful. She was happy that her husband got to be with their son now. Thelma said she couldn't wait to join them in heaven someday. River envied that kind of faith. It seems like such a positive outlook on life, especially in the face of unimaginable tragedy. But River knew there was no way she could contrive that kind of belief in things she couldn't see or at least prove, even if she wanted to. She wondered how Thelma could do it.

"Your faith amazes me, Ms. Thelma. I don't know how you do it."

Thelma could feel a distinct sadness in River from the moment she walked in the door. It was different from when she first saw her in church. She was carrying the kind of sadness that weighed enough to crush a human soul. Thelma recognized it. She decided to be transparent.

"When I got the call about Sammy I fell straight to the floor and didn't get up for two days."

River looked over, surprised that Thelma was talking openly about the death of her son. "I was in the grip of grief, I was. I could barely breathe. And I wouldn't have nothin' to do with God." Thelma stared past River into her living room. "God had abandoned me. And so, I abandoned him. The longer I pushed God away the more miserable I became. But I was doin' just fine ignoring an evil God until one day I realized that I was becoming the hate that killed my boy. Then I remembered the last thing Jesus said before he died. He said that God had abandoned him, too." Thelma's gaze landed back on River. "So, I cried out to Jesus, baby. I knew he would understand what I was goin' through. And when I cried out from the depths of my soul, a Jewish man stood right over there where I was, surrounded by light." Thelma pointed to the living room.

River swallowed.

"He really did, Ms. River."

Both women had gone completely still. Neither one was present in that room. They were somewhere else. "And I heard my baby's voice with my own ears, like he was standing right there in that room. He said, 'I'm alright, mama. I'm alright.' That's all I needed to know." Thelma's eyes were misty, "I still miss him every day, of course. I can still smell his precious skin, even after all these years. But he's in the hands of Jesus now and I know will see him again. 'N I can make it through *any* day knowin' that."

River came back to herself. She knew that Thelma wasn't lying to her about this experience. But River wasn't sure if Thelma's experience was anything more than a delusion of the mind, a coping mechanism to combat unimaginable grief. She would never say that to Thelma, of course.

"Wow, that's really incredible," she replied.

"Sammy was a couple years older than your mama. He would have been 46 this year. You know, he was datin' a

211

white girl when he was killed. I'm sure that's why he died. When I see mixed-race couples now, I think, that's a good thing. But I didn't back then. I didn't want Sammy datin' a white, partly 'cause it was dangerous. But you know, people don't give it too much thought anymore. And I think that's good. We're gettin' better at loving each other, I think."

River thought about the racial tensions in the U.S. that seemed to have increased along with the political climate, and wondered if things were getting worse again.

"Did you ever think about leaving Stillwater? I imagine it's difficult being a minority here."

"Well, this is my home!" Thelma sounded offended. "I buried my parents here, my sisters, my husband, and my son in the red dirt. Where else would I go?"

River felt like a complete jerk. An ignorant jerk! Of course this is Thelma's home and she has every logical reason to stay right here despite tragedy. "Of course," River said, shaking her head. "I'm so sorry."

"Life is sufferin', Miss River, it surely is. I haven't met a-one in my time who hasn't suffered greatly. But you know what the goal in the sufferin' is, don't you?"

River shook her head with a heavy heart and stared off into space. She loved goals. Goals were the only thing besides truth (when it could be found) that her life was oriented around. But she'd never imagined having a goal for suffering.

Thelma waited for River to look her in the eyes. "The goal is gettin' through the sufferin' without being corrupted by it, baby."

River liked that goal. "Well, I think if anyone has found the secret to that, it's you, Ms. Thelma."

"Well, God gets all the glory. He carries me through."

River felt like she was being dishonest with Thelma who had shared such personal information with her. "I really do admire your faith, Ms. Thelma. But I should be honest, I don't believe in God. Sometimes I wish I did, but I just don't."

"That's okay, baby. He believes in you."

River smiled.

"You know, there are different ways of knowing something? Not just with your mind. And I can see you have a strong mind."

"What do you mean? Like, with your gut?"

"With your gut. With your heart. With your feet."

"With your feet?"

"Well, how ya' gonna know where solid ground is when the lights go out?"

River nodded and smirked. "Okay."

"'N you don't know how to swim by thinkin' 'bout it, neither." Thelma added. "You know you can swim when you neck-high in water and you don't drown."

River knew what Thelma was getting at. *Bottom of your bucket*, she thought.

Thelma looked her in the eyes. "And, you know you believe in God when He's your only hope, and you run to him, baby."

River nodded, but she really couldn't relate to this kind of thing. A subject change was needed. "Is this a family recipe, or can I write it down?"

"Oh, this recipe ain't on paper! I'll do you one better. How 'bout you make it with me." Thelma pushed a bowl and measuring cup toward River. "Put three cups of warm water in there—*warm not hot*—and then add this yeast."

River was happy the subject had changed and also to make bread. She had never made bread before. There had rarely been time to do anything other than study since she left high school.

After the dough was made and set aside to rise, River said her goodbyes. At the door, Thelma told her that since Sammy was her only child, she would never have any grandkids, and she could surely use one right now. At first, River thought Thelma was just being nice, trying to take care of her, but then it occurred to her that Thelma might be the one who needs taking care of. River thought maybe their need was mutual. She didn't know how to respond, so she just nodded. But she determined to stop by and see Thelma semi-regularly to make sure she was doing okay. And when she made that decision her soul got a little lighter.

That evening, River drove to the hospital to visit Loretta. She longed for her mom to respond to her that night in particular. "Mama, do you believe in God?" she asked. "People 'round here talk about him like he's someone they know." She'd always assumed her mom didn't believe in God. But right then in that moment, she questioned her assumption. Her mother never wanted to talk about God. And Loretta refused to darken the door of any church. This made River wonder if her mother's obstinate resistance to all things God didn't equal disbelief but something closer to belief, plus disdain. If there was a God, River could see people might disdain him. After all, if life was God's idea, then it would also be his responsibility. It would be nice to have someone to blame for the fact that life exacts one lethal strike after another, eventually delivering one final blow.

CHAPTER TWENTY-EIGHT

There were times in River's life where motivation hid itself, despite a looming deadline. That Sunday morning motivation was not all that went missing. Clarity had gone missing too. Her mind was a fog.

That morning she'd tried to write sitting at the dining table but that location was a portal into hell, the place she'd stood gasping for breath. It was a present void calling from across the room, "Look over here. Something terrifying awaits your glance."

She put off finishing the article she'd started for *The Oklahoman* until the afternoon, assuming her mental fog would lift. But after lunch, not even coffee could bring her the necessary clarity to finish the piece. The words on her screen mocked her. They said, "We're just words. Meaningless words. Nothing more. We're not ideas. Not inspiration. Not art. Just words. You put us together. But you're no writer. And no one would care if you were."

She shut her computer and delayed the task further, until evening. Evening came and though she still lacked what she needed to get the job done, she forced herself to read through what she had written so far. The article fell flat in her mind. She couldn't figure out what Luke had seen in it originally. The will to build sentences just wasn't there, so she decided to transcribe the rest of Felker's interview. Felker's voice came through the speaker. She listened for something interesting enough to communicate to readers.

Nothing compelled her. She paused the recording and closed her laptop. There were still a few days before she had to submit the article. She would finish it later that week when something like inspiration returned.

River was happy to see Luke when he'd come back from his fishing trip that Monday. She was less jumpy and had gained some sense of normalcy.

That evening when they were closing shop Luke said, "There's supposed to be a meteor shower. How 'bout we take my flatbed out to Paxton's Field 'n do some stargazin'." He wiggled his eyebrows and said, "You can sit on my lap. We can talk about the first thing that pops up." He smiled and nodded, thinking his joke was funny.

It was funny enough to get a smile and a head nod from River. Actually, stargazing did sound fun. And so did sitting on Luke's lap.

She had a lot of good memories in the back of flatbed trucks. As a child, she'd helped her mom load pallets from the store onto theirs and deliver them to the Jefferson's Farm where they were used to make chicken coops. On the way home her mom would let her stand in the back where the tires kicked up dust along the country roads. Her mom would only let her do this if she promised to hold onto the cab. And so, she did.

That evening River wore her Daisy Dukes and Luke raised the bar for 'fun in a flatbed.' They had good sex in the great outdoors. When they got their clothes back on, they settled against the cab in a pile of blankets and pillows, waiting for nature's show to begin. She told him the only time she'd seen a meteor shower was in college, but she and her friends had to drive many miles outside of the city to escape the 'light-pollution.' River noted the strangeness of not being able to see the night sky amidst the buzzing lights of a city.

Luke said he couldn't imagine not seeing the stars every night. He said they were friends that would never leave you.

They kept talking about big-city life and about college and before they knew it, they were having a conversation that neither one of them expected to have.

"Take the situation with Carl," River said, "As grateful as I am that you were there to help (and I swear to God, Luke, I will always be grateful!) but the fact that you needed to save me just proves the existence of patriarchy."

"Does it? Or does it prove that men are stronger than women and some men take advantage of that?"

"But don't you see how that creates societies where women are owned by men?"

"Course I do. Look at history, men try 'n stake a claim on women for that exact reason—some men are brutes and women need protectin', especially when they are pregnant or have babies."

"Men claim women for more reasons than that—power and money are big ones. But are you saying that's just the way it is and how it should be?"

"No. I'm glad people are evolving. I mean, I'm glad women have freedom and they're treated equal. I know things could be better, but look around. This is the best we've come up with and it's not bad. Especially when you compare it to everything else that's ever been."

River looked at him and asked, "Would you say all that to me if Carl had raped me?"

Luke saw a piece of straw stuck to the flatbed near his foot. The old leather sole of his boot scraped it off. The straw stuck there, so he pulled it off. It needed straightening out, kind of like his thoughts. River could literally hear crickets in the night air. Finally, his lips moved sideways as he shook his head.

They sat in silence for a while before River said, "Being content with the way things are, even if it's the best we've done yet, is supporting patriarchy."

"Ha! Patriarchy! You mean, me."

"What? No! I mean, sexism."

"I went to college, River. I know who the patriarchy is. It's guys who look like me—white skin, with dicks that like to fuck women."

She hated the way he said that. "Luke, there are plenty of straight, white men who don't support unjust hierarchies."

Luke huffed. "How? By letting feminists put them at the bottom of their own hierarchy, as long as they hate themselves for being who God made 'em?"

"What are you talking about?

"I'm sayin', if I want the Olivia-types to like me (and I don't!) I have to agree that people who look like me are the lowest form of human life. (They assume everything we do is hate.) Then I have to agree that women, the blacks and the gays, and everyone else except whites and men has the truth about life. It's bullshit, River! I don't judge people by their skin, sex or anything else 'cept how they act. Fuck! Isn't that the whole point?"

She knew what he was trying to say but the words he used were all wrong. He would have been torn to shreds in any college class for saying 'the blacks, and the gays.' That alone would have confirmed that he was deserving of the labels "racist," "sexist," "bigot," "white supremacist," "homophobe." But she knew that he wasn't. So, she wondered why his choice of words alone would earn him these labels. It occurred to her that the rhetorical rules for engagement were getting so restrictive that they stifled any real discussion. But no one was around to call him names, so she considered what he was saying.

She considered whether the people who claimed to be solving racism and sexism were actually dividing people up by those categories and judging them. It had become clear to her that certain categories of people were not welcome in conversation about race, and they were getting the message loud and clear. But River wanted to have this discussion with him especially because of his demographic. She wanted to know what white men were thinking because it would take every person to make the broad-scale societal change that was needed. But still, Luke had learning to do, she decided.

"There are still real problems with prejudice and hate. Take Thelma's son, for example. That wasn't that long ago. He went to school with my mama. Things need to change in a serious way."

"I agree. But ain't nothin' gonna change when they call you a racist for sayin' words the wrong way. They wanna find a racist, they can hunt down the bastard who put a knife in Sammy's chest. People are aimin' at the wrong folks. Those so-called 'justice' types think all whites are the same 'n I don't care what they say 'bout me no more."

"'Those justice types' are working for equality."

"No, they ain't! They ain't interested in equality. They want revenge. And I ain't interested in turnin' patriarchy into matriarchy or changin' one color supremacy for another. And I'll never admit to bein' a bad person because of my skin color, or somethin' my ancestors did, or anything, other than how I act!"

"So, who's supposed to make the world a better place if not 'justice-types'?"

"Well, definitely not people yellin' 'Women Rule" 'n 'Black Power'. How's that equal? How's that different than sayin' 'Men Rule' or 'White Power'? They're sayin' some people are better than others, 'n everyone gets to be proud of their roots 'cept white folks. That's fucked up! They wanna punish me for history. They act like I created slavery and war, like it hasn't existed since the beginning of time."

Listening to Luke, really listening, made River feel like she was supporting all the injustice that had ever occurred throughout the history of the United States. But, why? There was an unspoken rule that she wasn't supposed to care about white-men's experience in the world. This made her think about college theories on race relations. She remembered her discomfort with using a version of Marx's economic theory. Marx talked about the poor versus the middle/upper class. He analyzed their access to the means of production and the control of capital. Other social theories like his also attempt to understand the imbalance of power and wealth in cross-sections of society. They took Marx's "poor" and renamed them "oppressed" and took his upper-class and renamed them "oppressors." But the problem was, they assign people to these power-laden categories by their arbitrary physical features like race and sex. Not economics! And Luke had been placed in the oppressor class, despite his humble state.

She was supposed to think about people as part of a group—guilty or innocent. She shouldn't sympathize with people categorized as the oppressor class. She should privilege the experience of oppressed groups... or at least the experience of individuals who say they represent those groups. But that brought River right back to the individual. The conversation she'd had with Jules came to mind, about how feminists say they represent women, purely by nature of their genitalia, not because they were elected by a majority. Then it struck her, the smallest minority *is* the individual and, so, the most protected class should be the individual.

Luke could see that River was stuck in her head again. He nudged her.

Finally, she replied, "I hear what you're saying about feeling targeted. I won't say I haven't noticed this. But did you know Ms. Thelma still gets watched when she shops in town?"

"Why?" The moment Luke asked the question, he knew the answer. And he felt like an idiot for asking.

River raised one eyebrow and tipped her head to the side.

He'd never thought about what it was like to have black skin and live in Stillwater before. He nodded his acknowledgement.

"If you let your guard down for a second, you might hear what reasonable people are trying to tell you."

Luke paused, "My guard's down with you, Delilah. Just don't tell me to hate myself, 'cause that ain't gonna happen. You can tell me what needs doin' and I'll do it." He looked down at her thighs, which were popping out of her daisy-dukes and lit up by the moonlight. He continued, "There's at least one thing I do that helps women." He grabbed one of her thighs and squeezed it.

She screamed and laughed. That was her worst tickle spot! He fell on top of her and squeezed her thigh again. She screamed and laughed. River didn't know how to feel about Luke. She loved to hate him and she hated that she liked him. He was so wrong and so right. He was ignorant and insightful. Frustrating and funny. And, oh dear god, the sex!

He kissed her mouth and she kissed him back. When the threat of tickling had passed, she asked, "Why'd you call me Delilah?"

He realized River had never heard the Bible story of Sampson and Delilah. "Cuz, I forgot you were a heathen, that's why." He told her the old story as they watched the ancient rocks finish their time-stamped journey by braking through earth's atmosphere and making this planet their home.

They sat in awe. At some point he asked, "So, how's your writing comin'?"

She sighed, "I lost inspiration for it. But I'll finish it before the deadline."

"You better."

"I will. Deadlines are a compulsion for me. Inspired or not, I get them done."

On their way back to town River stood in the back of the truck holding on to the cab. At some point she let go with both hands while the red dirt kicked up from the tires and her hair danced around her head in the warm breeze.

It felt good to be totally irresponsible for the first time since she was sixteen.

CHAPTER TWENTY-NINE

Luke assumed he'd be staying with River that night. He killed his engine and grabbed his duffel in the back of his cab.

"Hey," River interrupted. "I think I'm ready to stay here on my own. I've gotta do it at some point. And my mom has a gun in the house."

Luke said he'd agree to this plan as long as she knew how to handle the weapon. He came inside to make sure she that did.

The 9mm Luger was right where River remembered it being, on the top shelf of her mom's closet, along with a full clip of ammunition next to it. Loretta loved this gun. She mostly shot it for fun. But one time she needed it to take care of a rodent. His name was Jim. She thought Jim was the perfect gentleman when she met him, but she started seeing signs of control early on. Turns out, River isn't the first Novak who didn't take kindly to being controlled. Loretta's first and only fight with Jim happened when he demanded that she tell him everywhere she had gone that day. She didn't think she owed him this explanation and she let him know it. River could hear them yelling at each other from her room when suddenly things went completely silent. River wasn't sure why but it seemed Loretta had dropped the argument completely.

Later that day, Loretta dropped a few hundred dollars on a shiny new pistol. Jim came over that evening to find

Loretta standing on her porch. When he got out of his truck, she told him to get back inside it, unless he'd rather leave in an ambulance. He laughed at her and kept walking. She pulled the gun out from under her vest and didn't wait to see his reaction before shooting the dirt by his feet. His hands kept his knees from hitting the ground as he swung around and ran back to his truck. River ran outside when she heard the gunshot and asked what was going on. Loretta kept the gun aimed at his tailgate until his truck disappeared into the dust. Loretta said, "I'm just taking care of a rodent." River never saw Jim again.

The handgun in River's hand was heavier than she remembered it being. Its weight emphasized the gravity of wielding a deadly weapon. But she couldn't think of a better way to defend herself as a small woman on twenty-one acres outside of town. If there were danger, by the time the Sheriff made it out, River's story would have already been told. This gun would have to do. She gazed at the cold metal recalling the many times she'd heard Harvard academics decry "America's love-affair with guns." As a child, guns were just part of small-town life. But, as a student, she'd been convinced by professors that people don't need guns and that those who own them are morally suspect. In that moment, she found herself thinking, *I'd rather have a love affair with this gun than with Carl.* A newfound appreciation for her gun-totin' mama secured itself in her psyche.

Luke watched her insert the magazine into the handle and eject it with ease. He wondered if she would have the courage to pull the trigger if need be. He spoke up, "This gun will be used against you if you can't pull the trigger. So don't even hesitate. You've shot this gun before, right?"

"Not since I was a kid."

Luke emptied the chamber of bullets and double checked that it was empty. He placed her fingers around the handle where they should go and said, "Arms straight. Push forward with this hand but pull it back with the other. That'll stabilize your aim." He pushed down on her hips. "Bend your knees a little and lean forward. That way when it kicks back, it won't throw you back with it. That'll help you get it back to the line-a-fire, which is important if you need to take another shot."

As a child, Loretta taught River the basics of gun safety, but Luke reviewed it anyway. "Always know where the gun is pointin' and keep your finger off the trigger 'til it's aimed at your target. Always! There ain't no accidents with guns. Only idiots!"

He took the gun from her and inserted the magazine and then racked it. The loud click-clack announced its deadly purpose. He ejected the magazine again, showed it to her and asked, "Is the gun loaded?" She looked down at the round sitting in his hand and shook her head no. He pulled back the slide on the barrel and out from the top a bullet popped out.

River lost a bit of color.

"Always assume that your gun is loaded." He inserted the magazine again, racked it, gave it to her and said, "Empty it."

As she went to eject the magazine, she thoughtlessly aimed it directly at Luke. He jumped sideways yelling, "WATCH IT!"

River was so frightened by her almost lethal mistake that she nearly laughed with nervous tension.

"Always know where your barrel is pointin' and keep your finger away from the trigger."

This time, making sure the gun was aimed away from Luke, she ejected the magazine. It took her a couple of tries to pull back the spring-loaded slide but when she'd finally done it, the chambered bullet popped out. He put the safety on and showed her how to do a visual check to ensure it was empty.

"Good. Now load it."

She inserted the magazine and looked at him.

"It ain't loaded 'til you chamber a bullet, darlin'." She made sure her trigger finger was straight against the barrel and aimed away from Luke before racking it. The resounding click-clack declared its readied state. "This is a semi-automatic so you only need to rack it once; then you can shoot the entire clip." He looked down at little River holding a loaded gun properly. He nodded approvingly. If it weren't bad etiquette to joke around with loaded guns, he would have teased her for failing to be a proper liberal. Instead he said, "Now all you need is the courage to pull the trigger. Just remember, if that bastard's in this house, he deserves to die."

She nodded.

After Luke left, River emptied the gun again. She picked a target in the room and practiced getting out of bed while grabbing the gun and aiming it at her target in one fluid motion. Then after stabilizing her aim, pulling the trigger. With each practice, she built determination to shoot first and ask questions later. If she didn't want to rely entirely on the goodwill of strong men in the world, she would need to become a force to contend with. And she planned on it.

That night, her sleep wasn't very deep but in the morning her courage was. She'd made it through a night at the farmhouse with no company at all, except the resolve to use a deadly weapon.

CHAPTER THIRTY

She showed up at Penny's place that evening empty-handed and hungry for female company. On Jules urging, Penny offered a review of the progress she and Michael had made towards having sex. They had almost been successful, but not quite. Jules almost was impressed. But River had a new appreciation for the difficulty Penny faced in this area.

When Penny was finished with her obligatory speech, Jules turned her focus on River. "Well, sweetie, I imagine you know why you're here tonight."

"To hang out with friends?" River replied, sounding confused.

"Well, duh! But you know?" Jules paused before saying, "Carl."

The name hit River's ears with force. She sighed audibly and adjusted in her creaking chair. She hadn't shown up that evening prepared to talk about it. But apparently that's why she had been invited. River reasoned that their curiosity was warranted, but what she was supposed to say about it? She figured Jules wanted a blow-by-blow review of events and River wasn't keen on giving that.

Jules continued, "Luke said you were havin' issues and you needed girls to talk to."

That sounded like something he'd say. River felt as though gravity had suddenly doubled.

"He said you got hurt." Jules already knew how Carl hurt River, but she was giving her friend a chance to talk about it.

River didn't want to say what happened so she just pulled the neck of her shirt down a few inches to reveal a freshly sealed wound.

Jules shook her head and exclaimed, "I can't believe Luke didn't go after Carl when he saw blood!"

"He didn't. I made sure of that."

Jules jaw dropped. "I'm sorry River. God knows I love you like a sister but I really don't understand you sometimes!"

"Jules, what good would it do for Luke to go after Carl?"

"Well, for starters, Luke could have kicked his ass and you wouldn't have to worry about Carl comin' back!"

River shook her head. "I'll be worried about that long after he's dead!"

"WHAT?" Jules yelled, completely confused.

Penny spoke up, "I know what you mean, Riv. They always come back. In your head."

Penny's understanding tone brought a flood of emotion to the surface. River looked down trying not to cry. How could she cry in front of Penny who endured the worst possible kind of assault? Penny could see she was holding back tears so she stood up, walked over, and wrapped her arms around River. This made the tears flow freely and River cried right there in front of them. It was good for River's soul to be wrapped in the only arms that really understood what she was going through. Her hands shook as she wiped the tears from her face. Jules fell silent when River lost her composure. She'd only ever seen this once, when River saw her mom's body right after the accident. Jules didn't know how to help, so she stayed silent and let Penny take over.

Penny knelt by her chair and brushed River's hair from her face. "It gets easier, hun. Everything changes but you get used to your new normal. You might have strange fears sometimes. But as long as you know what's happenin', you can't feel too crazy."

When Penny said "crazy," River pictured herself locking her bedroom door the night Jerry stayed over. She sniffed, "I'm just... every sound makes me jump. It's driving me crazy!"

"Yeah. I know. That's here to stay. Just let it serve as a reminder of your strength. You have to put a positive spin on this stuff, okay?"

River nodded. When it came to dealing with the effects of trauma, she would take any advice that Penny had to offer. Jules was confused by the conversation but she knew her confusion was a good thing. It seemed the only way to truly understand this was to experience it.

River went home that night feeling stronger for having female support, but she was emotionally and physically exhausted. She flopped down on the couch, not intending to stay for long, but before she could lie next to the loaded handgun on her nightstand, she fell into a deep sleep.

Carl's last dime had been spent on his best friend—Jack Daniels. He tossed the remaining pennies on the ground. He drank half of one bottle on his way home from the liquor store while lamenting his complete failure to locate his delinquent wife. The usually straight road leading to his farmhouse swayed just beyond his dusty windshield. His swerving car eventually arrived at his fractured and empty home. As he entered his foot caught on the entryway sending him lunging forward. He protected the cradled bottles in his arms by landing on his side. He cried out in pain from the broken rib still aching from Luke's attack.

When Carl saw the kitchen, his stomach growled. He'd run out of food a long time ago. But Linn wasn't around to cook for him anyway. The piano seemed like the right place to line up his bottles, his last meal. This thought made him look up on the wall to see a framed print of Jesus eating his last supper. He laughed at the irony, but felt mocked. He grabbed the image and threw it across the room. He took a swig of the open bottle and slammed it down on the piano. *That felt good,* he thought. He swiped his arm across the top of the piano, relocating framed photos of his children onto the floor. He cursed each one of them by name before taking another swig. Still holding the bottle, he staggered over to the bookshelf and emptied its contents onto the floor. He lifted the bottle to his mouth but it was empty. He threw it on top of the pile that was forming in the middle of the room. On his way to the piano he remembered a riddle his youngest daughter had asked him last year. "If a tree falls in a forest and no one is around to hear it, does it make a sound?" He laughed at the thought that he was that tree and no one was around to hear him falling. He opened a new bottle and tipped it back. He steadied himself on the ragged armchair, the one Linn used to sit in. After taking a swig he flung the chair on top of the pile.

A stream of abuse began to flow from his mouth, as if Linn were there to hear it. She was a good-for-nothing whore. She was fat and she was lucky to have him. No one else could love her. In fact, her mama should have had an abortion. He growled the last bit as he pulled the bookshelf away from the wall sending it timbering down to the pile below. Winded, he leaned against the wall and thought, *this would make a good bonfire.* And then the story came to him, as if it had already been told. He would burn down the farm; it would be the biggest fire that town had ever seen. After lighting it, he'd find Sweet Cheeks and take her down to the grave with him. Carl reasoned that if Luke was with her, he'd gladly shoot that kid dead first. When he was done with the girl, he'd burn down the Novak farm, too. His last meal would be his revolver. He'd go out with a bang. He'd never really leave that town because everyone would say his name long after he was dead.

He stumbled past the rubble and into his garage and collected a couple rusted gasoline cans and a stack of newspapers. On his way through the kitchen he threw open a drawer and grabbed some matches. He dropped the newspaper on top of the pile then sloshed the gasoline around. Some of it landed on his shoes and pants but he didn't notice. He looked at his creation. He wasn't satisfied. Carl needed this fire to be the biggest one the town had ever seen. He took a wooden dining chair and tossed it on top. After stabilizing himself he picked up another chair and heaved it, too, a little too hard. It flew over the pile, headed toward the piano. Time seemed to slow down. He could see the tragedy unfold before it had happened. The airborne chair hit the corner where the whiskey bottles stood. Carl lunged forward reaching out, as if he were close enough to catch them. His foot caught on a frame and his head took a blunt hit from a chair leg sticking out of the rubble. The last thing Carl heard before the room went black was breaking glass.

CHAPTER THIRTY-ONE

That day had a sort of weight to it. Maybe it was the atmospheric pressure from the dark midday sky, which cast a dreamlike appearance across the Oklahoma landscape. The electric wind warned of an angry sky. The eventual rain made a muggy heat and turned the red dirt into mud. Folks were talking about a twister but the Weather Channel assured them the storm was due north.

Luke crouched as he unpacked a new shipment of cowboy accessories that had arrived in the store's weekly shipment. One of the buckles was particularly epic in size. It had an animal skull just under the words "Cowboy Up." He smirked and brought it over where River stood at the counter. He leaned in and said, "This thing could take our relationship to a whole new level."

River laughed about the buckle but her mind got stuck on the word relationship. "I hear ya' about that buckle." She paused and said, "But I'm not sure what we have is a relationship with a capital R."

The words cut to Luke's heart but he tried not to show it. "Why not. We're sleeping together and, as far as I know, we're exclusive." He really wanted her to confirm they were exclusive. Cheating would always be a sore-spot for him.

"Yeah, but you are married, Luke." The way she said "married" had a punch to it.

"Only on paper. Ellie broke that agreement a long time ago. The only thing she's got left of me is a signature. My heart's available."

The paperwork in front of River suddenly needed organizing. There were vendors mixed up with customer accounts. She was pretty sure the employee schedule and payroll paperwork had gotten mixed up in the pile. She sorted through it. Things with Luke were getting too serious too fast. They had only been sleeping together for a few weeks and she hadn't meant to get into a relationship in the first place. What the hell was she doing? Her mom was critically ill and her future was uncertain. Would she move back to Boston when her mom woke up? When would that be? Not to mention, this man wasn't easily civilized. There were too many unknowns with the whole thing.

River's silence spoke volumes to Luke but he played it off with a joke. "Well looks like I'm gonna need to buy a buckle with a capital R on it." They both laughed awkwardly and let the subject go. He walked away realizing he was more invested in the relationship than she was. And he needed to protect his heart. He wondered how people could give half of their heart away. He was the all-in type of guy. He consoled himself with the knowledge that at least she confirmed they were exclusive.

The moment Luke walked away regret washed over River. She wished she'd responded to what he said about his heart being available. She wasn't sure what she would have said to him but she did feel the tug of loving him. Something about him felt like home with a capital H. There was something about the two of them that created a symbiotic balance like the yin and yang, each having their own location but fitting together like two parts of one whole. And each of them had a bit of the other embedded inside, stopping them from flying off into oblivion with the centrifugal force of life.

They usually only slept over at each other's house on weekends but that Monday evening River invited Luke to stay at her place as a gesture of intimacy. He declined. He said he had things to take care of at home. So, they went separate ways.

Over the days that followed, Luke put some emotional distance between himself and River. He could see the situation he'd gotten himself into with River. In his mind's eye, she began looking less like a girlfriend and more like a potentially venomous snake. He'd been bitten once before, and it had almost killed him. At age seventeen, he'd thought there were only two kinds of women, the pretty and the ugly kind. But now, thanks to River, he could see with more dimension. There were at least two more kinds of women: the straight-forward and the manipulative types. Even in the short time he'd dated River, he'd appreciated her candidness, even when he didn't like what she said. She didn't expect him to read her mind. She required no interpretation, which for him was a welcomed change in female behavior.

It seemed she was reaching out when she invited him to stay over at her place again that Tuesday night, but he declined again. He realized he'd need to put some physical distance between them if he was going to develop some emotional distance. Even still, he found himself hoping that it was River who was knocking on his door that fateful night, because the truth was, he didn't want any distance.

He wasn't sure who would be knocking; his curiosity piqued as he opened it. Standing there instead of River was a real live viper. His wife. He had wished for this—the moment she'd return—so many times in months past. But with the passing of time he'd decided she was never coming back, so he'd stopped imagining how he'd respond if she did. He stood frozen like spotted prey. Ellie was shorter than Luke but her presence made him feel small. He got smaller each second.

Ellie stepped inside the house expressing regret for leaving him and requesting his forgiveness. She assured him she was done with Jeremy for good. She wanted to repair their marriage. Luke was so disoriented, he couldn't have quoted anything she'd said, just the sentiment. He closed the door and they sat on the couch. He wouldn't look at her. He stared straight ahead while she faced him and spoke softly. He had a hard time focusing on her words. They were just words. Empty words floating around him, barely able to reach his ears. The damage had been done. There could be no repair. Each word that left her mouth added weight to the air, pushing him deeper into the couch. He wondered if the cushions might swallow him entirely.

"Luke. Say something."

He shook his head.

He was trying to clear his thoughts when she tucked her baggy shirt around her bulging belly and said, "Luke, I'm pregnant."

He looked down at her belly.

"It's yours," she added.

"LIAR!" he yelled. But he wondered, could it be true? Would he be a dad in a few short weeks?

She put one hand on his shoulder and one on his thigh. She told him he was a strong man with a good heart. That he was the hardest working man she'd ever known. He had unparalleled character. And will make an incredible dad very soon. She rubbed his thigh. He didn't respond. She ran her other hand through his hair, brought her mouth to his cheek and kissed it. Her sweet scent brought a flood of emotion to the surface. He closed his eyes. She smelled like his first home. His first kiss. His first everything. She kissed his neck and moved her hand to the inside of his thigh. He didn't stop her. She aroused him and unzipped his jeans.

She had been his whole world since he was a kid. Teenage Ellie flashed through his mind. She was the picture of perfection that he'd chased all those years thinking he was chasing happiness itself. He wouldn't have admitted it, but he was crying. A tear rolled down his cheek. His heart was being ripped from his chest all over again and her touch was the only pleasure he could feel. He was lost in her gravitational pull and before he knew it, she had satisfied at least one part of him.

Luke left Ellie alone on the couch as he sat on the edge of his bed with his face in his hands and elbows on his knees. He knew he'd betrayed River's trust, however ill-defined their relationship was. And he knew what betrayal felt like. It's a cold steel knife in your back that can only be extracted by the hand of God. How could he tell her about this? Would he?

His mind shifted. The idea of being a father made his stomach flip, though he wasn't sure if the feeling came from fear or excitement. As much as he loved kids, he no longer wanted to have them with Ellie. But this baby could be Jeremy's kid. He considered Ellie's proposal of taking her back only briefly. What River had taught him without knowing it was the importance of hearing the truth, even when you hate it. He realized that Ellie never spoke the truth. She tells people what they want to hear, as long as it serves her purposes. He didn't want Ellie back; he was done with her. Done.

He went out to the living room to find her looking around at changes he'd made since she left. "I like this picture here," she said, not realizing the picture was covering a hole in the wall where Luke had taken out his rage when she left him.

"You need to leave," he said.

"What?" She sounded surprised.

He looked at her belly. "If you need a ride to your parent's place, I'll drive you, but you ain't stayin' here."

"But Luke…"

He interrupted with a raised voice, "This ain't your home no more, Ellie."

She wasn't used to him yelling at her. She paused before saying, "Luke, my parents won't have me." This didn't surprise him. He long believed her parents liked him more than they liked her. In fact, Ellie's mom took care of Luke as much as he would let her for the first two months after Ellie left.

"Find somewhere else to go."

When Ellie realized Luke wouldn't budge, she reluctantly pulled her phone out of her purse and made some calls to friends. But she failed to find a friend willing to take her in. They were angry at the way she left town, if only because she'd abandoned them, too.

When Luke could see that her phone calls were failing, he tossed a pillow and blanket on the couch and said, "I don't care where you go but you leave first thing in the morning."

"Luke, don't you want to talk about this?"

He interrupted again, "There ain't nothin' left to say, Ellie! You told me everything I needed to know when you fucked around 'n walked out on me." He went to his bedroom and closed the door. He imagined her climbing into bed with him in the middle of the night. That was something she'd do. He'd already fallen prey to her manipulations once that night. The lock on his bedroom door clicked. It was that moment when he realized for the first time that he would be happier without Ellie than he would be with her. She was a location proximal to hell.

He remained in his room for the rest of the evening playing his guitar well into the midnight hour. And he even cried a little. But he knew these were the last tears he'd ever shed for Ellie. It was like watching the end of a tragic movie, determined never to watch it again.

Carl woke up to the smell of gasoline and the sensation that a spike was being hammered into the back of his head. He looked up from the ground to make sure this wasn't actually happening to him.

Burning down the farm no longer seemed like an urgent task. He'd been unconscious for an unknown amount of time. He dragged himself over to the piano to see if any whiskey had survived the fall. Every vein screamed out for this potent liquid. He'd never needed hair of the dog more than he did right then. Both bottles had shattered and were empty. The ground around them was dry. He threw a stream of curses into the air and crawled to the kitchen sink to get water. He was sweating profusely and shaking violently. His heart raced. The pain in his head was nearly unbearable. A wave of nausea hit him when, suddenly, Linn appeared at the end of the hallway. She stood two feet tall and hovering in space. Her eyes shot laser beams at him before she bolted toward him at lightning-speed. The contents of Carl's stomach projected down the hallway. When his stomach had completely emptied, the dry-heaving began. This heaving lasted for many hours, until his stomach muscles ceased to flex.

He made it to the kitchen and gathered water; his hands shook so violently half sloshed out of the glass before making it to his mouth. He opened the medicine cabinet and swiped the entire contents onto the floor. He sat rummaging through the mess, then poured out a handful of Advil. He shoved it in his mouth and washed it down with the remainder of his drink. His head spiked, his heart throbbed and his skin was on fire. Sweat-saturated clothing clung to his fiery flesh. It took all of his effort to manage his physical discomfort. As evening approached, he faded in and out of consciousness and convulsions. While he lay dormant on the kitchen floor, his liver, kidneys and heart debated whether or not Carl would live to see another day. During his waking spells, he hydrated himself. During his sleeping spells, he peed himself.

As night fell, his mind became more alert and his body became less demanding of his undivided attention. And that's when the real pain kicked in—emotional pain. And nothing and no one was there to kill it.

CHAPTER THIRTY-TWO

When Luke came in to the shop the next morning the first thing River said was, "Did you sleep with her?"

"What?" Luke was surprised that River knew about Ellie staying at his place. He barely had time to process what had happened the night before, let alone figure out how to tell River about it. But apparently this conversation was happening right then.

Skippy cleared his throat reminding River he was present. She didn't care. Luke's eyes darted to Skippy and back to her. He didn't answer.

"Well?" she demanded.

Luke's gaze landed on Skippy, communicating that he'd better leave the room.

As Skippy was walking away, River said, "You should know how fast news travels in this town, Luke. Did you sleep with her?"

"No. I mean," he paused, "I told her she couldn't stay with me but she had nowhere else to go."

"Just tell me if it got physical, Luke!"

He looked down at the baseball cap in his hand and hesitated, "It wasn't like that, River."

"What WAS it like, Luke?" It was obvious to her that he was trying not to answer the question directly. She imagined them sleeping together and her face radiated heat.

The only thing Luke ever promised God was that he would always tell the truth, or at least he wouldn't lie. He kept his promise. "She gave me a hand job." He looked up.

River gave a bitter chuckle and a nod. There he stood, the Neanderthal, after all.

"I didn't," he began.

She Interrupted, "Well, Luke, Ellie can have your signature AND YOUR GODDAMN HEART!"

"River, stop!" Her arm escaped his grasp as she ran past him out of the store.

The bell on the door was a death rattle. The second woman he loved just walked out on him. This time, it was his fault and he couldn't fix it. His body stood like the walls of the Grand Canyon but his mind shifted like a tectonic plate under pressure. There were a million ways to screw up in life but only one way to get it right. There were a million roads leading into the abyss but only one way out. He had already been to the dragon's lair and barely escaped with his life. A new path appeared, calling him back into the abyss.

All he could hear was the rushing of blood in his ears. It was deafening. If he could stand outside of himself, he wouldn't hesitate; he'd bloody his face with his own two fists, no mercy. He'd gladly accept every blow as her revenge if only she'd take him back. The wooden countertop was a sorry substitute. He growled as he crushed his fist against the solid surface over and over again, picturing himself at the other end of these blows. He tried to hold back the tears but he couldn't help crying right there in the front of the store. The sound traveled into the backroom where Skippy sat on a box. Skippy stayed there for about twenty minutes after silence fell.

❖

When River got home, she texted Skippy, telling him she was taking the next three days off work. It was Wednesday so that gave her a good five days before she would have to see Luke's pathetic face again. She turned her phone off, skipped dinner and slept on the couch. She couldn't bear sleeping in her bed; it reminded her of Luke. The next day came and went and her stomach never once reminded her that people need food to survive. She kept water by the couch. "I'm a fucking idiot!" she yelled out aloud in the void. "What the hell did I expect?" Kathy's words came back to her, "The dust hasn't settled in Luke's life, yet," and she realized this was a warning, not a rejection. River figured this is why Kathy spoke these words to her instead of Luke. But Kathy wasn't the person to talk to about Luke. Neither was Jules. River couldn't bear to hear Jules defend him and she was pretty that sure she would. She imagined Jules saying something like, "Ellie's his wife, so technically Luke's been cheating with you, not her." Penny wasn't the right person to talk to either. She'd have nothing relevant to say about this kind of thing. And Olivia, even if she were still a friend, she definitely wasn't the right person to talk to about a Neanderthal. River stayed on the couch and slept through another sunrise and sunset feeling utterly alone on planet earth. She didn't even have the energy to go to the hospital and act like her mom could hear her voice.

On the second evening she had just enough energy to finish the article for the Oklahoman. It was due at midnight, and she'd never gotten this close to missing a deadline in her life. She still lacked inspiration, especially now, but she'd be damned if she'd miss the deadline. On her way to the dining table to get her laptop, she saw a file box against the wall, the one the hospital gave her with her mom's personal belongings from the crash. She decided this was a worthy distraction before the burdensome task of finishing the article.

She brought the cardboard file box to the coffee table to sort through it. There were miscellaneous items in the box: music CDs, a sweatshirt, a map of Oklahoma and Loretta's black leather purse. The corner of a white envelope sticking out of her mom's purse caught her eye. She pulled it out. It was a sealed envelope with a few words written on it in her mother's handwriting, "A Gift For River." Her heart jumped! Her mom was reaching out to her, even in her absence. She pictured a healthy pre-accident Loretta stirring a pot of beef-stew in the kitchen, calling out, "Hey baby-doll, I forgot to give you somethin'. That gift. You could really use this today."

"Thank you, Mama," River said aloud, "How did you know I needed you right now?" She opened the envelope. Inside was a multi-page handwritten letter. She held it to her chest, hungry for her mother's touch. It read:

Dear River,

This is the hardest thing I've ever had to do. I need to tell you something important. I'm afraid it will change our relationship. Please don't let it. The only reason I haven't told you until now is because I didn't want to lose you.

When you were young, I told you I didn't know your father. Well, that's sort of true. I don't know him personally, but I know his name and where he lives. When I found out I was pregnant with you, I realized it would be hard for him to be involved in raising you. He lives an hour away from Stillwater. I figured I was strong enough to raise you myself, and I was, especially with help from people around town. But at some point, I realized you wished you had a dad. I didn't expect that. I thought my love would be enough for you.

I'm telling you this now because I know you're old enough to understand my decision and old enough to decide if you want him in your life. I'm giving you this gift—the gift of knowing your dad.

The night we met he was playing in a band at The Farm. Since we didn't use any protection, he gave me his information and the name of the reservation he lives on. He's Cherokee. He lives by the Arkansas River. Actually, that's why I named you River, because of him.

I know you'll probably be bothered for a while that I didn't tell you sooner but you have to understand and give me credit for telling you at all. Parenting is hard. You have to make a lot of hard decisions. You'll understand someday. Please see this from my perspective.

Loretta finished the letter with contact information for her father—Joseph (Joe) Adair—and further requests for understanding. River put the letter down on the coffee table and her mind went completely blank. The ground dropped out from beneath her and the walls sank in around her like they were on quicksand. Her past, the history that made her who she was, shattered into a million irrelevant pieces and fell into the abyss behind her. She was falling into the void as well and no one was there to catch her. A distinct emptiness hollowed out her soul. Her eyes became boulders. She curled up on the couch and closed them. Her body felt as though it weighed a ton and yet she was floating into space, as if no couch lay below her. Her mind was just as empty as the space she'd set adrift in. Eventually, she fell asleep, going in and out of consciousness for an unknown amount of time. The sun came up and went down at least once, but she didn't notice its coming or going. Eventually, she got up and went to the bathroom, then gulped a huge glass of water.

She looked at the letter laying on the coffee table, her mother's signature at the bottom. Anger came bubbling up from the depths of her soul like lava, the heat of which she'd never known. This sensation began below her stomach but it rose up. Higher. Higher. Her breathing picked up pace. Her mother had stolen her father from her. Little River thought her daddy was out of reach and yet he lived in touching distance all of these years. He didn't even know she existed. What would he have done if he knew? Would he have loved her? Would he have been a part of her life? Would she have camped with him those summers at the lake instead of other families? She felt the absence of her father's presence acutely and she realized that she'd been missing him all along.

Her heart raced. Her breathing sped. Loretta stole her native heritage from her, too. Would her father have taught her Cherokee traditions, their history and their sacred stories? Anger boiled up to the brim of her impoverished soul. She jumped up from the couch, fists clenched to her sides and screamed to the sky with every fiber of her being. All the air emptied from her lungs. She drew in another breath and with all of her soul she screamed again, swinging her arms through the air, as if hitting someone. Her eyes were wild with rage. She stomped over to the side table beside the couch and threw its contents to the ground with one swing of her arm. The lamp broke on impact with the floor. A picture of her mom flew sideways to the ground and a glass of water splashed across the floor. She picked up the picture of her mom and threw it across the room while heaving another scream. The frame's blunt edge took a sizeable chunk out of the wall before shattering on the ground. She moved across the room where another picture of Loretta and River hung. She raised her arm and smashed it repeatedly with the ball of her hand. She felt a shard of glass slice all the way through her muscle to the bone. The pain was excruciating and welcomed, a distraction from the anger burning a hole inside of her like acid on tissue. Blood spurted out from her hand; she didn't care. But her subconscious directed her back to the couch where she sat pressing the wound against her waist.

She sat breathing wildly and rocking back and forth for a bit. But then the sound of primal weeping flowed from her open mouth. This noise was unrecognizable to her own ears. *Is that me?* she wondered. She listened to herself like an outsider, curious about this unusual display of emotion. It was a foreign sound. She could almost see herself sitting on the couch from a distance. At first, she didn't feel the emotion connected to the sound.

But then she did. All of life's tragedies came rushing over her in one drowning wave; there was no escaping its impact. Her mother had been mortally wounded. Her mama betrayed her. Her father was always absent and yet ever-present. Her native heritage had been stolen from her. There was a Luke-sized hole in her heart. And she had become trauma's fool. Her past went missing. Her present was dizzying. She saw no future in sight.

CHAPTER THIRTY-THREE

As River's rage subsided, her crying became more recognizable to her own ears. Greater waves of sorrow rushed over her, each one pushing her further away from the shores of hope. She felt as though she was being pulled toward a black hole with inevitable darkness and isolation ahead. The lonely void was accentuated by the present silence, only pierced by the ticking of time on the wall. It mocked her tragic existence.

She sat in this haunted space wondering if she was as dreadfully alone as she felt. She thought about Thelma, how Thelma cried out to Jesus in her despair and how she was granted relief, if only by way of hallucination. Or maybe, River wondered, maybe God does exist. But even if he does, he seemed farther away from River than the nearest galaxy. Or maybe God was close, and why she was suffering. Maybe belief in God warranted disdain. After all, if God is responsible for life on earth, and life is tragic, what does that say about God? *Maybe God is evil.* The thought that God intended this kind of harm made the crushing weight of grief even more unbearable, something she didn't know was possible.

River wanted God to exist, and she wanted him to be good, and she wanted him to be close. This was her only hope. She was even willing to hallucinate about an ancient Jewish man. Her soul cried out and River did something she never thought she'd do. She looked up and spoke to God as if he were real. "Help," she cried out. "I can't do this. Please, help me."

River felt warm water pouring down over her head. She looked over one shoulder, then the next, expecting to see someone standing behind her. But there was no one, only liquid peace spreading over her entire body, from her head all the way down to her toes. It was a present kind of peace, almost tangible. She reached out thinking she might touch it with her hand but she only felt the ethereal contrast perfect peace to the dark despair she had experienced only seconds before. The contrast was so stark she imagined these existed in different galaxies. *Heaven and hell,* she thought.

It had been a few decades since Carl took a sober look into his own eyes. The mirror reflected his image, but there was no familiarity there. Luke's attack still marked his face. And, he didn't recognize himself without a bottle in his hand. His face told the story of living life hard and fast. He ran his hands over his stubble and thought, *who is this old man?* Inside he felt like that fourteen-year-old boy who believed the future was bright, that is, until the unthinkable happened. He never told a soul that he was raped. He couldn't bear the shame of it. But right then, a sober understanding that he had spent every moment since that event sabotaging his life and the lives of everyone else around him was too heavy a burden. For a fleeting moment he was happy that Linn had escaped his grasp, he loved her. But his celebration was short-lived. He knew if Linn were standing in the room right then he would kill her. Even sober. He'd kill her. She was his wife, an extension of him, not a separate person with her own life to live. When she said "I do" she was saying she belonged to him, and he would stake his rightful claim on Linn to the very end. If he could find her.

He told his reflection: the whiskey is dry, there isn't a person alive who loves you, not an ounce of food in the cupboard, not a dime to your name and there is no hope of finding Linn. There was only one thing left to do.

He walked to the safe and tapped out the code on the keypad. It opened. All of his guns had been sold to finance his unsuccessful mission of finding her, all of them except his revolver, the gun his dad gave him on his twelfth birthday. He would need to do this right with one shot.

River's body went limp on the couch and her vision went white. She saw a light that was brighter and whiter than the sun but strangely it didn't hurt her eyes. She could look directly into it. The beautiful brightness surrounded her and then filled in all the space around her, even matter itself. There were no shadows.

As her vision acclimated to the light, she saw that she was standing waist high in a crystal river that was streaming down from the source of this light. It felt as though trees lining the riverbank, but she kept her gaze on this transfixing light. It was unlike any she'd seen before. It was mightier than the sun, yet had a common feeling to it, like home. Its nature was personal. Actually, the longer she looked at this radiance, the more it seemed that this light were merely a garment. As though something, or someone, adorned itself with it.

Hundreds of previously unseen colors reflected in this unmatched brightness. Hundreds of previously unheard pitches reverberated through the sound of rushing water. She had the understanding there would be no limit to her movement, should she wish to move. But she didn't. She wanted to stand in the crystal river and look into this source of perfect peace. In this place, there was no care in her soul, no hunger in her body, not even an itch on her skin. Only peace. She could simultaneously see the past, present and future with unmatched clarity, as if she were seeing in high resolution for the first time. Being there made the husk of physical embodiment seem like a bounded and primordial puppet for the soul. Time didn't exist, it wouldn't pass by, spreading its decay. In that moment she knew the remainder of her life on earth would feel like a lucid dream compared to this experience.

The bullet was slick and heavy. It was unlike any Carl had ever seen. It looked like the devil himself, the only thing on earth that could take him out. Carl slid the silver devil into the cylinder and walked out the back door of his house toward the barn, leaving the screen door swinging in the wind. He'd meant to oil that creaking hinge a long time ago, but he never did. This sound used to nag him about tasks undone. That day, it announced his final task.

Carl slid the heavy barn door open. He walked inside and sat down on a stack of hay by the stable. Everything seemed brighter, louder and potent now that his senses weren't dulled by the fermented dragon. Even then he couldn't stop thinking about it. He leaned his elbows on his knees and gazed at the cold, dark metal in his hand. Somehow making the animals witness this moment made him feel less alone. He had nothing left in this world, not even courage to do the one thing he had left to do. But he would sit there until he found the courage. He had nowhere else to be.

Standing in the presence of perfection and love emphasized for River all of the imperfection and hate that resided inside of her. She didn't deserve the love of God that was saturating her soul. And yet, he gave it so freely. She reasoned there could be only one response to this kind of gift: gratitude. She determined she would live a life of thankfulness to God for this moment. She tipped her head back and fell back into the water, accepting every ounce of this undeserved love. The water rushed over her head and she could breathe, even under water, she could breathe. Maybe even for the first time. She could breathe.

❖

Carl sat motionless for so long, field mice had begun scavenging nearby, but he didn't notice them. He'd been pondering whether the shell of his body might actually contain a soul, or something like it. The void in his chest screamed, NO! He realized that even if he had a soul, no one in would miss it when he was gone. And he knew he deserved that. He brought the gun up to his face and held it there shaking for a while. Something pulled the gun down. It was his mother's voice. She was singing the song she'd sung at his bed each night when he was a child.

> Amazing grace, how sweet the sound
> That saved a wretch like me
> I once was lost, but now am found
> Was blind, but now I see
>
> 'Twas grace that taught my heart to fear,
> And grace my fears relieved.

How precious did that grace appear
The hour I first believed.

Believe. Carl scoffed at the idea. He figured if God were real, he would have struck him dead by now... he would have struck all child-rapists dead. And anyway, Carl reasoned, even if God were real and gracious, "I don't deserve grace," he finished his thought aloud.

He brought the gun up to his face again. Another voice tried to stop him, but he kept the gun at his face. He could hear the preacher's gravelly voice yell, "The wicked are forever damned to burn for eternity in the unquenchable fires of hell!"

Will I burn in hell? Carl desperately wondered. *I deserve to. But will I?*

The animals jumped at the sudden sound of weeping that spilled out from the depths of Carl's soul. The gun slumped down between his knees as he sobbed. He recalled another hymn he'd sung as a child, Grace Greater Than Our Sin. In between heaves and groans he asked God silently, but with little hope, *is your grace greater than all of mine?*

After an unknown amount of time, the sensation of being under water evaporated and the light faded. Gravity set in and River became aware of her body lying on the couch, but she could still feel lapping waves of liquid love and peace rushing over her, though less and less every second. She didn't move, hoping it wouldn't end. Her heart leapt upwards in the attempt to stay in a location where feet didn't get dirty and hearts didn't crush in the ruthless grip of grief. But God seemed to say that feet could be washed and hearts could be mended, even in a location very near to hell.

The wound on River's hand announced itself as a harsh welcome back to her earthly existence. Other than her hand being sensitive to touch, all of her senses were dull compared to what she had just experienced. She looked down to find blood on her clothing, the couch, and the floor. She examined her hand. The wound was sensitive to touch but it was sealed entirely. River stared in amazement; she knew this wound should have needed stitching.

There is healing in the river, a voice inside of her said. This voice wasn't hers. She recognized it as God's.

God is with me, she thought. *In me?* She realized the nagging loneliness that had made its home inside of her was gone and everything felt brand new. Her lungs seemed to fill to capacity for the first time. There was a strange sensation that her hands were full. And the cavity in her soul had been filled with liquid light, illuminating places she didn't even know were dark. But more importantly, she knew she was loved. And definitely, definitely not alone.

Loretta's letter lay on the coffee table summoning her attention. She held the rough-textured stationary in her hand. It was the feeling of sadness and betrayal. But she wondered what that other feeling was. A new one. Compassion? Yes. She ran her finger over Loretta's signature and felt compassion for her mother's impoverished soul.

It had been several days since she'd eaten and her stomach finally announced this. As she stood spreading jam over bread, she realized that she felt light, like the spongy dough in her hand, a welcomed relief to carrying the weight of the world on her back. It occurred to her she was grinning.

The dining room grabbed her attention, specifically the haunted place where Carl had attacked her. The place she'd stood terrified and choking. Moments before, it was a dark presence, an open portal into hell, always calling her back. But that location no longer held power over her; she gazed commandingly at it. Compassion called out from inside of her soul, compassion for the broken man that Carl was. This feeling was not her own. It was God's. She didn't know it was possible for God to love Carl, or that she had the capacity to experience God's love for him. But then again, only moments earlier, she didn't even know God was possible.

A great calm settled over Carl. He watched the leaves on the old oak tree swaying in unison, being moved by an unseen force. He could hear the rustling of hay being eaten behind him. The familiar smell of his barn filled his nose. And the cold barrel of his gun filled his mouth. In a flash, his lifetime of experiences appeared to him: his mother's smile, his dad's suspenders, sloppy kisses from his childhood dog. His fifth-grade teacher. Linn's laughter, the laugh she had that first year of their marriage. The rising sun over his crops during harvest. The softness of his babies' skin. The horror on their faces when he beat their mother. Drunken bar fights. Whiskey bottles. So many bottles.

His lungs caught one last breath before every moment collided, when his finger released the silver devil who shattered his skull and sent pieces of it flying throughout the barn. The animals stomped and reared and vocalized their protest at the ear-splitting sound of his revolver. Field mice scurried under piles of hay and a flock of birds took flight from the old oak tree sitting against the morning sky.

Some time passed before the animals settled. But when the farm had finally fallen as silent as the grave, the flock of scissor-tails returned to their broad oak branch and finished the song they'd begun singing when Carl was still alive.

River took the last bite of her sandwich and she stepped into the shower. The warm water did its dutiful job of cleansing many days' worth of blood, sweat and tears. However, as it poured down over her head, she noticed how dulled her senses were. She couldn't feel the water with the same kind of intensity that she felt the crystal river against her skin. Once again, she longed for a place where feet don't need washing. But it was enough to have a strange assurance inside, assurance that she would endure any grief this realm had to offer.

After showering River laid down on her bed where the smell of Luke's shampoo still lingered. She pulled his pillow in close and hugged it. The bed cradled her shape and before she knew it, she'd drifted into a peaceful sleep.

CHAPTER THIRTY-FOUR

River struggled to speak loudly enough, frustrated by the encounter she was having with Loretta. Every second she struggled brought more awareness she was coming out of a dream. Once fully awake, she remembered the encounter she'd had with God the day before. The memory was more vivid than the swaying grass outside her bedroom window, but this dream seemed just as real as that rugged landscape. In this dream she'd gone to the hospital to confront Loretta about the letter. But the hospital bed was empty. River came back home to the farmhouse and found the un-mangled version of her mother cooking breakfast, acting like nothing had ever transpired. River expressed anger at Loretta for withholding her dad from her all of these years. Loretta interrupted with a statement that ended, "You'll get over it." River tried to make her mother understand the loss she was experiencing, but Loretta spoke over her saying she was making a big deal out of nothing. The angrier River became the quieter her voice got and the slower her mouth moved. Meanwhile Loretta swiftly spoke about how River was being selfish, not thinking about her mother's needs. River's heart began to race, even as she lay awake in bed recalling this virtual encounter with her mother. She wondered if that was really how her mother would react when confronted. Would she ever have the chance to tell her mother how angry she was, how this letter was not a gift but an exposure of her deep selfishness?

River got out of bed and stepped into a pair of jeans lying in a heap on the floor. She wasn't consciously aware of the fact she was getting dressed to pay Loretta a visit. She just knew she was slipping on her boots to take a walk. A very long walk.

She headed east on the dirt road leading into town. The sun shot colorful beams of light through a cluster of clouds near the horizon, giving simple grasslands the effect of looking more mysterious than they actually were. The nature of this unseen artist came through in his art, which she now expected to find in unexpected places.

The smell of earth grounded her in the realm that her body inhabited, though she felt less and less attached to it. She would always have the sense that there was somewhere else she'd rather be.

River considered what she really knew about her past. Just like the dirt displaced by each step she took along that country road, each recollection stirred up questions in the atmosphere of her mind. She could see her ten-year-old self in her mother's flatbed truck delivering wooden pallets to the Jefferson's farm, but were they driving away from or towards her father's home near the Arkansas river? She remembered her friends braiding her hair on either side of her head and telling her that she could pretend to be Pocahontas during their imaginary play. Turns out, she didn't have to pretend. River wished she could hear her mother's thoughts when they'd stopped by that native arts gallery outside of town one year and brought a dream-catcher home to hang in River's bedroom. Did Loretta consider telling River about Joe at this time, yet still keep this knowledge to herself? The answer was obvious. River's high view of her mother dropped a little more with each rewritten memory.

She recalled people's sympathy when she told them she didn't have a dad. They acted like she was missing something, so she would say, "You can't miss something you've never had." She realized now this wasn't true. Seeing Mr. Thompson kiss Jules head those summer nights at the lake and say in a baritone voice, "Sleep-tight, don't let the bed-bugs bite," poked at the hole in River's thirteen-year-old heart. She wondered what it felt like to have a father's hand cover her entire head as he patted it. Getting a man's love was distinct from a woman's. Not better, but distinct. And River admitted that she felt this loss all along.

She remembered that time in Jr. High when Ms. Thelma assumed her dad was Native American and River corrected her. A wave of embarrassment flooded her to think this might have been obvious to everyone but her. She felt like a fool. She'd lived her whole life as a white person, psychologically anyway. Her psyche was missing half of who she was. Even now, knowing she's part native, she still didn't feel native. Was it even possible to incorporate that part of her ancestry into her psyche at this age? She'd spent her entire life feeling guilty for being white, the oppressor class. But now she was also "the oppressed," as they say. Was she the perpetrator or the victim? Oppressor or oppressed? Obviously, both. This narrative carved a trench through the middle of her psyche, like a tornado through farmland, drawing a distinct line, splitting River into two warring halves.

She thought about the native people who were exterminated from this land. And then she thought about the native girl that was exterminated from her own mind by Loretta. She knew her mom wasn't prejudiced toward native people, that she'd made this decision to keep Joe out of her life because of her own selfish needs. But this choice had racial consequences, whether Loretta admitted it or not.

River could have grown up on a reservation, being influenced by the native side of her family, absorbing customs and stories into the fabric of her being all of these years. She felt the tug of resentment. Maybe she was oppressed after all. When she considered embracing this narrative and claiming 'oppressed class' she felt resentment taking hold. Her soul felt a little darker. She needed help. Ms. Thelma came to mind. It took her awhile to recall what Thelma had said about suffering. It seemed relevant now. It had something to do with corruption. Yes! Not being corrupted by suffering. Ms. Thelma's words had struck River as important when she'd heard them, but now River deeply understood their meaning. She was at an impasse of deciding whether she'd let her pain corrupt her or whether she'd overcome it.

In her new illuminated state, she wanted nothing to do with resentment or oppression. The past had brought her to the present, horrible as it was, and she couldn't change that. But she could craft her future, so she decided that she would. The oppression narrative didn't leave room for all of who she was. The story denied at least half of who she was no matter how she looked at it. It only allowed for her to be the oppressor or the oppressed. Neither sounded appealing. In the end, the narrative itself was oppressive.

So, what story would River tell about herself if not this one? She didn't know. Not yet anyway. But one thing was sure, she would embrace all of her heritage, both native and white. It seemed like a futile endeavor to hate one and love the other.

Two hours later River walked into her mother's hospital room with dust on her boots. As usual, Loretta was laying there, still as the grave. River sat in the corner chair. The distance felt appropriate. She kept her gaze at her feet. Some morning light streamed through the window, illuminating the dust that had stirred up around her. Eventually, River looked up. Loretta's body was a picture of her soul—broken and atrophied. Impoverished and void of awareness. One could hardly say she was alive. River looked at Loretta for a long while before speaking.

"I read your letter, mama. I'm not sure what to say." She paused before saying, "If I was sure you could hear me, I probably wouldn't tell you about this. I had a sort of... spiritual experience." River thought this sentence sounded especially strange coming out of her mouth. She really wasn't the same person. "It changed me. I can handle this news better than I could before. But I'm still hurt. I'm mad about not having a dad my whole life, even though I could have." An angry huff of laughter escaped her lungs. "I mean, the man lives down the fucking road." A tear ran down her cheek. "You could have given me a daddy but you took him away!" Her chest heaved and her tone rose when she yelled, "YOU CALL THIS A GIFT? YOU'RE A FUCKING THIEF! THAT'S WHAT YOU ARE! You stole a daddy from a little girl and you stole MY ancestry, too!" She gasped and heaved, "None of this is a gift! Do you understand that? You didn't give me anything! You returned what you stole; that's what you did! And you stole TIME, mama! You can't give that back! You can't give back time!" She cried from her gut and she didn't care if hospital staff could hear her. She had to say all of this to Loretta, even if she couldn't hear it.

River's crying calmed to a sniffle before she said, "If it weren't for that spiritual experience I had, I don't know when I would've ever talked to you again. I'd probably have let you rot and die all alone in this god-forsaken hospital bed. That's what you deserve, you know, to die alone." The thought of not deserving goodness made her touch the newly sealed wound on her hand. River looked down at this slash of raised flesh and then added, "But, sometimes we get things we don't deserve, I guess. That's what a gift is, mama; that's what a gift looks like." She paused, still rubbing her wound, then said, "I got unimaginable love that I didn't deserve. So, I guess I could give you some of it." River paused, considering the fact that she didn't have to give any of it to Loretta. She didn't want to. She wanted to stay angry. The thought of releasing this anger felt like condoning the harm that Loretta did. But the thought of keeping this kind of hate in her heart weighed her soul down. A familiar feeling. And the thought of withholding this love that was so freely given to her plucked at her conscience. When she'd stood absorbing God's liquid love, she'd determined to live a life of thankfulness. Now resentment threatened to stand in her way.

Finally, she said, "I know what it's like to have an impoverished soul, mama, and you do. You do." Her tears began again. "I still love you, mama. It just hurts to love you right now." River stood up and left Loretta's room determined that she would not return until she'd met her father in person.

That is, if he wanted to meet her.

River woke up in a panic, sitting straight up with sweat on her brow. She had dreams like this in college, where she would show up for the first day of class but it was actually the last and they were in the middle of taking the final exam. But this was no dream, she'd missed her article's deadline. Her heart sank along with her head onto the pillow. She groaned and slapped the blankets. But despite her utter failure, she knew that hope for impossible circumstances actually existed. So, she got up and finished the article and sent it off anyway. Maybe the deadline got extended or they'd make an exception for her. Who knows? She'd be shocked if they accepted it. In fact, she'd be surprised if they'd want to work with her ever again.

When she'd finished the piece, she brought her mug of coffee to the window chair where morning sunlight streamed in and warmed her all over. It made her think of the crystal river and the source from which it flowed. Earth's sun couldn't warm her soul in the same way. She thought about Thelma. It occurred to her that Thelma was someone she could talk to about this experience, maybe even the only person on earth who would believe her. She determined to drop by Thelma's house that morning. But it was Sunday; Thelma would be at church.

The past few weeks had left River's heart raw, like a piece of tenderized meat, no fiber remained intact. One tragedy after another had unfolded: her mother's body mutilated and her mind absent, the trauma of being assaulted, losing Luke, the news of having a father after all these years. And then there was the otherworldly experience of meeting God. She felt it would be comforting to be around the folks at Stillwater Chapel who had supported her through these treacherous months. River looked up at the oversized clock on the wall and realized she could make it to church on time if she left soon.

The church bell rang at the top of the hour with ten resounding gongs. It was the sound of her youth. Growing up she could hear the steeple bells ring a couple blocks away from Loretta's store on Sundays. River was happy to see a seat in the back next to Thelma again. Thelma did a double-take when she looked at River. This wasn't the same women she'd had lunch with recently. River's face was lit up, like life was worth living.

Before the congregation sang the first song, the worship leader said, "This hymn is familiar to all of us. Even though it was written in 1876, it endures today as a regular worship song in churches across the nation. Some of you know the story of the person who wrote it. He was a man who lost everything. He experienced complete financial ruin, his two-year-old son died, then he lost all four of his daughters in a shipwreck. As he sailed over the part of the sea where his daughters drowned, he wrote these words."

> (Everyone sang)
> When peace like a river, attendeth my way,
> When sorrows like sea billows roll
> Whatever my lot, thou hast taught me to say
> It is well, it is well with my soul
> It is well with my soul
> It is well, it is well with my soul

Tears flowed freely down River's face. She could have written these lyrics herself. Thelma put an arm around River's waist. Both women stood in amazement that the human experience of reaching out to God in the worst possible circumstances produces the same unexplainable peace across time. River thought maybe the author of this song saw the same crystal river that she did over 140 years ago. Or maybe he just experienced the current of peace that flows from it. River considered that maybe people don't go to church to find God. Maybe they go to church to remember when they did.

After the singing quieted the congregation remained standing for the reading of scripture. The preacher said,

"Today's sermon is about Eden being restored and the curse of sin being broken. Our scripture reading is Revelation 22:1-3. As you know, Revelation is a vision the apostle John had and recorded when he was banished to the island of Patmos. Let's read together." A chorus of voices arose:

> Then the angel showed me the river of the water of life, as clear as crystal, flowing from the throne of God and of the Lamb down the middle of the great street of the city. On each side of the river stood the tree of life, bearing twelve crops of fruit, yielding its fruit every month. And the leaves of the tree are for the healing of the nations. No longer will there be any curse…" Revelation 22:1-3

As they read this passage, River saw the crystal river in front of her again, clearly and with her eyes. An overwhelming wave of liquid peace rushed over her and she stumbled backward a bit, regaining her vision.

Thelma put her hand on River's back and breathed, "Ho-ly! Ho-ly!" and River wondered if Thelma felt that, too.

She didn't understand much of what the preacher said that day but one thing stood out like a flashing neon sign. Someone asked Jesus who he claimed to be. He simply answered, "I Am." She recognized this as a claim to being God and she wondered if this could be true.

As the service concluded with a final song, River noticed that Luke was sitting many rows ahead of her to the right. He was alone, looking down.

CHAPTER THIRTY-FIVE

Luke walked down the aisle of Stillwater Chapel palming his hat. Catching sight of River in the corner of his eye, he stood like a deer in the headlights. Church wasn't the place he'd imagined seeing River. A pleading look spread across his face, begging, *please, River.*

River expected to feel unbearable pain when she saw him, but she found instead that a longing for his companionship outweighed his betrayal. A familiar compassion welled up inside her, a foreign love, the kind God has. But what surprised her was that she could feel her own love for him, as well. Maybe even for the first time. She walked to him and took his hand. He hesitated; his grip was unsure. But he took her hand as they walked out of church together. Luke questioned whether this moment was actually happening or if he was imagining it. The strange looks they got from people they passed convinced him that it was real. Did God really answer his prayers? And so quickly?

"Wanna get some lunch?" River asked as they stepped outside.

Luke stopped and squeezed her hand. He looked her in the eyes. "Every day for the rest of my life."

She smiled and said, "One day at a time, Luke."

They walked a few blocks to The BBQ Pit and found outdoor seating, enjoying the warmth of the late morning sun on their backs.

The raised flesh on River's hand caught Luke's attention. "What's this?" he asked, turning her hand over.

"The bottom of my bucket."

He looked down ashamed. "I'm so sorry I had anything to do with that."

River paused before saying, "I looked up."

They locked eyes for a moment. "I guess so. You're sittin' here with me."

Neither one of them wanted to have the inevitable conversation, not in public anyway. They made small talk about the food and the new management at the restaurant but neither one of them was really thinking about the restaurant or its management. They had other things on their minds—Luke was thinking about the possibility of being a father, and River, about the possibility of having a father.

At a pause in the conversation she asked, "Have you ever heard of people being…" she didn't know how to say it. "Never mind. I don't know what I'm saying."

"What?"

"Well, you know… having an out of body experiences or, what the pastor said, visions?"

"Dan Stein said he had a vision once. Guess he saw Jesus leadin' him up a mountain, or something like that." He shrugged, then looked at River. "Why?"

"I'd just never heard of visions before," she said dismissively, hoping he wouldn't ask any more questions. She knew her otherworldly encounter was the most real experience she'd ever had, but she also knew it was the most abnormal. People like her former self would think she was a crazy person if she told them about it.

Her mood shifted a bit after lunch when they arrived at the farmhouse to talk. Luke walked in and saw the damage done to the living room.

"Bottom of the bucket," she explained.

Luke nodded, as a pang of guilt shot through him.

They sat at the dining table and Luke told her about that night with Ellie. "I messed up by letting Ellie touch me, River, but I swear on my baby's grave I didn't touch her." River had never heard Luke mention his baby before. She believed him. And decided she'd never bring it up again, unless he gave her a reason to worry. "Also," he added, "Ellie's pregnant. She's due in a few weeks. She says the baby's mine. I guess it could be but I'll need to make sure, of course." He studied River's face hoping this wouldn't change how she felt about him. River had no reason to assign any value to fatherhood. Luke wondered if she'd understand.

"Of course," she replied. "A kid needs their dad."

Luke's eyebrows shot straight up. He didn't think she could shock him anymore than she had already that day.

"So, speaking of dads," she left the table to pick up Loretta's letter from the coffee table. "This emptied my bucket completely. I found it in my mom's purse." She thought the news was best delivered in Loretta's own words, so she handed the letter to Luke. He kept eye contact as he took it from her. He paced the floor shaking his head as he flipped through the creased stationary.

When he was done reading it he walked straight over to River and pulled her head against his chest, "I'm so sorry, Riv." She wrapped her arms around him and cried in his arms. "You don't have to do this alone. Can I take this curve with you?"

She nodded between his chest and his arms while realizing that two months ago he would have said, "I'll take care of you," or something like that. It occurred to her that she was having an effect on him. *Men evolve best in the context of love*, she thought.

God interrupted, *so do you.*

She smiled and nodded, *yeah, me too*.

When River nodded, Luke asked, "What?"

"Nothing. Just talkin' to God."

He shook his head in total disbelief that River was able to set her beautiful, brilliant mind aside long enough to experience God.

CHAPTER THIRTY-SIX

River had been avoiding her email for days. She'd opened it long enough to see a rejection from the Oklahoman sitting in her inbox. The preview-text of the email said, "I'm sorry to inform you." It was obviously a rejection letter. But she couldn't ignore her growing inbox any longer. She clicked it open:

> I'm sorry to inform you that the deadline for submission in the Music Festival series has passed. We cannot accept this piece for our A&E segment.
>
> However, we are starting a History series in our Life Section that your article would be perfect for. No one has written a proper history of Red Dirt music and its Oklahoman roots. You have made an incredible start. We would like you to dig deeper, do some investigation into the development of this genre, and submit your article for review in our Oklahoma History series. I've attached information about this.
>
> And, please observe the deadline. It is fixed and nonnegotiable!

❖

River stayed at Luke's place most nights. Maybe it was just his physical mass, but being around him made her feel stronger than she was. His presence made it seem as though she were courageous enough to map the most uncharted territory of her life. Taking that first step, calling Joe, felt to her like a step into Chaos itself.

For the third day in a row, River stood holding her phone in one hand and Joe's number in her other. That day she entered his digits on her screen but didn't push the call button. Various scenarios played out in her mind and she imagined herself surviving each one. What if the contact information she had for him was bad? She imagined herself coming to terms with not actually having access to her father, after all. What if he were actually a terrible human being, like a rapist or a wife-beater or something? She imagined how she might deal with that. But the hardest scenario for River to imagine was that Joe wouldn't care about her at all. What if he took no interest in her? It was hard enough not having a dad because she didn't know who he was. It was quite another thing not having a dad because he doesn't care that you exist. She wasn't able to come to terms with this possibility; it was the only thing stopping her from contacting him.

The sound of Luke's footsteps moved closer to the kitchen. She shoved the phone in her pocket. He gave her a sideways glance and poured his coffee. He had learned over the past two weeks that asking River when she was going to call Joe wouldn't help her actually do it.

Luke often found River stuck in her head, thinking about the challenge ahead of her. One evening as Luke put leftovers in the fridge, he suggested they go dancing. Her mind was tired from constantly laboring so she reasoned she could use the distraction, even though she didn't feel like dancing.

When they got to Outlaws, Luke led her through the door by the small of her back, a gesture she'd come to appreciate. She decided to quiet the feminist voice in her head that demanded she be offended by this. Instead, she allowed Luke to define his own gestures. For him, this was just one way he told River, "I've got your back, darlin'."

They only danced a few songs, then watched people from the bar, but River was still stuck in her head. Luke called her out by putting his arms around her waist, pulling her close and singing in her ear.

> I came to life when I first kissed you
> The best me has his arms around you
> You make me better than I was before
> Thank God I'm yours
>
> The worst me is just a long-gone memory
> You put a new heartbeat inside of me
> You make me better than I was before
> Thank God I'm yours

She recalled the first time they slept together—how he said, "You're mine now," and she protested. But now, he sang, "I'm yours." She decided that the ownership was mutual. Some tears fell down her cheeks with the realization that she loved this man, this gorgeous, brave, evolving man. He wiped a couple tears from her face realizing he'd broken through the seemingly impenetrable shell that protected her heart. And he recognized the vulnerability that only love can bring. She kissed him on the lips and leaned into Luke, filling more than his arms. She sank deep into his chest and filled the cavity to capacity.

Over the previous few months, they had enjoyed plenty of sex, but that night, they made love. As they were falling asleep River said, "Hey, Luke. Have you ever thought that if we can make this relationship work there might be hope for the whole damn country?"

He chuckled, "No pressure." And, then it hit him, the R-word. It sounded so good coming from her mouth.

She added, "I'm gonna love you like this makes sense."

He pulled her closer, wrapped an arm and leg around her, then whispered, "And I'm gonna love you like you ain't dangerous."

Another week went by and she still hadn't contacted Joe. Luke could see she needed some nudging. His previous attempts had failed so that morning he took a different approach. As she moved through the kitchen, he gestured for her to join him at the table. He made small talk for a bit before saying, "Did I ever tell you about the best day of my life?"

She shook her head.

"It was the day I found out I was a dad." His lips contorted. Luke was suddenly on the brink of tears. She'd never seen him like this before, never once seen Luke come close to crying. She couldn't take her eyes off him. He said with wavering voice, "If my baby-girl was out there somewhere," his Adam's apple rose and fell, "I'd wanna hear from her." He removed a tear from his eye before it had the chance to roll down his cheek.

And just like that, River saw the heart of a father. It was beautiful! It mirrored God's heart for her. She decided, if

Luke could love a daughter he'd never met, then maybe Joe could love her, even at age twenty-three. She decided, if her dad ended up loving her with even half of the love that Luke was exuding, then it was worth the risk of Joe not loving her at all.

That was the day River called Joe. She didn't know how to do this kind of thing, so she just told him the truth as concisely as possible and let him decide if he wanted to meet her. Joe didn't hesitate to invite her to his home by the Arkansas River. She felt some relief knowing that he hadn't rejected her outright before meeting her. She made plans to visit him the following Saturday.

Luke was eager to join River for this meeting, but she told him she needed to do this alone. His protective instinct was in full gear, but it wasn't just that, everything inside of him wanted to watch her story unfold. But his gut told him she'd be okay and she was right. She needed to take this step alone.

That Saturday rolled around and Luke noticed River didn't say a single word the entire morning, not even to answer his questions. Her only communication was a nod or shake from her head. When it came time to leave, she single-mindedly jumped into her Jeep.

Luke leaned his arms on her open window. "Will you at least call me when you're leavin' his place?"

She nodded.

"I'm proud of you, River. You're the bravest person I know."

She started the engine and then finally spoke. "What a coincidence. That's what I think about you."

She kissed him, then drove down the long, dirt drive. Luke put his thumbs in his pockets and watched her drive away. And he stayed there, until all of the dust had settled.

.

CHAPTER THIRTY-SEVEN

Halfway through the drive to Joe's house River remembered she wasn't alone. "I'm so nervous," she said to her new unseen friend.

God seemed to reply, *I got you this far, didn't I?*

She wasn't used to that quiet voice, so unlike her own, sharing the recesses of her mind. But it was comforting to know she could engage with the deepest form of love whenever she wanted to, even if less dramatically than she had at first.

As she approached the Arkansas River, a baby deer stood at the end of the bridge looking directly at her, almost like it was expecting to see her. She slowed her Jeep to a roll. Its light brown coat had a splash of pale white going across its back and down one leg, the beauty of which amazed River, especially the closer she got. The baby deer decided she'd gotten close enough and sprung from the road into the forest in two playful bounds. She liked this neck of the woods. The earthy-air skimming past her windshield carried the same iron-rich smell as the air in Stillwater did. Just more potent. Beyond the scent, the area had a strange familiarity River wasn't expecting, even as she moved into uncharted land.

She drove down the long, dirt road leading to her dad's house, which she could see up ahead. The house was small and shaded by trees. River determined that despite her fragile emotional state, she would not fall apart, she wouldn't make a fool of herself in that way. She would push through this awkward introduction until it was over with, as if it were perfectly normal to meet her father for the first time in her twenties. She took a deep breath, got out of her Jeep and began toward the house. She stopped. Joe was standing on the porch looking at her. They stood looking at each other for a moment before she finished the trek toward him. He looked familiar, she thought, like she'd seen him before. And it struck her, he looked like her. Or more accurately, she looked like him. He had long dark hair pulled back in a ponytail, a high forehead, high cheekbones and a penetrative look in his eyes. He was taller than she was but shorter than Luke. River climbed three old wooden steps and was surprised when he pulled her in for a hug, without saying anything. The feeling of hugging her dad was so foreign. Who was this person? He didn't smell like family yet, but she was glad to finally touch the man who had something to do with her existence on earth.

Before her arrival, she couldn't conjure an image of what her father might look like, but his attire surprised her somewhat. He was wearing cowboy boots, jeans, a white blouse tucked in and bolo tie with an arrowhead pendant that featured a large turquoise stone. She wondered if this was his formal look.

Joe's house was small and dim, very little daylight came through the couple of small windows in the room. She was surprised to see a rugged wooden cross standing on one windowsill, above which hung a dreamcatcher; feathers hung from a ring of interlocking circles where daylight streamed through. Against one wall leaned a fishing pole and against another rested a guitar. Loretta had mentioned that her father was a musician. River was curious to hear him play and she hoped that Luke and Joe might be able to bond over this common interest.

Joe asked her if she wanted some tea and she gladly accepted for lack of something else to say. He told her it was made from traditional herbs, which made her excited to try it. When he went to the kitchen she took in the rest of her surroundings. River found herself thinking that hipsters would be jealous of the good condition his old furniture was in. A couple slim-legged swivel chairs sat opposite a 1960's-looking couch. A framed photo of two young girls and a boy hung above the couch. It occurred to her that she might have siblings. This possibility had never crossed her mind for some reason. The picture looked dated and she wondered how old those kids were now, or if she was even related to them. It seemed to her like Joe might live alone. The home lacked feminine touch. She was eager to find out what his story was.

Joe came back in with a cup of tea. She took the steaming cup and sat on the couch. He settled on a chair across from her with his own cup. He opened his mouth to speak but then paused. He didn't know how to start a conversation with this sudden-daughter. Like River, he wasn't much for small-talk, so he pierced the silence by saying, "My mother's name was Adeyvasgv Ama. That means flowing water." He looked up in time to see River swallow her tea. "Names don't come to you by accident, you know? They have a purpose. We Cherokee, we're rooted but not fixed. We're like the water," he pointed to the stream running alongside his house. "A large stone can't stop us from going where we need to be. It just changes our path."

River sat amazed at the depth of her name's meaning and that everything Joe was saying held such deep truth about her.

"When we talk about water, we actually mean river. In fact, our people still have a ritual of "going-to-water," where the elders stand waist-high in the river and cover their heads with the water, washing away everything that keeps them far from God."

River's jaw dropped open a little as he continued.

"Have you ever gone on a Vision-Quest?" he asked.

River felt as though she were watching this conversation from a distance. She couldn't believe what Joe had just said. And especially couldn't believe that he'd just said the word "vision." "Uh... a Vision Quest?" she finally replied. "I don't know. What is that?"

"You go on this journey alone, usually in nature. You prepare by fasting, not eating anything for a few days, and you center your mind on what you seek. On this quest, you ask The Great Spirit to give you understanding. If the Spirit gives you a vision it changes your path in the world."

River's face contorted, trying to stop herself from crying openly. Joe hesitated, seeing her reaction. It was clear to him she'd been on a quest without knowing it. He continued, "When I was twenty-two, I did my first Vision Quest. The Great Spirit gave me a vision of a young doe standing on the opposite side of a river. She was looking at me. I knew she wanted to cross the water. I wanted her to cross it but Spirit said, 'Not yet'."

River couldn't stop the tears from falling when she'd heard that her father's vision included a river, as well, but she kept her emotional response as quiet as she could. It frustrated her that she was already making a fool of herself on their first introduction.

He turned away from her a bit so he wouldn't be distracted by her and continued, "The Great Spirit brought me back to the place where I sat waiting for the vision and I knew I would understand the vision someday. But I didn't know when." Still looking away, he said, "I turned 45 last year and I still hadn't figured out what this vision meant. I went on another quest because I was frustrated that Spirit hadn't shown me the meaning. Spirit gave me another vision. He brought me back to the river, where the doe was standing. She was bigger, but weaker. She stepped into the water and it swept over her head. I wanted to save her but Spirit stopped me. He said, 'She can breathe'."

Jarring sobs shook River. She was overcome.

Joe paused at the outburst and looked at her. It was clear to him that his vision resonated with her deeply. He waited until she quieted down before continuing. "I waited for the doe to come out of the water and when she did, she was on my side of the river. And she was stronger. Then Spirit brought me back to myself and I knew I would understand the meaning of both visions very soon. You called me a few weeks later. That's when my visions were clear. Spirit was telling me about you." He looked at River and said, "My doe."

River heaved more sobs at the endearing nickname her father had already given her. And the ownership he claimed by using the word "my." She wiped her dripping eyes and nose with her arms and hands, rubbing them frequently across her jeans. Joe gazed at her for a while before collecting tissue for her.

A whirlwind of thoughts swept through River's head. First, amazement that her father had had a vision of her stepping into that crystal river. Second, that God had prepared him to meet her, even before he knew that she existed. She felt overwhelming gratitude to God for taking her nightmare situation and weaving it like a dreamcatcher into the most beautiful and meaningful moment. She felt God say, *you chose this path. I illuminated it.*

She looked over at this native man, her father. He spoke so confidently and openly about his experiences with God and his words instilled a kind of pride in her for her native heritage. River felt the two halves of her psyche merging, native and white. She wasn't two-halves but one-whole. The Great I Am had breathed life into every part of her.

Briefly, she stood outside of the moment in which she existed. If the person she had been only months before had met Joe, she would have assumed that he had mental problems after speaking with him. Furthermore, if someone had told her that by summer's-end she would be a gun-toting Native American who would fall in love with a Neanderthal, find Jesus and her long-lost father, and, what's more, they would have shared visions, she would have laughed in their face. She wouldn't have believed them, not even if her life depended on it. But it was all true. She simply wasn't the same young woman who had been a city-dweller immersed in academia only months before.

River had experienced the river of life. And as she stood in that crystal water, immersed in liquid love, she knew that no matter what the future would bring, whether life's currents would be torrid or calm, whether the water was waist-high or over her head, it really wouldn't matter. She knew she would breathe.

EPILOGUE

If you're lucky in life you'll have very few opportunities to journey into the abyss. If you are blessed, you will have at least one. To the degree that you suffer is the degree you can experience God's regenerative love. This makes despair an opportunity you don't want to miss.

Don't waste a single tragedy.

About the Author

Gracie West's debut novel was inspired by a desire to hear real and difficult conversations between very different kinds of people, a lost art in our politically-polarized climate, now replaced by name-calling.

Gracie got a B.A. in Women's Studies and an M.A. in Sociology of Religion. She's determined these degrees are little more than an indoctrination into progressivism (far-left identitarianism), which sells a potent hatred for westerners, white people, men and other groups of "power," which is the heart's desire of this doctrine. After deprogramming from these programs, Gracie has been re-enchanted by her first love: Jesus Christ, a belief in truth, individualism, science, and her fellow man (and anyone still willing to use the word "man" in reference to all of humanity).

Luke and River have helped Gracie sort through the culture-war raging in western civilization today. So has Jordan B. Peterson, Thomas Sowell, Larry Elder and thinkers associated with Intellectual Dark Web. But nothing has guided her thinking more than a sustained intimacy with the powerful and loving God.

Gracie grew up skipping rocks across a river in rural northern California with her parents, her sister and three brothers. She and her husband are raising two kids in the Portland, Oregon area.

www.ReadGracieWest.com
Gracie@ReadGracieWest.com

Made in the USA
Coppell, TX
18 March 2020